Dead On Time

Meghnad Desai

Beautiful
Books

Beautiful Books Limited
36–38 Glasshouse Street
London W1B 5DL

www.beautiful-books.co.uk

ISBN 9781905636730

9 8 7 6 5 4 3 2 1

First published in India in 2009 by Harper Collins Publishers India,
a joint venture with The India Today Group.

A catalogue reference for this book is available from
the British Library.

Cover design by Ian Pickard.

Printed and bound in the UK by CPI Mackays, Chatham ME5 8TD.

To Kishwar,
who made it possible.

Author's Note

All the characters and events described in this work are fictional. For the sake of verisimilitude, the names of some real-life radio and TV personalities have been used but the words and actions ascribed to them are imaginary.

1

6.59 a.m. London

This is the Today programme with James Naughtie and John Humphrys.

Ian groaned as his radio alarm clock woke him up. So it was the Old Big Two this morning. What are they up to?

Pip Pip Pip Pip Pip Peeeep.

Good Morning on Monday the tenth of May. Here is a summary of the news.

International tensions are rising between Libya and the United States of America as an American attack on Libya seems imminent.

As Scotland gears up for the first elections for the devolved parliament, an opinion poll shows the Scottish Nationalists closing the lead. We talk to Gideon Crawford, the Secretary of State for Scotland.

Negotiations for Cyprus's entry into the European Union enter a crucial phase. Is enlargement a step too far? We talk to the Foreign Minister of Greece.

And what is the Prime Minister's recipe for the Millen-

nium? We ask the experts: 'What is the Free Way'?

Today's newsreader is Corrie Corfield.

Ian drifted back into sleep as the soothing, well mod–ulated voice washed over him. He was trying to get back to the dream which had just been interrupted. He was surrounded by newspaper files and trying to open a door. Someone, he could not make out who, was trying to get him to drink.He lost the dream, turned over. Hilda had, of course, got up at half past six. She did not need an alarm clock.

It was James Naughtie's voice now.

It is eleven minutes past seven. The enlargement of the European Union when it is finished will add eleven new members to the present fifteen. But not all are alike. While Poland, Hungary and the Czech Republic are on everyone's list of favoured new members, there are problems with Cyprus. Our European Affairs Editor reports.

Ian forced himself out of bed. He would normally linger until 'Thought for the Day' came on at around ten minutes to eight with some Bishop rabbiting on about Jesus and cannabis. But he had something else to do today, something he could not immediately recall. Something which meant he had to break his routine. It will come to me, he thought, as he splashed cold water over himself. He grabbed the large furry blue towel to dry his face.

On the line from Heathrow before he boards a plane for the EU Council of Ministers meeting in Vienna where Cyprus is being discussed, we speak to the Secretary of State for Europe, Terence Harcourt.

'Good Morning, Secretary of State.'

'Hello Jim. How nice to hear from you…'

Ian remembered. Just the sound of Terence Harcourt's voice, that polite unctuous voice full of totally false bonhomie brought Ian back to reality. Yes, he had to go in and do a spot of political journalism today. Not foot-pounding through the streets or the corridors of power. He was too old for that. He had to wrestle with newspaper archives. Now where was his tooth brush?

7.20 a.m. London

When Gideon Crawford arrived at the White City complex of the BBC, he was greeted immediately by a young woman who was immaculately dressed in a well-pressed white shirt and a skirt which was just a few stripes short of tartan. Gideon did not quite hear her name but he thought she had said she was Celia. He noted how bright and pretty young women were nowadays. As to what Celia thought of this tall and lugubrious Scotsman with a large beaky nose and thinning hair we shall never know. You don't get anywhere in the BBC revealing your thoughts about the great and the good. She showed just a shade of respect for a Cabinet Minister but no more. She whisked him through the door using her BBC pass, upstairs to the first floor to the *Today* studios and sat him down in a small waiting room with transparent walls. It had the morning's newspapers and a machine for dispensing coffee and tea. There was a large jug of orange juice. Celia asked him whether he would like a cup of coffee or tea.

'Coffee please. Milk and sugar, two please.' Gideon

was not into healthy habits.

A voice from behind *The Guardian* said, 'Hello Gideon. What are you doing here so early in the morning?'

It was Andrew Merton, the well known sociologist. He was thin and wiry with a sallow complexion and wore an old-fashioned NHS frame for his spectacles. It was his idiosyncratic way of telling the world that a Professor at Cambridge he might be, but he was still proud of his working class origins. The frames available on the NHS had improved in range and quality but he only wore them because when the Beatles were all the rage, John Lennon had made the wiry NHS frames trendy. Andrew had adopted them then and now it cost him a fortune to have them reproduced. Gideon had known him for many years. Andrew had been in and out of the Party as his conscience or his latest sociological theory dictated but Gideon always regarded him as one of their own. After all, a Scottish lad can't go too far wrong, or Right for that matter.

'Well, this is a surprise, Andrew. I didn't think you Cambridge dons had to get out of bed till your first tutorials after lunch. Are you here facing the dulcet duo as well?'

Facing John Humphrys and James Naughtie early in the morning on *Today* seemed to many people an exercise in self-flagellation. Whatever you did and however clever you were, they came out on top. But it was still worth it, since the programme set the day's political agenda. To be tongue-lashed by John Humphrys or being hopelessly lost in the labyrinthine questions of James Naughtie was the fate of anyone and everyone who ventured on the programme, but they still kept on coming. To be asked to appear on *Today* meant you had arrived in the political village of Westminster.

'I have been up since half past five to get here on time. It's the Millennium Commission that the PM has set up. They want to have some fun with me about that, I think.' Andrew did not want Gideon to be confirmed in the popular view that Cambridge dons enjoyed a sybaritic life style.

'Oh, Harry White's great dream project. His cure for the world for the next millennium. Well, I take it you will tell Harry what to think and he will agree, surely.'

'Oh, don't you believe it. Harry White is not so simple after all. He takes his Millennium Commission very seriously. He is genuinely keen to arrive at some philosophical agreement which can guide us through new challenges. I have really come to admire him while working with him on this.'

'Well, I am glad to hear that. Don't let those two make too much of a mockery of Harry.'

'It is twenty six minutes past seven and here is Gary with the sports.' It was James Naughtie.

'Morning Jim, Morning John. First the Old Firm game at Ibrox. It is a cliffhanger since the championship of the Scottish Premier League hinges on the outcome. Celtic have to win outright if they are to win the League. Rangers, who are level with them on points, are ahead on goal average. So they only need to draw.'

'Isn't this the match the Prime Minister is attending?' John Humphrys asked.

'Well, for the fans of the Old Firm game, that will be the least important thing, I can assure you,' Gary laughed.

7.28 a.m. London

At the mention of Harry White, Sarah threw off her bed clothes and leapt out of bed.

Sleep or no sleep, she had to get ready for work.

7.30 a.m. London

Celia came in to the waiting room and asked Gideon if he would come with her. Gideon heaved aloft his tall gaunt frame and prepared himself for the ordeal he was going to face. He waved goodbye to Andrew Merton, who was still waiting to go in. The studio itself was next door to the waiting room. Celia opened the heavy wooden door gently and silently ushered Gideon in. There was a very large round table which occupied much of the room. On one side, there were some empty chairs with chunky red and blue microphones nearby on the table. Gideon was directed to one of the empty chairs. John Humphrys, with ear phones around him, was being fed some information from the producers on the other side of the large glass window at one end of the room. He was nodding and waving a sharp pencil in the air. There were papers and newspapers strewn in front of him. He saw Gideon and waved the pencil in a greeting. James Naughtie put down the polystyrene coffee cup from which he was taking a sip and bid a silent hello to Gideon. There was a woman sitting further to his left just finishing the news summary.

'Thanks Corrie. It is now seven thirty five and with me in the studio is Gideon Crawford, the Secretary of State for Scotland. Good Morning, Secretary,' John Humphrys said.

By some mysterious and long forgotten rule of the BBC, Scottish matters went to John Humphrys since he was Welsh and James Naughtie was Scottish. That, however, did not make things easy for Gideon.

'Good Morning, John. Good Morning, Jim.'

'Now Secretary of State, are you in trouble in Scotland? The latest poll shows the Scottish Nationalists catching up with you. How will you manage?'

'You don't want to take a single poll too seriously, John. I am pretty confident that when the day comes...'

'But we don't know the day because the Prime Minister will not set the date. Is he afraid of losing?'

'No, let me finish, John. I was saying that when the day comes, and, indeed, it is the Prime Minister who will set the day, we are confident that the voters in Scotland will remember that it was our Party that delivered devolution.'

'But was it? It was Stan Davies who did much of the work, along with Terence Harcourt. But Harry White is not the same thing is he? Is he not very unpopular in Scotland?'

'I wouldn't say that, John...'

'But the polls say that in Scotland Harry White has only twenty nine per cent support while the Scottish Nationalist leader...' John Humphrys was quick.

'The election will not be fought on personalities, but programmes. We have a positive and radical programme for Scotland in its first Parliament. It is good for Scotland and good for the Scottish people.' Gideon had not been in politics for nothing. He could waffle his way through the few minutes which he knew was all he would be allotted.

'You call it radical, but it is the Scottish Nationalists who are promising to take North Sea oil into public ownership, and perhaps ScotRail as well. You have avoided any talk of nationalisation.'

'All that is empty talk. That is the old way, and around the world it is being abandoned. We have to do the same. What matters is health and education and jobs for our people.'

'Are you sure your Party members in Scotland agree with this new fangled philosophy of the Prime Minister? Isn't this just the old Tory radicalism?'

'Well, this is what the Party fought the last General Election on and we won at Westminster the largest majority anyone can remember.'

'So what is good for Westminster is good enough for Scotland. Then why devolve?' John kept the pressure up.

'No, I am not saying that at all. Devolution is the great and glorious achievement of our Party. The Scottish Nationalists don't want devolution. They want to break away. We will protect the Union.'

7.45 a.m. London

'Oh give up, Gideon,' Ian shouted at the radio. He had

10

now gone through his morning routine of a shit, shave and shower, as he called it and was getting ready for the outside world. Now what was he to wear? What did the day foretell? He drew the blinds and looked out. It was a glorious morning on the hills of Hampstead, so by midday it would be sweaty in the lower marshlands of Westminster. So: no suit, but a light combination with a tie would be de riguer. He might end up in the portals of Parliament, after all.

9.00 a.m. London

England was not made for hot summer days. They used to be rare. That is why the poets celebrated them. But now in the final decade of the twentieth century, what with all the global warming, such days came often and yet no one was prepared for them. No air conditioning in cars or offices or houses, let alone on the bus or in the underground tube. New York was better equipped, as Sarah recalled her holiday there this time last year. The subway was air-conditioned, not like the Victoria Line on which she was stuck.

Ian, on the other hand, was walking down Hampstead High Street to his bus stop. He would have preferred, if he was to swelter, to be in Provence, which is where hot summer days are meant to be spent. But they always went in July to their Provence cottage. It all began when, in the nineteenth century, River Thames stank by the summer months and Parliament could not function due to the foul smell. So it recessed. Thus started the practice that everyone had to have a holiday during the English summer. This was why, when the children were at school, they could not get away on holidays till the end of June. Now, even though the children had grown up and the grandchildren were keener to go to America than France for the summer holidays, Ian and Hilda still went every July. Such, Ian thought to himself, is the power of History; or perhaps just the force of habit.

It was a fraught Monday morning for both, but to look at them you would have thought that it was a life-threatening event for Ian and no more than a common cold for Sarah. Ian was furious, muttering about the incompetence of people who had inconvenienced him. That was it. Ian hated being inconvenienced, at having to break his routine, even if that meant getting paid handsomely. Sarah was stoic. As she had put on her make-up for the day ahead, she was the complete professional that her colleagues had come to expect. Whatever her problems, she had to look her impeccable best. That meant coordinating her printed shirt with her flaming red hair and a discrete but fashionable skirt. Sandals rather than high heels, but the pair with bold colours matching her top and the beads that she had picked up in Monsoon. She had decided to put on her no-smudge lipstick—'easy for that forbidden kiss,' as the poster said. She painted her nails and toes and threw on the silk scarf she had bought in New York. She was prepared for whatever may happen. After last night, anything could.

Her life had been undermined, her happiness destroyed. She had come home Sunday night, having spent the weekend with her sick mother, in Warrington, as she had done for the last few months. Her mother was getting more difficult each week. Sarah had never got on with her. She was really her dad's girl. She had adored him. His tall handsome face came back to her often. She was distraught when he died as she was just getting her first job. He had been her solid support when her mother never thought she would amount to much. For her mother, Sarah was the poor substitute for the son she never had. Once her father died, her mother just fell apart. She became physically frail but more querulous than ever before. Yet Sarah was her only support and Sarah bore the burden of tending after her mother stoically. Anything as long as she did not have to live in the same house as her. She had to think about finding her a safe sheltered accommodation. A costly option though. She would have to consult Alan, as he was the financial whiz kid.

When she had entered their flat in Islington, she had found it strangely empty. Alan was not back yet from his five-a-side football game, and there was no hot pasta dinner awaiting her with his freshly made pesto. No message on the answerphone, no note. She checked her mobile for any missed calls or messages. She changed into her floppy salwar kameez, picked up in Delhi last Christmas on holiday, and began to think about food and why Alan was not there.

Something was amiss. Not quite as it should be. She had put the kettle on. She was no good at food. She left all that to Alan. She put the TV on, but paid no attention and wandered about the flat. When she got to her study and, out of habit, turned on her desktop, she was intrigued. Logging on, she saw it there. A simple e-mail from Alan:

I am leaving. Jo and I are hopelessly in love.

Now, in the morning, facing the tube ride from Highbury and Islington to Victoria, she had pretty much overcome the shock. All night she had tossed and turned, trying to understand what Alan had done to her. She was in tears and wracked with much self-doubt. What had she done wrong, where had she hurt him and how? What was to happen to her life on her own? What of the flat they had bought together on a joint mortgage? Why had this happened to her, and why now? There she was, all of twenty nine, looking forward to a long relationship with a caring man, perhaps to have children with and marry in good time. What would she say to her mother?

As the crowded and hot Victoria line train speeded from one station to the next, the anger was just beginning to rise inside her. Jo, of all the people! She had no idea Alan was gay. Their sex life, while never volcanic, had been normal, and Alan had always said he loved her and found her attractive. Jo, that fresh faced Cambridge lad—a Double First and Boating Blue—had been recruited to the Policy team 'for photocopying and coffee making,' as Alan had said. Why would he take Alan away from her? Alan had talked of how nifty Jo was in their weekly game of five-a-side football. She had thought that all that Alan's friends were capable of, even while playing their boyish games, was to bore each other about the latest transfer of a football player and the salary he had negotiated. Sex in the after-game showers among Whitehall high-flyers! Whatever next?

9.05 a.m. London

Ian never got into the Underground if he could help it. Despite a lifetime in journalism, however, he was still not used to taking taxis and charging expenses either. It all came from the penury of his childhood and his early experience in journalism. His first proper job had been with the Manchester Guardian. In those days, that staid newspaper was deeply imbued with the values of C.P. Scott, its greatest editor. Thrift and idealism were the watchwords. As a fresh graduate from Oxford, he was added to a small army of leader writers…that was the old class divide. Graduates wrote leaders, and those with just a school certificate or even less education went out to gather stories. Writing editorials bored Ian silly. So he had chosen instead to go out into the field as a newspaper reporter. The job of a journalist was a noble one but badly paid. Good pay and fat expense accounts were to come in his later years. His first home was a bed-sit in Kilburn. He had now graduated to Hampstead where he and Hilda had a five-bedroom house in Frognal, a five minute walk from the Hampstead Heath tube stop. Yet he walked all the way downhill to the bus stop at the bottom of Pond Street and took the number 24 bus to his destination.

It was too early to go to work, especially for a man who had retired from active journalism twice already. After all, it was not as if this was America where they had working breakfasts. Ian had loved being the New York correspondent for *The News* but never took to those early hours. Life had to be lived at a more gentle pace. But they still called him up for special assignments and Party Conferences or at times when the younger set had failed to deliver due to a hangover from alcohol or worse. Mustn't grumble, he said, as he cursed young Marcus who had become Deputy Editor in charge of Letters and Obituaries. Not hot stuff but then he had to be found something to do as he would inherit the paper when Old Marcus popped off.

Could Ian come and do an obit of the PM? No, no there had been no accident, no news. Just that he had not updated his obituary since Harry White became PM. Yes, he was only forty five and not remotely likely to die soon. Yet Marcus liked keeping to his new fangled system, his Automatic News Updating System. Ian could, of course, input the obit from home, but he was not on the network. Ian did not even have a laptop. What a pity!

9.30 a.m. London

Getting angry was not very professional, Sarah told herself. Not even on the crowded, smelly Circle line in which she had to travel the two stops to Westminster from Victoria. She began to think of the day and the week ahead. That was her Monday-on-the-Underground routine.

Life at 10 Downing Street was quite hectic anyway but nowadays it had acquired supersonic speed. Parliament was frantic this week but, in any case, Harry White did not care much for the House of Commons. As the PM's diary secretary, Sarah had to be well-informed about his movements. She was just a minor cog but in a machine that was fascinating as well as scary. When the PM was in London, life was busy but easy. It was when he was abroad or going from one summit to another, dropping by only to repack, that life got really tough for Sarah.

She was now at Westminster and was propelled out by pushes from commuters eager to alight. The bright sunshine hit her. For once, she would have preferred the day to be gloomy and overcast to match her own mood. But then, she thought, maybe my day will be upbeat and happy. She was surrounded by people who all seemed to be buoyed by the nice weather. Hundreds of Whitehall civil servants, foreign tourists and idle Londoners with nothing better to do than shop and stroll converged on Westminster. There was a Babel of languages being spoken by the snakes of small children clutching their guides, being hectored by their polyglot teachers as they gawped at the Big Ben and turned left towards the Westminster Bridge. The smart-suited civil servants showed no curiosity about the sights and turned right to their various ministries and offices. Sarah had her own route. She turned left out of the station and then left again along the Embankment. Now on firm ground and with the river air inside her, she began to regain her poise. The familiarity of her routine was reassuring. Some things in her life hadn't changed. Her job, her daily commute to the job, her own special way to her office. This way there were fewer pedestrians and a sight of the Thames. She walked along the Embankment and then passed through the narrow gap between the Norman Shaw building and the Ministry of Defence. Few used this gap but it allowed her to emerge on Whitehall just across from Downing Street. This way she could say a silent hello to the great generals whose statues adorned the ground of the Ministry of Defence. There was Montgomery, the hero of Alamein, whose enormous statue caused as much controversy as the Field Marshall did throughout his life. There was Viscount Slim, the hero of the Burmese campaign with his jolly jaunty hat which cheered Sarah every time she saw it. Poor Walter Raleigh was also there. Sarah always felt a bit sorry for the Elizabethan hero, since his statue was tiny compared to the other two. Was he being punished because he brought tobacco from America to England?

She could, if she was careful, take a slight detour and cross at the traffic lights. But Sarah enjoyed scrambling across, dodging the traffic and ending up exactly at the iron gates guarding the Prime Minister's house and office. She slung on her security pass round her neck. There were a few people stopping by the gates but the policemen on duty kept them moving along. She said 'Good Morning' in as cheerful a voice as she could manage. They waved her through with a smile. Her usual self-consciousness at the privilege of working at such a posh address swept over her. She may be only a lowly secretary, but the opportunities at 10 Downing Street were not given to everyone.

She had landed the job the first week after the new government was installed. After many years in opposition, the new team in power did not trust the old staff to keep their mouths shut. They were paranoid about the tabloids picking up gossip. They needed loyalists they could trust. Sarah's political sympathies were known to her friends. After all, she had first met Alan at a Labour Party dinner in Islington. She had gone along with her flatmate Judy who was active in the Party. It was a way of raising funds for the Labour Party while having good food and fun. The dinner was at Fredrick's in Camden Passage. Michael Cramer, the Leader of the Labour Party, was the Chief Guest. Judy had known Alan at University and introduced them over pre-dinner drinks. They had shared a large table and got talking. When Alan won a dinner for two with Michael Cramer at the House of Commons in the raffle, he asked Sarah to go with him.

Bloody Alan. Would she run into him today? The thought almost choked her.

From the iron gates, the walk to 10 Downing Street is longer than it looks on TV. In the old days, before the IRA security scare led to the iron gates being set up, there would be visitors to London standing along the pavements waiting for a glance of someone famous coming or going. Children would be having their picture taken in front of the famous black door of No.10. Now the street was deserted except for the few people who worked at one of the offices. Only when there was a Press Conference or some dramatic development like a sudden Cabinet resignation would the place be crowded with cameras and journalists.

It was an odd choice for a house for the head of the government—or rather, the First Lord of the Treasury as the plaque on the door told the world. A large shapeless house stuck in a cul-de-sac off Whitehall where tall and stately buildings stood next to each other. As a building the house had no merit whatsoever. Why did the Prime Minister not have his office in the Banqueting Hall across the road? Now there is a building, Sarah thought, with a beautiful painted ceiling by Inigo Jones and spacious rooms. But then, history was full of odd quirks, since Banqueting House was the place where Charles the First was beheaded. He had made Parliament angry and they had revolted. Oliver Cromwell was the Parliament's outstanding leader. George Downing, the man who gave the street its name, had helped Oliver Cromwell defeat the tragic King. Then, as an astute politician, he changed sides after Cromwell died and his son proved an incompetent successor. So George Downing helped Charles the Second get back to the throne and earned as his prize the large plot with the buildings standing on it. More trouble followed, as within thirty years of the Restoration, the Stuart line ran into trouble with James the Second, Charles the Second's brother. He was a Catholic and thus not to the liking of the Parliament. He began to give dispensations to the Catholics from laws passed under his brother's reign. Something had to be done with him.

This time Parliament did not hang the King but only deposed him. The nearest successor was Mary, James's daughter, whose husband William was a Dutch Prince.

So William of Orange was brought across from Holland to take the throne of his wife Mary's father. But they died childless. Mary's sister Anne, who succeeded them, also left no heir. So a minor German prince, George from Saxe Coburg Gotha, descended from the Stuart's female bloodline, was invited to be King. Seventy years after George Downing had been given the house, another King, George the Second, offered the property to Robert Walpole as a personal gift. But as the first modern Prime Minister, Walpole had a sense of history. He told the King he would only take it as the perk of his office as the First Lord of the Treasury, not as his own property.

In the eighteenth century, not many Prime Ministers followed Walpole's example. They were aristocrats and had large mansions in London and houses in the country. But there were exceptions. The hapless Lord North, who lost the American colonies, lived there as Prime Minister and would not quit even after he was sacked. William Pitt, who became a MP at the age of twenty one and Chancellor of Exchequer at twenty three, had nothing better than his chambers in Lincoln's Inn for living in. He told his mother he would love to live in 'the best summer town house possible' if only the Lord North would vacate. He only wished for a part of the big house. It was only when he became Prime Minister a year later that he began to live there and spent the next twenty of his twenty four years there. No one had lived there for a longer period since.

So at times the Chancellor of the Exchequer lived there, and the Prime Minister at other times. Some

Prime Ministers like Pitt and Gladstone of course combined both jobs. Gladstone did not like living there to begin with when he first became Prime Minister, preferring to live in the more elegant Carlton Terrace. He gave 10 Downing Street to his Private Secretary, Arthur Godley, who spent his first few years of married life there. For this kind favour, Gladstone was rewarded by the young bride Sarah Godley with a large cup of tea and a slice of bread and butter every time the Cabinet met. The rest of the Cabinet had to watch Gladstone's evident enjoyment with envy.

After Gladstone, no one tried to do the two jobs at once. The Chancellor of the Exchequer began to live at No.11 while the Prime Minster lived at No.10. This arrangement was not conducive to harmonious neighbourly relations. In most cases, the Chancellor was a rival of the Prime Minister who, in his turn, suspected the Chancellor of trying to oust him. Thus in almost every Cabinet, the two could barely stand to speak to each other.

Harry White had revived the practice of holding both the portfolios. He had seen how every government in the previous thirty years had been wrecked by the rivalry between the Prime Minister and the Chancellor. At first, everyone thought he would fail at it. But Harry's early training as a Cambridge economics student had stood him in good stead. Yet he retained the tradition of having an enemy as his neighbour. Terence Harcourt had been his rival in the leadership contest and was sore at losing to Harry. To keep him happy, Harry created a brand new department Terence could head. Given Terence's pro-European leanings, this was to be the Department of European Affairs and Terence was to be the first Secretary of State of this new Department. To boost Terence's ego further, Harry threw in No11 as a consolation prize. Harry tried his best to live next door to Terence Harcourt though he loathed him. Luckily for him, nor did Terence like Harry as a neighbour so he kept his family in Edinburgh and used 11 Downing Street only for his receptions and dinner parties.

Sarah remembered that Terence Harcourt would have been en route to Vienna with Alan in tow. Alan was Harry's favourite economist. Harry had hoped to have him advising on Treasury matters, but Terence knew how vital Alan would be in the European negotiations. So he insisted on having Alan as his Special Adviser; a bag carrier, as Sarah used to tease Alan. So the boys' brigade would be off to Vienna.

Did Terence know about Alan and Jo? Did he, an uxorious man if ever there was one, madly in love with his wife after all these years of marriage, approve? Would the papers find out and make a fuss? No one cared in these tolerant days, Sarah thought. Bonking someone else's wife was much more scandalous for a politico than a gay liaison. And Alan was not a politician, but a Special Adviser. So perhaps the tabloids would leave him alone.

It would be an easier day at 10 Downing Street as Harry White was leaving soon after lunch to go to Glasgow. He never liked the place, neither Glasgow nor Scotland. But the elections for the very first Scottish Parliament were looming, and he had to show he was willing. Then came further requests for a popular gesture. Could he be at the Old Firm game—the Rangers Celtic Derby—which was taking place today? Harry hated football and he kept himself away from all the persistent talk about football matches which politicians indulged in. He had no favourite team to follow and paid no attention to scores and positions in league tables. He was a cricket fan. Indeed, had it not been for his myopia, he could have played for Cambridge. But ever since England won the World Cup in 1966, football had become a popular sport even with the middle classes. MPs had to follow the fortunes of their local team and be seen to be fanatically supportive. They tried to get some local publicity by putting an Early Day Motion in the House of Commons congratulating their local club for some recent victory. No Early Day Motion had any chance of being debated so it was a fatuous exercise. But that did not stop them.

But most towns had only one team so the MPs of that town could agree, despite political differences, to back the team. In big cities like Birmingham, Manchester, Sheffield, they had two teams, often bitter rivals of each other. So MPs had to choose which one to back and the rule was, you followed the club whose ground was nearest to your constituency. Glasgow was the same. It had the Rangers and the Celtic football teams, bitter rivals along sectarian lines. So Glasgow MPs had to take sides between the two teams. The Old Firm Game was just what it said—a very old tradition, and in many ways Scotland's version of tribal warfare between two sides, one Catholic and other Protestant. Harry was not looking forward to this. There had been much twittering about his Catholic inclinations. He had taken communion recently and there were always rumours that he might become a Catholic. So the match was even more fraught than usual.

'If anything goes wrong, Gideon will have his head chopped off,' Christine had said. As the Secretary of State for Scotland, Gideon Crawford was an obvious candidate for the fall guy if Harry was to have any trouble in Glasgow.

Christine Brown was the brains in the PM's office. She knew everything before anyone else, perhaps even the results of last night's five-a-side football game, and told Harry sooner than the rest. She was fiercely loyal and had been for the fifteen years they had worked together.

10.00 a.m. London

Ian was astonished yet again, as he went over the newspaper files, at how slowly Harry had started, but how fast he had accelerated since the previous election in which his Party had lost. Checking his previous drafts of the obit, he could see that had Harry died in an accident ten years ago, he would have hardly rated a column. Young MP, worthy but dull career, climbing steadily. After the usual stint as Parliamentary Private Secretary (PPS)—the most junior job as bag carrier to some Minister, even worse when it was just a shadow minister, not even the real thing—then in the Whips' office, he had just become Shadow junior minister on the Treasury team. His lucky break had come when Stan Davis, the Shadow Chancellor, had to be in hospital for a few days. He had fallen while climbing Snowdonia.

Stan was a mountaineering enthusiast and, despite the obvious dangers, he refused to give up his hobby. England did not have any serious mountains for climbing but he had climbed the Ben Nevis in Scotland. He wanted to do the same with mountains in Wales and so Snowdon was his objective. On a wet foggy day, he made the attempt, lost his step and fell. He was out for five weeks. Harry had to take over at short notice and proved brilliant. All the economics he had forgotten since his Cambridge days came back to him. His chance came on the weekly Treasury Question day. He had prepared well for this. He tripped up Roscoe Hartley—the lazy incumbent Chancellor—in a question about the yield curve. They may not have grasped the subtleties of the economic argument on the benches behind him, but they had laughed and cheered and thrown the order papers in the air. Harry had arrived.

The Party kept on losing the elections, however. Their leader Michael Cramer had tried his best to make the Party popular again but the Press remained hostile. The Polls were favourable as never before as the General Election approached, but at the last moment there was a surge of support for the Government. It was all due to a scare about taxation and budget deficits.

Michael could never understand economics and, at the Press Conference which launched the Manifesto, he got into a tangle about whether his Party would raise

National Insurance contributions. Poor Michael. He was a real horny-handed son of the soil—or rather, coal mines. He had a romantic view of the Welfare State. As far as he was concerned, the 1945 Labour Government had single-handedly established it. His father had been a miner, and the nationalisation of coal mines had saved his life. He was able to get a good pension and health care for his emphysema. For his father's generation of workers, National Insurance contributions meant a weekly stamp purchased and stuck on a card. This told the world that the man had been in paid employment and had paid his contribution towards the State so he could get his pension. For Michael Cramer, the world had not gone beyond that, although he had not done a day's manual job ever. To a modern generation, it was just another tax on income and no one licked stamps onto their cards any longer. All Michael could talk about was how his dad had always paid his stamps, and how these contributions were the backbone of the Welfare State. He missed the point of the question, which was whether his Party would raise taxes if it was elected.

So, when he was asked point blank whether that meant an overall rise in the tax burden, he said 'yes'. Then, he denied it, as he had been told by his spin doctors to do. The result was confusion and denials and retractions. He was savaged by the broadsheets and humiliated by the tabloids. Stan Davis was furious. All his efforts to establish the Party's credentials as 'a friend of business' were nullified. The label of a high tax, anti-business party stuck. When the Government squeezed back in with a majority of twenty five, everyone blamed Michael for blowing the election. He had to resign.

Stan Davis became the leader, Harry was promoted to the Shadow Chancellor position. Terence Harcourt resented that very much since he was senior to Harry by a decade. It was he who was the darling of the Annual Party Conference, and got elected to the National Executive Committee (NEC) with more votes than anyone else each year. Terence bit his tongue and bided his time. Stan gave him the Deputy Leader's job.

Terence reckoned Harry would regret the promotion. Being the Shadow Chancellor was not the best job, not in the Labour Party, not while the Party was in Opposition. It was more of a poisoned chalice. The Party was imbued with old fashioned thinking about taxing the rich and higher public spending. But the times had changed. Now Harry had to tell them that high taxes were unpopular and any spending they promised had to be vetted by him; and in any case, the answer was no to all their demands for more money for their pet projects. The normally genial Harry became a sombre person. It was a recipe for unpopularity. But Harry made a success of his Shadow Chancellorship. Here the continuing incompetence of Roscoe helped.

Harry acquired the reputation of a serious economic thinker, thanks of course to Christine. She had used all her charm and old contacts at Cambridge to put together a team of advisers who fed Harry good material. Alan Carling gave up his job in the Faculty to come and work full time for Harry.

10.05 a.m. London, 10 Downing Street

'Bloody Alan,' Sarah said.

Christine put a sympathetic arm around her, but then neither said anything further. There was much to be done. The Rangers Celtic game was being played on a Monday rather than on Saturday afternoon which was the usual time. Weekday games started in the evening at 7.30 p.m. This one, however, was starting fifteen minutes later at 7.45. What with a reception and a dinner afterwards, Harry would not finish till after 11. But Harry being Harry did not wish to spend the night in Glasgow. No matter how late, he wanted to go straight to Belfast. There was still trouble between the Protestant Loyalists and the Catholic Republicans, as there had been for thirty odd years if not the last three hundred. In Belfast, he had a breakfast meeting scheduled with officials and ministers.

The Irish Problem had haunted British governments for decades now. The Liberal Party under Gladstone's Prime Ministership had split when he offered Home Rule in 1886. After another thirty-odd years of trouble, Ireland was given independence but split into a largely Catholic Eire and the six counties of Ulster in the North which, predominantly Protestant, had stayed with the United Kingdom. The troubles did not stop there but abated for a while. Republican Nationalists wanted a united Ireland which meant a merger with the Irish Republic. The Protestant Loyalists wanted to continue the Union of Northern Ireland with Great Britain. As the ruling majority, the Protestants excluded the Catholics from jobs and housing. The resentment finally welled up in the 1960s. The Army had been sent in by Harold Wilson when he was Prime Minister way back in 1969. Yet off and on the sectarian violence had continued. Then secret negotiations began with the IRA who defended the Republican cause with guns and bombs. A ceasefire had been declared unilaterally by the IRA. Much hope was placed in an open democratic Northern Ireland emerging from a many-sided peace process. But it was a relentless saga. No British Prime Minister could afford to take his eyes off the Ulster question.

So Harry had to be in Belfast tomorrow morning. There was some rumour that the ceasefire, which had been in place for a few years now, could break down. There was a lot of anger among the Protestant loyalist paramilitary groups. They reckoned the IRA were being given special treatment. There were mutterings about Harry being a crypto-Catholic. Harry had to tread carefully. The Belfast meeting was meant to gauge the chances of a permanent peace agreement. For this, he needed cooperation with the Republic. So he would head to Dublin for a lunch meeting with the Taoiseach, his Irish counterpart. There had been good relations between Dublin and London for a while now, and the Americans were hoping that this might lead to a better life in both the North and South of Ireland. But at the bottom, this was a problem for a British Prime Minister. If the Northern Ireland problem was going to be solved by any British Prime Minister, Harry White was determined to be him.

Elisabet (no z, no h, remember or you are dead) could

not go with Harry to Glasgow and Dublin as she had to be at the dress rehearsal for her play. It was her own translation of Alfred Jarry's *fin de siecle* comedy, *Ubu Roi*, and she was directing the all-women cast at the National. The effort in getting a First Night on a day Harry was in town had meant a major crisis between 10 Downing Street and the National but they had sorted that out. Harry was to come back from Dublin tomorrow in good time for the 7.30 p.m. curtain rise.

Elisabet's diary was not their concern. She had her own staff who liaised with Sarah, but being temperamentally theatrical, they did not always appreciate political pressures. Everyone forgave Lisa her terrible friends because she was so stunningly beautiful and charming. All Sarah needed to know on any day was whether Lisa was in town or not, and if in town, available for the PM's outings or busy performing elsewhere. But Lisa was a trouper. She had clawed her way from poverty and her parents' messy marriage to go to Oxford and had done brilliantly—a First in English, and a play at the Royal Court before she was twenty-one. She and Harry had married quite young but had no children. Elisabet pursued her theatre career, despite much muttering by the Press and other politicians. She did not care. As far as she was concerned, she could combine her career and her duties as the PM's wife. And Sarah was certain Lisa could always be relied upon to turn up trumps.

10.10 a.m. London

Ian left the paragraphs on Harry's marriage for another

day. He was ready to do the politics in full detail, but not yet the chase through theatre reviews to write about Harry White's wife. There was so much to do. He was almost grateful that young Marcus had asked him to come in. He had just come up to the time of Harry's succession to the leadership after Stan's tragic death in the Alps in a second mountaineering accident. The shock was palpable throughout the country. Indeed many people were surprised to find that, even after fifteen years in the wilderness, the death of an opposition leader could bring forth such a widespread cry of anguish from all around the country. When voters had become cynical about politicians, here was one man whose loss was felt by many as if someone in their family had died. Newspapers gave acres of coverage to Stan's life and his integrity and probity as a politician. They mourned the loss of a potential Prime Minister. It was common agreement among the pundits that whoever succeeded Stan was guaranteed to win the next Election, whenever it took place.

Terence Harcourt just presumed that he would succeed Stan as he was the Deputy Leader. He insisted on staying in London and at the House of Commons. He wanted to be in the Chamber when tributes were paid to Stan. He sent Harry to collect the body, while starting his own campaign for leadership immediately. Harry knew why he was being sent away from Westminster but gamely agreed. This act of selflessness proved providential. He had hours of TV exposure as he was seen with the bereaved family bringing the body back. It was his face that appeared on the news headlines every time the clip was replayed.

So when the leadership election came, no one was interested in Terence Harcourt's experience. The Party wanted a new fresh face, the face they had just admired on their TV screens. It did not help that Terence's team tried to insinuate that Christine was in a ménage-a-trois with Harry and Elisabet. It was something about Lisa's parents being Polish refugees that never sat easy with the Comrades in the Party. Harry was able to reach for the high moral ground and refused to say anything about his own marriage, but instead had nothing but praise for Terence's family. That was clever because the picture of Dorothy and her three daughters was so cloying that it put people off. The time for the old-fashioned happy family had gone, and the trendy post modern marriage of Harry and Lisa was what people preferred. Life plays strange tricks.

Ultimately, the patrician Terence Harcourt lost to the young pretender. Harry was disturbingly handsome. Anyone who came in his presence felt the force field of his charisma. And there was more. It was when Harry began to speak that people forgot how young he looked. He could move mountains as well as Parliaments. They didn't care that Lisa never had the time to campaign nor that she was a Catholic. Harry won not only the leadership but, when the election came, he carried the party to a spectacular victory.

Once in office, Harry dealt with Terence Harcourt very deftly. He knew how much Terence cared for status and the perks of office. Europe was bound to loom large in any British government's life. The previous lot had skewered themselves on their split on matters European. Harry had promised a new deal on Europe with Britain at the centre of things, with a positive attitude rather than the Europhobia of the previous lot. So he created a special Department and made Terence Harcourt the Secretary of State for Europe. As Shadow Chancellor he had learnt that the Treasury could destroy Labour governments. So he hived off all European economic issues from the Treasury and gave them to Terence's new department. He gave all the foreign aid issues to the Department for Human Development that he also created. The reduced Treasury was thus manageable and he retained it for himself. Terence not only had 11 Downing Street but Harry gave him Dorneywood, the posh weekend residence, as well.

Any decent obituary of a Prime Minister had to have comparisons with previous Prime Ministers and an evaluation of the man's place in history. Ian did not think he had to do much on that. The poor man had hardly had two years so far in office. He had not done badly. Having Terence Harcourt on board who resented his very existence was not a recipe for a happy government. But Harry was his own Chancellor and made quite sure that Terence would behave himself by encouraging Alan Carling to become Terence's confidant. Terence was very pleased he had stolen Alan away from Harry.

There had been some controversy when Alan 'defected', as Ian recalled, but it was something got up by the hacks. In public, there was sweet unity in the Cabinet. Most of them had never enjoyed the fruits of ministerial office, being too young to remember the last time the Party was in power. It was only a few oldies like Terence and Gideon, who had been ministers then. They were the leaders of the Party's old mafia whom Harry had to watch.

Yet, once Harry became Prime Minister, it was pretty much life as before. Ian had seen them come and go. They always started with a lot of hope, a promise of renewal, an obeisance to the middle classes, a distancing from the traditional heartlands. This was the hopeful beginning. Ian well remembered Harold Wilson, who shared not merely his initials with Harry White, but also so much of his penchant for the new. They both had a gut feeling for the worries and hopes of middle England that was uncanny. Poor Harold Wilson's reputation had started high, but despite four election victories, ended up in the mud. Today Harry faced very little opposition within his Party just as Harold Wilson did in his first Government. But then had come defeat in 1970 for Harold Wilson, with much discontent and dissension among the MPs. Even when he won power back in 1974, Wilson did not enjoy either the authority or the popularity of his first years in office. Would Harry go the way of Harold? Ian wondered. Who still remembered Harold Wilson? he muttered to himself.

10.30 a.m. London, 10 Downing Street

Christine could, even now, after all these years, feel a tingle in her nerves when Harry came down from the flat upstairs to the office down on the ground floor.

She heard him coming and instinctively looked in the mirror on the desk to make sure her long blonde tresses were neatly in place. She had put on a pale yellow shirt with golden highlights which went well with her hair and her favourite scarf which set off her smooth fair skin and her almond eyes. She knew he noticed what she wore everyday at work, but, even if he had not, she wanted to show him her best side. He always stopped by the various offices and said hello. It was a small gesture but it made all the staff feel valued. The first stop of course was Christine's office. He was, as always, impeccably dressed. He had remembered that his day in Scotland meant no blue suit, no blue tie. He was in a pale Armani shirt, with a Versace tie which had hints of red rather than pink in it. He gave her a peck on her cheek as he always did, putting his arms around her. This was the routine. This was the limit while they were in public. Christine's office door was always open so she could keep an eye on what was going on around the place. As she watched everyone else, her office was like a fishbowl. So Harry stuck to the minimum. Then he moved on to other offices.

He said hello to Sarah, and asked how Alan was. Sarah just made a face, and shrugged. Harry moved on, but he did make a note that Sarah looked quite fetching that day.

Christine gave Harry a couple of minutes to settle down in his office, to log in and check his e-mail. Then she knocked gently and went in. Harry looked at her and said, 'Nice scarf.'

Christine blushed. She had put it on specially because it was his present for her when he came back from Italy, on his first visit as PM. This was not his first present to her, nor even the latest. But Harry's first visit to Italy as PM meant a lot to Christine, whose father, Piero Bruno, had come to England from Italy soon after Mussolini made his pact with Hitler. He knew then that as a Communist his days of freedom in Italy would be numbered. He still spent his war years as an enemy alien working as a hospital orderly and that is how he met Lydia, who was a nurse. After the War, they got married, and Piero was able to resume his academic career as an economist. Their first and only child was named Cristina but then when she went to Cambridge, Cristina Bruno anglicised her name. Yet things Italian were close to her heart, but then, so was Harry.

Harry did not let her dwell on the compliment but merely asked, 'What's with Sarah and Alan?'

'He has left her for Jo, that young Blue from Cambridge.'

'Alan? Never knew he was gay—well, there's a surprise for you, isn't there?'

'Yes, but it only puts him more in Terence's grip, doesn't it?'

'Terence could hardly blackmail Alan after what we know about him,' Harry said.

'You still believe that old canard?'

'I have heard nothing against it yet. Thank heavens no one has raised it. But then Chris would physically beat them up if they dared.'

Terence's PR man, Chris Mott, had an awful reputation. He had been a bouncer in his youth before he got into the trade union movement. He fancied himself as an amateur boxer, especially when he was not sober, which was frequently the case.

Christine did not even smile. She had no time for Terence and even less for Chris. She did like Alan though. I hope he is not totally lost for us, she thought. But there were more urgent things. This was their quarter of an hour, every morning, to discuss the day's agenda. Christine handed Harry the brief on the Scottish situation. It was all there, down to the number of times Celtic and Rangers had played each other and the outcome each time and the cliché jokes which he would no doubt be told ad nauseum. He had to be neutral and not be seen cheering either side too much. This was easy for Harry, since he preferred cricket anyway. Still, it would be better for his image to look as if he was interested in the match.

'Has Gideon got any special problem with this visit?' Harry asked.

'Nothing special. Just the normal problem that we were only five points ahead of the Nats and you saw yesterday's poll. They are catching up fast. Gideon was crap on Today, and of course, he is universally hated inside the party there.'

The Scottish Nationalists were a big problem for Harry's Party as they were pushing for total independence for Scotland rather than just devolved power. They were also a Left party, full of radical policies and posed as the leading alternative to the Labour Party.

'Why is that?"

'Well, he did rat on Terence when he voted for you

in the leadership election'.

'He says he voted for me, but how can I be sure about it?'

'That is what he says.'

'Would you trust him?'

Christine raised an eyebrow, but remained quiet.

'I think he may have voted for neither of us. He was hoping for a second round in which he would run himself. Remember, Gideon's grandfather narrowly missed being leader. He wants to reclaim what he believes is his heritage.'

'Over my dead body.'

'Or mine,' Harry said.

Christine was superstitious and she immediately reached for the cross she always wore and said a silent prayer. Harry got out of his chair, came around and held Christine in his arms. Without a word, he kissed her eyes and then her mouth. They had not been this close since before Harry and Lisa went on their vacation to the Seychelles.

'Why are you not wearing your new contacts?'

Christine's question was a gentle but firm way of getting back to businesslike behaviour. Ever since the leadership campaign, Harry's myopia had posed a problem for his image-makers. At that time he had refused to give up his thick bifocals and dark black frame. But, slowly, his dedicated spin doctors tried to wean him off his thick glasses. They got him varifocal lenses and rimless frames. Still, they thought his blue eyes needed to be shown to their full advantage. So his team asked him to switch to contact lenses. He hated them. He kept on losing them; his nightmare was dropping them on the floor and having to scramble around looking for them. They finally got him disposable contact lenses. But still, while he was in his office, Harry liked wearing spectacles.

'Later,' he said, 'when we are within camera range.'

'But will you remember?'

'You will be there to remind me if I don't.'

'No, I am not in the Scotland party today.'

Harry looked at her quizzically.

'Too much to do. We haven't yet sorted out the pile from Easter and I must start work on coordinating the various bits for the Queens Speech. If we don't start...'

'Rhubarb.' He put his finger on her lips. 'You are afraid, aren't you?'

'Not afraid, worried.' Christine always felt that every time she was seen in public with Harry, she had to be sure no one would gossip. Their public relationship had to be seen to be strictly professional. An overnight trip together was fraught with danger both due to her own weakness and the ever vigilant tabloid press looking for dirt on Harry. No one had forgotten how the Press had hounded Harold Wilson for the way he listened to his secretary Marcia Williams about political matters. There was not even a whiff of an affair between the two, but still there were endless stories about whether she had power over him and why. Harold Wilson became paranoid about these stories. He came to hate the Press but could never ignore it. One had to be careful that Harry's relations with the media did not go that way.

'Well, don't be. But I will let you off this time.'

Christine was almost at the door when Harry asked, 'So, who is coming with me?'

'Well, Oliver of course. But Gideon said he would bring a team from the Scottish Office to brief you.'

Oliver was Harry's Press Officer. He was clever and ferociously loyal. Harry could be quite sure that his trip would be well flagged in *The Scotsman*, *The Herald* and *The Record*. Oliver would no doubt tell him much more about the mess he was going to face in Glasgow.

11.00 a.m. London

Scotland, Ian thought, would show whether Harry White would end up as a great Prime Minister or not. As an Englishman, Ian held the simple view that nothing would ever make the Scots happy. They will always want more and hate to pay for it. Harry had little choice in the matter. Stan Davis had sold the pass when he became leader. He had needed the Scottish votes to win and so he had come to an arrangement with Terence. Scotland would have its own Parliament with a First Minister. After Stan's death, Harry could not go back on the promise. So one of the first pieces of legislation that Harry proposed was a Scotland Bill giving a limited autonomy to Scotland. There would be some areas such as Health which were devolved entirely to Scotland and others were shared, such as Agriculture and Rural Affairs. Scotland even had its limited freedom to change the basic rate of income tax up or down by a few pence in the pound. The trick was to give

Scotland some autonomy without going as far as creating a Federation in the United Kingdom. Whatever the demands of the Scots, Harry was convinced that the Union of Scotland and England forged way back in 1707 by Queen Anne could not be broken up. That is what the Scottish Nationalists wanted and every other Party was against. So Scotland got a nice deal about the amount of public spending, much more generous than England or Wales. That way Harry hoped in the first elections for the Scottish Parliament coming up in the autumn, his Party would get a majority. He may not like Scotland but it was vital to win it. He was willing to do a lot, even go and watch a football game, to win Scotland.

Anyway, it was time for a break. Ian had worked solidly for nearly two hours and made copious notes. But he was dying for a smoke and in these modern times that meant that he had to go out of his office. It was either the Cafeteria, which he could not face—what with its plastic chairs and formica tables—or out of the building. It was hot outside but at least there was some fresh air, unlike in the office. So that is where Ian found himself lighting his cigarette.

What he did not wish to find, however, was Rodney Page, an addict of news and gossip, a constant fixture in what was once Fleet Street. Rodney had made the rounds of practically all the London newspapers. He had never wanted to do anything else. Neither radio nor TV had any attraction for Roddy. The once handsome large face had now become ravaged by too much drink and too many late nights. Yet the thump he gave

Ian's shoulders was hefty and startled him.

'What on earth are you doing here, Grandpa? Shouldn't you be sitting on a hot beach in Costa del Sol at your age?'

Before Ian could even open his mouth, Roddy put his arms around his shoulders and Ian found himself dragged to the pub next door. The Raven and the Bat was the local pub for journalists working on *The News*. Every newspaper had its own favourite pub where the journalists would hang out. In the bygone days when the printing presses used hot metal, the printers were an aristocracy in themselves and would not drink where their middle class colleagues did. Fleet Street was full of pubs and each had its distinct clientele. Now with computers and online printing, there were no printers to hold publishers to ransom by striking at the final hour and going off to the pub in protest. Newspapers had moved away from Fleet Street. Now offices were clean and so were the employees. The pubs were also modern and more like cafeterias. The Raven was an exception. It was in the Long Acre. It was still a large pub with large Viennese mirrors and some lovely old prints of Victoriana. There were pools of sunlight where there were tables by the large window facing the main road outside. Away from that front, the pub was dark and cool. Roddy left Ian at the sunny side while he went to order the drinks. It was too early to drink but Roddy was not one to take orders from anyone. Ian got a large malt whisky with Roddy booming in his ears—even in an almost empty pub.

'So what are you up to, you miserable lefty troublemaker?' Roddy had known Ian for many years but never forgave him his radical past.

'Young Marcus has asked me to come and touch up the PM's obit.' Ian did not rise to Roddy's bait about his old days.

'What's happened? He has not, has he? I didn't hear.' Roddy was looking agitated.

'No, he is alright. This is just a routine updating. I expect Harry will be around, man and boy, for another few years. Who knows, he may even break Maggie's record of ten years as PM.' It was Ian's turn to wind Roddy up.

'Now there is a depressing thought early in the day. Is there no hope of getting rid of Harry? Is there no chance of an internal revolt on the backbenches? God, the Party is so gutless and the Opposition isn't any better. Perhaps Nature will do its magic work and he will have a heart attack. Maybe someone will take a contract out on him, you reckon?' Roddy's imagination began running away with him.

'No one is going to kill Harry White and he is unlikely to have a heart attack, though I admit that is more likely than a party revolt against him. As for the Opposition, they are all still in denial.'

'God, politics has become dull. Mind you, even if you get rid of Harry, there is hardly anyone you would find to put in his place.'

'I thought you were a Terence Harcourt fan.'

'Me? Never.' Roddy was emphatic.

'You mean not for the last twelve or fifteen months or so. Didn't you write a fiery article in his favour in the

Spectator at the time of the leadership election?'

'They pay handsomely at the *Spectator* and all they wanted was to foment more trouble in the People's Party.'

'That is what they used to call the Party. Now it is the Pretty People's Party. So what are you up to nowadays, Rodney?'

'Investigative journalism: consultant to his Lordship for his many newspapers.' Many journalists referred to Matt Drummond as Lord Drummond as some sort of in-joke. He owned the largest selling tabloid, and the oldest Establishment newspaper, plus a television channel. That was just in the UK, but he also had a media interest in Europe and America. Since many newspaper owners had titles, people began to refer to Matt Drummond as Lord Drummond to join the gallery of Lords Beaverbrook, Rothermere, Thompson. As an American and a Republican, Matt Drummond neither cared for a title nor did he qualify. He wanted influence, not titles, and to buy influence, he was willing to spend money. Roddy was quite happy to come by some of that money to help him along.

'You mean, gossip columnist anonymous.'

'Dirt digger and muck spreader more like. Gossip is much too pleasant a name for what I do. But the money gets better, the shoddier the news. I must give you lunch at Nico's in Park Lane.'

'You have gone upmarket, Roddy.'

'It is the expense account that my Lordship affords me. Fancy a bite today?'

'I better stick to a pint and a pasty. I have work to do.'

'Oh, don't be such a miserable old sod. Look, young Marcus will pay you twice as much if you knock off now and come back another day. He would never dare insist that you work after lunch as well.'

Ian was tempted. He had done the basic work, but he had been short on the colourful bits which might come in useful and Roddy was bound to know some. But still, a three-hour lunch at Nico's, even if Roddy was paying, was bound to wreck his regime. He thought guiltily about his Significant Other. Being a GP, Hilda never stopped warning him about the need to avoid rich foods and heavy lunches. But he convinced himself that this was really in the line of duty.

'OK, but only if you give me the lowdown on Harry to use for my obit.'

Roddy was about to say something when he felt his pager vibrate in his pocket. Taking it out, he looked at it, his face serious, and said to Ian, 'Stay here. I must make a call. Back in a tick.'

With this, Roddy put his pager back and pulled out his mobile. He went to a spot just outside the pub. Ian could see him. Roddy looked grim, but excited. His eyes kept shutting and suddenly his head would shake. Ian could lip read to the extent that he guessed Roddy was at the receiving end of some juicy gossip. Ian could also see that there were others who could not abide *The News* cafeteria, and were now trickling into the pub desperate for a smoke. Ian waved at one or two, making clear that he was happy sipping his whisky alone.

He saw Roddy hailing a taxi. Then, as he was about to get into the taxi, Roddy seemed to remember that he had left Ian behind. He rushed back in.

'Sorry lad, must hasten. Something big has come up. This is going to be the grandmother of all bust-ups when it hits the fan.'

'Tell me quick.'

'No way. This is mega. This is the sort of stuff that Cabinet crises are made of. Tell you later. And I owe you a double lunch next time I see you. Cheers.'

And with that Roddy rushed off at a pace Ian thought was athletic. Saved from a large lunch he did not quite want, he abandoned his whisky. He went back to his labours with the life of Harry White. Try hard as he could, he could not guess what it was that took Roddy away so suddenly.

11.30 a.m. London, 10 Downing Street

Christine turned around and said, 'Would you like Sarah to come with you? It would give her good experience and cheer her up.'

'Not a bad idea,' said Harry. 'Can she get ready on time?'

'I am sure. I will get her on the tarmac. The rest is up to you.'

Christine gave Harry a look as she went out. He just smiled. He had a crowded day as usual and no time for decoding Christine.

No sooner had Christine departed than Oliver burst in. He never came in gently, never knocked and certainly never wasted any time.

'OK, item one, the no-hopers of the Keir Hardie

Group want to see you, mainly to talk about US policy in the Middle East. You agreed before going off on the hols. Mistake then, waste of time now. Fob them off. Next is the completely disastrous Pamela, your Culture Secretary.'

Oliver spat out the words, Pamela and Culture. Harry wasn't quite sure which he hated more. Pamela Meade had been the failure of the Cabinet. Harry had been warned about Pamela's competence but then she had been crucial to his campaign for leadership. When the women MPs had accused him of being a chauvinist pig, Pamela had stood up for Harry and swung the sisters around. Then there were only nineteen of them; now there were one hundred and forty women MPs. Pamela had airbrushed out his chauvinism and a softer, gentler Harry, devoted to his wife, had been constructed. They loved Harry—all hundred and forty of them, or at least the new recruits did, since the older bunch, now labelled the Seven Sisters, had seen through Pamela's ploy.

The one thing Harry dreaded was tears and Pamela always threatened to flood the place. Harry looked at Oliver helplessly.

Oliver chuckled.

'But thanks to the Libyan crisis, you have to be in a video conference with the Presidents of USA and France and the Secretary General of NATO. So, if you want, we can tell Pamela to get lost—very gently of course.'

'But she will come back.'

'Yes, but tomorrow is another day. You are in Belfast

in the morning and then you go to Dublin in the afternoon. Then you are at the play at the National. Luckily it is a short play. There will be a reception but we have made arrangements, so you can pop back at Division Time, if you wish. So Pammy can only see you in the Division lobby. OK?'

Harry went into the House of Commons as little as he could manage. But every evening at ten o'clock there would be voting on some of the day's motions. As a motion came up, those in favour would go in the Aye lobby to be counted by the tellers. Those against would crowd into the No corridor. This ritual brought the Party together and gave many backbenchers an opportunity to see Harry or some other Cabinet Minister whom they wished to importune for some favour, a job or some contract for their constituency businessmen. That was one reason why they all voted the way their whips told them. Maybe not all, but most of the loyalists in any case. There were some perennial trouble makers in Harry's party, such as those in the Keir Hardie group, but thankfully Pamela was not one of them.

'Then I can sack her from the Cabinet in public.'

'I will hold you to that.'

Oliver was one of the few, and Christine was another, who knew the real Harry. Even Elisabet was not on that list. It had all started soon after Harry got into Parliament. Oliver had been sent to do a hatchet job on new MPs by his Editor. He had all the chips on his shoulders—no university education, not even A levels. Left school at thirteen, went to a borstal and as soon as he was eighteen, he returned to prison. It was there that he was obliged to put in some time working in the Prison Governor's office. This changed his life. He was trusted, given responsibility. He had to sort out the incoming post, open it and make separate piles according to subject. He also had to arrange for the letters going out to be posted with the appropriate stamps so he had to practise his literacy—to read and write. He came out and got a job at *The Herald* as a messenger boy. From then on, he rose fast, moving from one to another paper till he landed a plum job with the *Daily Mail*.

Oliver was expecting Harry to be a stuck-up toff, with his public school and Cambridge education. He had read up what he could get on him. But, on the day of his interview with Harry, it all went pear shaped. Oliver's car broke down. It was raining and he couldn't find a taxi. Then, as if by miracle, Harry was driving by on his way to meet him at Westminster. He saw Oliver and gave him a lift. Oliver was surprised that Harry even knew what he looked like. Harry just turned his car around and took Oliver back to his terraced house in Clapham and helped him dry out. They even matched shirt sizes. Oliver was not only well dried but also restored with a good malt whisky. He saw in Harry the mark of a real drinker to have good malt whisky available. From then on, Oliver was sold on Harry.

Harry was obviously pleased to have made Oliver a friend. He even helped Oliver write a mildly negative portrait which showed him to be not a fire-breathing socialist but a man fond of the theatre and good food and opera, which is to say, almost a Tory. The *Daily Mail* was not read by millions of women for nothing. Oliver and Harry managed to hit the G-spot, as it were.

From then on, Oliver and Harry conspired to build Harry as if he was the latest perfume—pretty, precious and potent to the real purpose—in the case of perfume, seduction and in Harry's case, power. The quiet, unassuming, obliging Harry was a hard ambitious plotter. Oliver was stunned to find out much later that Harry had been following him that morning of their first meeting—just watching his every step. Harry left nothing to chance. Even the bottle of malt whisky was the label Harry knew Oliver liked. He himself was a martini man.

Just as the polls closed after the last Election, Oliver had asked Harry the one question he had been curious about for a long time.

'Why did you join Labour Party, Harry? Didn't the Tories offer you a seat?'

Harry did not even smile. He accepted the question as a serious one. After all, he knew he was about to become Prime Minister, and Oliver was bound to be keeping a diary of all conversations and events.

'I looked at the position in 1980. I examined the age distribution of Tory MPs and then of Labour MPs.'

'No liberals?'

'I wanted power, not a warm bath. I saw that the Tories had a much younger age profile, full of Cambridge and Oxford graduates only a couple of years my senior. But Labour had many who had entered in 1945 or 1950 and were still around. They had come to power too soon and then couldn't stop quarrelling after 1951. Even when Harold Wilson brought them to power in

1964, they kept on fighting each other. I reckoned I needed at least two Parliaments to get near the top. The chances were much better among the Labour dinosaurs than among the prowling Tory cats. And then Maggie, bless her soul, gave me even more time.'

'So no ideology, then?'

'Only as an aftershave to stem the blood and keep off the true scent. I am after power, I want to do things. I can buy ideology from any of these think tanks which are full of sincere chaps. Cheaper that way.'

Oliver did not know if he loved Harry more than Christine did. But their love was different. Christine had sunk her emotional and physical energies in helping Harry get to the top from his early days as an MP. At Cambridge, they had been friends and briefly even lovers. But after graduation, they had gone their separate ways. Harry was not seriously into politics, much though he spoke in Union debates. Christine was a passionate socialist. He went to work in the City and she joined various political movements on the Left fringe. They lost touch. Then suddenly one day, years later, Christine got a call from Harry. He was going to run for Parliament and would Christine like to help him. Christine was surprised that Harry even knew where she was. But she was happy to give up her dead end job on the staff of *Tribune*. It was a small circulation Labour weekly but very much in the dissident tradition. There was never enough money to pay workers proper wages. They all worked for the cause, but no one could tell what the cause was. The paper monitored endless quarrels of various factions in the Labour Party.

After all, *Tribune* was born in dissidence when Stafford Cripps and Aneurin Bevan founded it in 1938. They had both been expelled from the party, only to bounce back as Cabinet Ministers and, in Bevan's case, even Deputy Leader. That was the complex maze of Labour politics. Christine was steeped in it, but quite happy to quit when Harry asked her. He valued her extensive network in the Party. She had other ideas. This way she would direct Harry to the left wing of the party, or so she thought. She became the core of Harry's staff, the first and the foremost. But working for Harry was for Christine more than just a job. She still had her political ideals, her pet dreams about reshaping society and Harry was the instrument. But Harry was more than that. Her fling with Harry at Cambridge had been brief but passionate. She was emotionally committed to her ideals and to Harry. It was not just a job for her; it was her life.

For Oliver, working as Harry's PR man and press officer was a superb career move. Like Harry, he had a sceptical, if not cynical, outlook on politics. He wanted the authority to control the flow of information in and out of Harry's office. He wished to make Harry invincible against attacks from the journalists. They were all reptiles. He should know. He had once been a reptile himself. Had he stayed in the media, he could have been editing a tabloid by now. But he wanted a change and an adventure. It was Harry as a person rather than as a politician who interested Oliver. It was a gamble that Harry could be at the top and when he got there Oliver would be at his side, indispensable for media control. They were of a similar age and even similar in size and looks. Oliver was a bit rough while Harry had a smooth baby face. Theirs was a great bond between two robustly heterosexual men, all smells of jockstraps, showers after the match, and whiskies and martinis to sink into late into the night and even till the morning after. Oliver knew all Harry's secrets, or at least so he thought. With Harry being such a charming bastard, you could never quite be sure.

But of one thing, Oliver was certain. If Harry had any scandals to cover up, it would be about women. Harry was a sex addict. When he was travelling in those early days, Harry couldn't keep away from prostitutes. He was hopeless. When the pubs shut, Harry seldom went straight to bed. Oliver soon told him to stick to escorts and avoid the floor mops in the back streets. And as Harry rose in the public eye, even that had to stop. So Christine always accompanied him if Lisa wasn't there. It was all very discrete. Lisa did not mind. She needed the security of Harry for her life and her career. Fidelity was not important to her. She had made it clear to Harry—no divorce ever. As a Catholic, she was willing to live with a harem of mistresses but not divorce. Christine was also Catholic. Harry was happy with the arrangement, so was Oliver.

Oliver's mobile rang.

11.45 a.m. London, 10 Downing Street

Christine went round to the cubby hole where Sarah sat. It used to be a broom cupboard in the old days, but

now that the staff in Prime Minister's Office had expanded, every bit of space had to be harnessed. So the
cupboard was now an office. It was enough for Sarah's
state-of-the-art computer, which sat at the other end
from the door on the wall-to-wall desk. Sarah was a
paperless office woman, no mess, no files. All in dis-
kettes, neatly arranged in a box. A slim, but expensive
glass vase with one rose in it was an interesting new ad-
dition. Christine wondered who had brought the rose
today. Alan always sent one over—perhaps he hadn't
cancelled the order.

Sarah turned around as Christine came in. Christine could see that Sarah had obviously tried, especially
today, to dress well as if to show Alan what he was
missing. Not sexy or vulgar, just someone you would
want to take to lunch in an expensive restaurant in the
hope of future favours to be bestowed.

'Hi. Sorry to disturb you but this is important.'

'No problem. How can I help?'

'Can you go with the PM to Glasgow and then on to
Belfast and Dublin. Back tomorrow evening?'

'Aren't you going?'

'I must stay and do the Queen's Speech stuff. It has
been mounting up. The Libyan crisis has taken up too
much time. I'd be ever so grateful if you could. It might
even be fun.'

'I'd be terrified. Who would be there? What would
I wear?'

'Nonsense. You know all of them. Oliver will be
there and Gideon with his gaggle of young Scots lads.
You will be in the Director's box at Ibrox and then at

the reception. Belfast early next morning and Dublin for lunch. Back in time for supper in London.'

Sarah looked both thrilled and petrified.

'But…'

'Oh, just go and buy some new stuff at lunch time. Charge it to us. Buy a suitcase as well, handy for such a short trip. We have all got to get used to quick changes. OK?'

'Oh yes.'

Christine smiled and turned to go when Sarah said, 'Oh, and thank you for giving me the chance.'

Christine's smile became positively enigmatic. Sarah's phone rang. She picked it up. It was Oliver.

'Can you come in for a minute, Sarah?'

'Yes, of course.'

Christine looked on questioningly, as Sarah quickly explained that it was Oliver. She was about to head off to the stairs to Oliver's office, when Christine said, 'He is in with the PM.'

Sarah had not been into Harry's office, except when he had a large formal gathering. She had no time to check how she looked. It would be too embarrassing in front of Christine, but then the latter did something very sweet. She put her arm around Sarah for the second time that day and whispered in her best French falsetto, '*Courage*'.

12.00 p.m. Belfast

The English think it always rains in Ireland. The French of course think it always rains across the Channel. It is a subtle form of one-upmanship. Sunshine civilised, rain backward. Yet today it was as bright and hot in Belfast as it was in London. But inside the Orange Billy pub, it was dark and cool. At this time of the day on a Monday there was just the one odd regular whose job did not start till after one o'clock. Alice Mason knew Derek and she also knew that he was about to do his delivery jobs but then one pint never did any one any harm, she thought. She had just finished polishing up the brass handles of the beer pump she would be pulling several times later at the bar. For now, her job was to tidy up and get the place ready for the crowd that would come in by lunch time. The door opened and there was a sudden brightness from the street which briefly came in but went away as the door closed again. When Alice adjusted her eyes, it was Kenny the young plumber from the Ardoyne. Kenny was hardly seventeen and had dropped out of his school. His dad used to be in plumbing before he got blown up in one of those quarrels which went on in the province. His uncle found Kenny his apprentice job as a plumber. Alice knew that, even so, Kenny's heart was not in plumbing. He had hardly lost his acne and with his pale skin and sallow hair he still looked a kid. She knew he was up to no good, but then she was not his mam, so why should she care? He asked her silently the question which she was expecting. She just nodded her head and pointed to the back where the staircase was.

Upstairs Kenny knocked gently on the door and a gruff voice said, 'Aye'. Inside, there was a long table, bare except for a revolver, in front of which sat a man who was clearly the leader of the four others who had gathered for some purpose. Those four were solidly built with clean shaven heads and tattoos visible to the naked eye. Their leader was of medium height and stringy. He had thin lips and lanky red hair. He was wearing a black shirt under a light grey jacket. On his right hand there were rings on the two middle fingers and one on the index finger of the left hand as well. On his open neck you could just see the beginnings of a tattoo which went over his shoulder.

'Kenny boy, did you get it?'

'Yes Red, I got it.' Kenny held out the rucksack he had been carrying on his back.

The man smiled.

'Good lad. Are you ready then to come with me?'

'I am looking forward, Red. It's not often I get to go to see a big match like this.'

'It is not just any big match, lad. It is the Old Firm game. It is our civil war against the papists in just another fashion.' Red was laughing now.

Ken produced an envelope from his rucksack. Red took it and examined its contents. There were airline tickets in it for the group of six people who had gathered. They all got up and started putting on their jackets silently. Each knew what he had to check he had it with him.

'We'd better give Kenny all the hard stuff. All the guns and knives and the dope you may wish to get rid of at the other end. He will go through security separately from us. His Nan works there so she will see us alright. Let's go.' Red was decisive as he led out the group. No one said anything as they got out of the back door of the pub, so the few more stragglers now giving Alice something to do wouldn't see them.

Red got into the driver's seat in the van. Safely away from any danger of being overheard, Ken asked,

'So what's the plan, Red?'

Red looked back and glowered at Ken. Ken realised that he had overstepped the mark. He was not supposed to ask such questions.

'Sorry, Red. Forget I said anything.' Ken's heart was thumping rather loudly.

The four others in the van just laughed.

'Don't you fret, lad. Red won't kill you. He is gentle that way with his kind. Not as if you are a papist,' Ritchie, who was large and obviously the man for heavy duty, said. He wore a blue flak jacket even in the heat and beneath, an open neck orange shirt.

'Well, as you are new, I should tell you something or we could get into trouble if you get caught on the other side and the bastards shake you out. You, Kenny, don't know the names of Eddie, Ritchie, Rob and Des if the Police ever ask you. You never met them until the game. You are all going to enjoy the game, the most glorious game in the annual calendar. It is us against them but in Glasgow and not here. Here we do it with bombs; there they stick to footballs. My purpose is a simple one. I shall not be so much watching the game as going after my quarry.' Red was expansive now.

'Don't ask who. He will tell you if he feels like it,' Ritchie warned Ken.

'No, I'll tell you. It is that bastard Harry White. He

is coming here tomorrow and as we now know he will be signing his surrender to the PIRA. He calls it a ne-gotiated settlement but we know he is selling Ulster to the boys down south. He has swallowed their prom-ise that they will decommission but he is a fool as we know. They will just hide their real weapons elsewhere. He canoodles with the boys in Dublin. I didn't mind for a long time. Each of them when they get in power in London starts selling out. That is till we lay down our marker and then they come to their senses. I thought Harry White would be just the same. But once he had taken communion along with that foreign wife of his, I knew he was beyond hope. He will be there tomorrow at lunch time after a meeting here, and if he gets there, that we can kiss Ulster goodbye.'

'Except that he won't get there,' Ritchie helpfully filled Ken in.

'Aye. I intend to stop that papist bastard in his tracks tonight… The time has come for some hard measures.' Red turned around as he said that and nearly drove off the road.

'Whoa, Red. Wait till tomorrow before we go off the road,' Ritchie shouted.

'Aye, lads. Tomorrow we will celebrate the decom-missioning of the Prime Minister.'

'Don't ask how lad. Wait till you see what Red has planned as part of the after-match celebrations in Glas-gow. You just make sure your rucksack makes it to the other side and Bob's your uncle,' Ritchie said.

Ritchie had known Red for nearly twenty years now. They had been in many scrapes together. They had been bloodied in the big strike when the Protestant shipyard workers of Belfast stopped any compromise of the London government with the nationalists. In those days, things were quieter than they got later. It was just the SDLP and they were a lily-livered lot. It was later that the PIRA got into the act. They were a seriously murderous lot. The only way to fight them was with gelignite and bullets. So Red became the leader of their gang. They called themselves Carson's Irregulars after his hero Carson who had saved Ulster from being swallowed by the Catholics. They freewheeled across the province as they saw their chances. Ritchie and Red had been in and out of the Maze a few times. They were marked men but they were also dedicated loyalists.

Redvers McGann had dedicated his life to the fight against the Catholics. He had grown up in Londonderry as a child and gone to watch the Apprentice Boys parades. They were glorious occasions and he wanted to be one of them when he grew up. There were also the Twelfth of July parades in Belfast which the Orange Order regarded as the climax of the year, almost as important as Christmas. Red's father, also called Redvers, had been accepted in the Orange Order and Red thought he would follow one day. But Londonderry became a difficult town for the Protestants to live in. The Catholics mounted their civil rights movement and soon the world began to believe their lies that his people the Protestants were bastards who were nasty to the Catholics. But the violence did not stop and one day, while he was quietly drinking in a pub, Redvers Senior was blown up. He was well known for his

Orange sympathies but few thought killings would be so coldblooded. So the McGann family moved along with a lot of others to Belfast. Red decided that it was no good belonging to the Orange Order and marching in parades. He had to do more than that. His people had to retaliate bullet for bullet, bomb for bomb, if their way of life and their province was to be saved. So he formed his own group and called them Carson's Irregulars. Just as Edward Carson had stopped the sellout of Ulster by the Asquith government eighty plus years ago, this time they had to repeat his success. What he did with his speeches and his Ulster Volunteers, they had to do again but this time with bloodshed and mayhem. As far as Red was concerned, every Catholic was a nationalist and thus his enemy. The news that Harry White was flirting with becoming a Catholic was proof enough for him that the man deserved to die.

Red drove on. He did not want to have another accident like he had just avoided. Getting caught in a traffic accident would do him no good. The RUC would love to lock him up even for a minor offence. They said it was for his own good but Red did not believe them It was not like the old days when you could rely on the RUC to protect their own people. Now it had gone soft. It was all performance pay and the diversity bullshit. Mind you, things had started going bad even before Maggie had gone. It had all to do with fear. When the bastards blew up the Tory Conference at Brighton, even Maggie relented and gave in to Dublin. Now it was galloping along at a very fast rate towards Armageddon. Red had to do something desperate. Something which would be as big as what the bastards had done to the Tories and generate real panic in the London mob. That way they would come away from their foolish ways.

He had to get Harry White somehow. When he heard that Harry White was coming to Glasgow and even to the Old Firm game, he could not believe his luck. Glasgow, and especially the Ibrox crowd, were his family. He would much rather get at Harry on the mainland than in Ulster. So what is wrong with a bomb deftly planted under the Prime Ministerial car? The INLA had managed to do that to Airey Neave in the carpark at the House of Commons; surely Red could manage it in the open parking lot at Ibrox. Especially with such a big game on so everyone would be watching the game and not the car park.

12.15 p.m London, 10 Downing Street

Oliver's phone had brought some good news but there were problems. Apparently, Matt Drummond was in town for just the day and wanted to lunch with Harry. Matt Drummond was not around London, or Britain for that matter, very often. He had to stay out to escape taxes, but he still kept a close eye on his empire. He had flown in from his yacht near the Balearics for the afternoon and he wanted to speak to Harry.

Harry was annoyed. He had arranged lunch with members of his Commission on the New Millennium. The Commission was Harry's favourite project. It was to give the British people a new ideology, a new map for the Millennium. It was another ploy to secure Harry's place in history. The Archbishop of Canterbury and the Chief Rabbi were co-chairs. The Duke had gracious-ly accepted to be Chief Patron. Andrew Merton, the Max Weber Professor of Sociology at the University of Cambridge, was to be its principal theorist. Maxine Murtagh was the token woman. She had spent her life in the probation services. Abu Obiah was the fiery Black poet whose streetwise pronouncements were popular among the politically correct. Barry Carrick was the David Hume Professor of Moral Philosophy at the University of East Anglia and a leading human-ist, just to balance off against the religion lobby. Harry had been looking forward to this cerebral gathering and now Matt Drummond had turned up.

But Matt was insistent. He had something urgent to talk to Harry about, and no, it could not be said on the phone. No, he was not free at any other time but lunch. No, he could not be in Glasgow, Belfast or Dublin. To-morrow he had to be in San Francisco. Matt was not to be denied. He had secretly funded Harry all these years. He had paid for all those escorts and undermined Ter-ence Harcourt's campaign by spreading rumours that he was a paedophile in his younger days.

That is where Sarah came in. Harry had his contact lenses on now so that his blue eyes could work their magic.

'Come in, Sarah. You know Oliver, of course.'

'Yes, Prime Minister... And...'

'Listen, Sarah, you have to do something special for Harry,' Oliver said.

'Hang on, Oliver. What were you going to say, Sarah?'

'Just a simple thank you for the rose you sent me.'

Oliver tried his best not to look at Harry. The bastard, he thought. Here we go again.

'Don't mention it. I just thought it would cheer you up after what Alan did. But Oliver is right. We are in a bit of a fix and I would like you to do me a favour.'

'Whatever you say, Prime Minister.'

'Oh, call me Harry, please. No formalities here. But you know, the lunch today?'

'With the Commission?'

'Yes. Can you cancel it?'

'Now?' Sarah looked at the big clock in Harry's office. There wasn't much time left. 'Of course, whatever you say. Though I am not sure I can find all the invitees to inform them.'

'Well, try your best. If they turn up, we will just have to send them away. But Sarah, it is very important that you don't tell them I cancelled it.'

'What can I say?'

'Well, the simplest way, though not the most pleasant for you, is to say that you got my diary wrong. Tell them any story you like but, if you don't mind terribly, can you say you goofed it up?'

'If you say so Prime… Sorry, Harry.'

'That's marvellous; look forward to having you with us on the Scotland trip.'

Finally the penny dropped for Oliver. So this was the new recruit.

'But…'

'What, Sarah?'

'I hope it won't go on my record.'

'Not at all. No one will mention it after today.'

12.20 p.m. London, 10 Downing Street

Christine saw Sarah coming out of Harry's office. Sarah was white as a sheet. Christine got to her door and silently waved her to come in.

'What's the matter, Sarah?'

'Well, I have to cancel Harry's—I mean the Prime Minister's—lunch.'

'Which lunch?'

'The lunch today with the Archbishop and all the other members of the Millennium Commission.'

'Why?'

'He didn't say. He said I was to tell them that I had got the Diary mixed up.'

'Really? But who is he seeing instead?'

'I was not told. I had better get on with it. There are many people to contact.'

'Yes, of course. Do you need help?'

'No, this is my job, I'm afraid.'

'Yes, of course. Anyway, don't stay on the phone forever, remember your shopping.'

'Well, who knows about that now...'

Christine was curious. What were those two concocting? Who could Harry be seeing that he was standing up the Archbishop and the Chief Rabbi? Something was cooking and Harry wasn't going to tell her. It was something that Oliver had obviously hatched. She was going to find out, but how?

12.25 p.m. London, The Slug and Lettuce, Docklands

The noise in the bar was deafening. But the noise was essential to Roddy's transactions. He was looking at some photos in the dim light thrown by the garish juke box. The Honourable Adrian Andrew, the seedy toff, was standing by with a sherry. He was tall and stood a head above Roddy. His lank, straw-coloured hair had not yet thinned, and his handsome good looks, once ravaged by drugs, were back since his detox. He had given up drugs and even hard drink; hence the sherry. Roddy was aware of Adrian's history and despite that still liked him.

Adrian was the younger son of Lord Summerfield. He had a title but no money. He went to Rugby because his father had been there and refused to learn much. On leaving school, he had an attitude but not much aptitude for anything. So he tried the City and then he tried exploring for oil and diamonds and had a go at running specialist tours of remote parts of the world. Nothing worked to earn him the sort of money he thought he was meant to have. But he had a lot of charm and met Rachel Stoner of the family which owned the Stoner supermarkets. She had signed up to one of his exotic tours of India. Rachel was devastatingly beautiful, a porcelain doll. She had a wild upbringing having been sent off to a finishing school in France after the usual routine of being expelled from several schools. In Adrian, she met her match for wild living. A maiden aunt had left her money in a Trust, with peculiar conditions attached to it. She had to be twenty one before she could get her hands on it, but only inter vivos. She could not pass it on to anyone else. So as soon as she was twenty one and could claim the money, she married Adrian and took off for travel round the East. Their interest was not in the religions or the arts but in the drugs they could buy, and they blazed a trail from Goa to Varanasi and Kathmandu and Bangkok. In India, one could freely get charas and ganja and bhang, all variants of cannabis. But soon they were into heroin in Kathmandu and by the time they reached Bangkok, cocaine as well. Rachel could not cope with it as well as Adrian. Her drug habit killed her before she was thirty. Adrian's life was in shambles. He had no wife, no money and no future. He had to do something to get himself out of the hole he had dug.

He came back to England and tried to make a living. He had picked up photography as a hobby when he was at Rugby. His family knew many of the rich and famous and he exploited his connections. He became a celebrity as a photographer snapping other celebrities. When the glossy magazines took off, he was in clover supplying them with pictures of posh weddings. He could get to weddings from which most ordinary fashion journalists were excluded. For a while he had spending money, if not serious wealth. But then his cocaine habit drove him to a crisis. He was referred to City Roads, a 24/7 drug rehab charity. It was located in Islington near the Angel tube station. A small outfit, it had a dozen beds in which to treat drug addicts and rehabilitate them. This was his saving.

He came out of rehab and found that the magazines did not want him back. It was one thing to be on drugs but quite another to be plunged into a crisis and need treatment. So he had to explore other avenues. This is how he met Roddy. There was a lot of money to be made, Roddy told Adrian, if he could get pictures of the famous in compromising positions. It was every paparazzi's dream to catch the famous singer with someone other than his wife or the police commissioner's car parked outside a brothel. Footballers were even better quarry. The newspapers paid enormous sums, multiples of what magazines did if they could run a scandal.

This is how Adrian became Roddy's instrument.

He knew that Matt Drummond had a total hatred of Terence Harcourt. The origins of this hatred went way back to the 1970s when Terence was a junior minister in the Board of Trade in charge of competition policy and he had thwarted Matt in one of his takeovers. Matt got what he wanted from the Tories who came back into power when the government fell but he never forgave Terence, who had refused a large bribe to bend Matt's way. Terence did not need the money, thanks to his wife's largesse and so could afford his left wing conscience. Matt Drummond began a whispering campaign against Terence. He had had a tip-off about some sexual peccadilloes of Terence but was short of evidence. Once Labour came back to power, Matt could not wait any longer He had let his papers hint for some years off and on that Terence was a paedophile. But then he went big with a full Sunday spread. Terence sued and the case was rumbling on through the courts.

Roddy had taken on the job of finding the evidence and this is where Adrian had come in. He promised he would get some evidence on Terence, though he would not say how. Roddy did not care about Adrian's methods or his morals. He wanted the bullet to get at Terence Harcourt. It was pay-off time.

'This is dynamite. But it is filth.'

'Yup. You buying?'

'I think so. Can I talk to the Boss?'

'Only from here. Now that you've seen the pictures, I can't let you out of my sight.'

'You can trust me, Andrew.'

'No way, if you can't even remember my first name.'

'But you have two first names, you bastard.'

'Be that as it may, you call your lord and master from here. And don't give me any bullshit about not knowing where he is. He checked into the Ritz at 11 this morning.'

'How do you know?'

'Never you mind. Call him.'

At that moment Roddy's phone rang. It was Christine. Roddy put a hand to one ear and shouted.

'What is it?'

Christine and Roddy had been lovers briefly long ago in their Stalinist youth when Christine was ready to go to Vietnam to fight for the Viet Cong and Roddy was the intellectual of their local branch. They never spoke of it.

'Is Matt Drummond in town?'

'Happens he is. Why is everyone interested in his

whereabouts?'

'Don't worry. Thanks. You're good as always.'

Christine rang off. Adrian looked at him with contempt.

'Now will you call that American toad and get me a proper price.'

Roddy had no choice.

12.30 p.m. London

As soon as Ian got back to his office, he ran into Edward Shorthead, the young tousle-haired editor of *The News*. Edward was of course young only compared to Ian. He had been in journalism for some twenty five years now. He had built a reputation for knowing how to combine quality journalism with some fiery political editorials. He had revived the fortunes of *The News* and made old Marcus very happy indeed. Edward was clearly agitated. He needed to speak to Ian.

'Ian, so nice to see you are here. Are you free for lunch?'

'Yes, of course, but is this not a little premature?' Ian made a hopeless gesture at getting back to work.

'No, I need a rather long chat with you. I will give you lunch at the Garrick. You are a member, aren't you?'

The Garrick was the club of the journalists and the actors and the media types. Located in a street with its own name, it had stood on the edge of the Covent Garden for decades. It was a convivial watering hole for its members who were partial to long, boozy lunches.

Ian had gone off the Club ever since the public fracas about women not being admitted to its membership. He had not minded till the issue had been raised but now he felt a trifle embarrassed.

'I do not like its misogynism,' Ian said.

'Oh sod that. I have to speak to you about this mad policy Harry White is pursuing about Libya. You know his mind, I am sure, and you were so brilliant on Vietnam, as we all remember. You can tell me how to think about it.'

Ian could see that he may have escaped Rodney's big lunch but there was no way out of Edward's invitation. Libya was beginning to look worrisomely like Vietnam did thirty years previously. British Prime Ministers had a weakness for things American and especially the White House, regardless of which party was in power. Which made sense, since American policy was bipartisan when it came to oil or the Middle East.

The Americans were always looking for cheap and reliable suppliers of petrol to drive their big, fancy cars. Towards the end of the Second World War War, they had made a deal with the Saudi princes that in return for American protection, they would supply oil for ever. Soon the entire Arab Middle East and North Africa was being used as a source of oil. The Arab princes and sheikhs were happy to pocket the millions of dollars that the Americans spent on petrol. Then came Colonel Gadhafi, who overthrew the King Idris of Libya. He was a fire-breathing Arab nationalist. There had been others like him before: Egypt's Nasser, for instance. They wanted to fight Israel and help the Palestine cause. Nasser was defeated soon enough but Gadhafi had oil and hence a guaranteed flow of money. Soon he was the leading anti-American Arab leader. When oil prices quadrupled in 1973, he just became even more of a nuisance. So Americans were looking for some way they could remove him or at least contain his influence. They were looking for an excuse to start a fight.Colonel Gadhafi, being what he was, did not make their task difficult. There was the sad killing of a young English policewoman, Yvonne Fletcher, outside the Libyan Embassy in London. It was suspected that the bullet which struck her came from inside the Embassy. Then followed the crash of Pan Am 103 in the Scottish village of Lockerbie where, again, Libyans were suspects. Even though attempts to have Gadhafi murdered came to nothing, they were pinned on the Americans, and promptly denied. And so it went on.

This long-running soap opera of Colonel Gadhafi and the USA was having another one of its episodes. The President was convinced that Gadhafi was trying to wean the Saudi princes away from the USA by getting them to endorse extremist policies. If the Saudis went against the Americans, the oil market would just explode. This was not a risk the Americans would take lightly. There were accusations of terrorist activity originating from Palestine but with Libyan financial support. It was a murky issue with many doubts about the bona fides of the CIA which was issuing the reports, naming Libya as the source.

But the Americans had little patience. They needed a casus belli one way or another. Then the military satellite picked up activities in the Libyan desert which looked suspiciously like preparations for a nuclear explosion. The Americans traced the nuclear connection to Pakistan where there was a sizable technological and scientific expertise. It was obvious that blueprints of nuclear bomb technology had passed from Pakistan to Libya. The CIA had picked up contacts in Zurich where the deal was closed. There was a clear need to do something quick and effective.

Harry White was in on the loop from the very beginning. Given the death of the policewoman Yvonne Fletcher and the Lockerbie connection, he knew that the British public would back him on any tough action regarding Libya. Some in the US State Department wanted to go to the UN Security Council. But Harry advised the President against that, since by the time the UN Security Council had a debate and came to its usual inconclusive resolution which would then be vetoed by France, China or Russia, Libya would have moved the facilities elsewhere and the element of surprise would be lost. He was urging immediate bombing of the site and facing the UN later. President Robert Royston (Rob Roy as he was called) was impressed by the UK Prime Minister's resolve.

'Come, there is no time to lose. I have told Andrew Merton we will meet him there. You know Andrew. Don't you?' Edward grabbed Ian by his shoulder and hurried him on.

'By reputation, though not personally. I read his book on Post Marxism way back when no one was even thinking about it. But since then I have only read him in the weeklies rather than between hard covers.' Ian was trying furiously to recall what he had read most recently of Andrew Merton.

'I think Andrew is one of the great thinkers we have today. Harry White has inducted him on his Millennium Commission. I guess he hopes Andrew will write the report for him.'

'If the Archbishop and the Chief Rabbi allow him to get a word in edgewise, you mean.' Ian had his cynicism in tact.

'They can do the three-minute package on Thought for the Day but surely not any sustained thinking. Doesn't God always get in the way?'

'So you think the Millennium Commission Report won't be just Thought for the Day over three hundred pages?' Ian was not letting go that easily.

'You have to ask Andrew that when we see him in a minute or two. Actually it is a happy chance that Andrew is free for lunch. He just called me. We go back quite a bit to our college days so we keep in touch as and when we have the time.'

They were in the hall of the Garrick now. Ian always thought that while the Reform had a better and bigger space on its ground floor where people could meet, its stairs were dark and dingy. The Garrick had a smaller hallway but a splendid sweeping staircase with brilliant portraits of the actors and writers of the past which gave it a very bright outlook. They were now getting up to the bar where you met up with your friends. In case your guest had arrived before you, even he would be found there. And so it was with Andrew Merton. He had clearly arrived earlier and found someone who was a member to buy him a drink. In Ian's view, Robin Capstone was an obsessive bore. Robin had a brief career as MP and even became a junior Minister in a previous Labour government. But his hopes of going higher up had been frustrated. He had lost his seat and no one had thought of putting him up for a Peerage. So he had recycled himself as a columnist and for reasons Ian could not fathom, editors and publishers went on giving him space to display his prejudices on any and every occasion. Perhaps the only thing to be said about Robin was that he could write 1200 words on any given topic in quick time and hard pressed editors love anyone who can do that.

'So you have found yourself a drink, Andrew. Thanks, Robin, for looking after my guest. You all know Ian, I take it. Ian what will you have? Robin, Andrew are you ready for a refill?' Edward took over the occasion in a commanding way. He was, after all, the host.

'Thanks for agreeing to meet me at such a short notice, Edward. A very strange thing happened. I was supposed to be given lunch by the PM and we were going to have a meeting of the Millennium Commission. And at the last minute it turns out his diary secretary, some daft woman called Sarah, cancelled it. Apparently she had got his dates completely wrong. Such bloody incompetence, I tell you. We have a lot to improve in our bureaucracy.' Andrew was quick to get that off his chest.

'Anyway, it is Harry White's loss and our gain, Andrew. I bet the food is far better here than at Number

10. Thanks a lot,' Edward said, collecting the drinks from the bartender.

'Mind you it could be like a diplomatic cold. I recall when Henry Kissinger was in Pakistan in the early Seventies, I recall 1971 but I could be wrong, there was a news item that he could not attend the dinner given in his honour by the then President, Yahya Khan, if I am not mistaken, and it turned out later that he had just hopped across to Beijing to meet Mao. That was the beginning of the Nixon Mao relationship. Mind you, had he gone without putting out a press release about it no one would have noticed. So he was obviously giving a signal, don't you think?' Robin could go on like that forever.

'Let us hope Harry White has not hopped across to anywhere far away. Shall we go to our table? Why not join us Robin, if you are not lunching with anyone in particular,' Edward said, much to Ian's dismay.

'You are a generous host and who knows, I will learn something from your discourse.' Robin fell in with them.

12.30 p.m. London, 10 Downing Street

The bastard. The filthy bastard. Christine was beside herself with rage. She had never liked Harry's arse-licking of Matt Drummond. It was not so much that years ago, the Drummond rags had attacked her active role in the Campaign For Nuclear Disarmament and pried into her private life. That had all been long forgotten. But Matt Drummond was a poisonous, evil person whose agenda was money, money, more money and

Matt Drummond. In the run-up to the election, Harry had suddenly shifted his media strategy and opened a hotline to Matt. This had led to a big split in the campaign team. Christine was for the first time ranged against Harry and on the same side as Terence Harcourt. But Harry had sweet-talked her around by taking her off with him on an eight day trip to the USA. Their 'honeymoon', as he called it. He had wined and dined her in style. Oliver had protected them ferociously, provided perfect alibis. Even the White House staff had been squared so they could spend a night together in the Lincoln Bedroom. The President was prone to such behaviour himself. He was the last to cast stones.

But when the sweetness continued after the election, Christine suspected that Harry's relationship with Matt Drummond wasn't just strategic. The bastard may actually agree with Matt. Christine looked for any chance to deflect Harry gently from Matt's clutches. She encouraged him to talk to other papers like *The News* and *The Guardian*. Harry would indulge her for a while but she could never be sure.

So Matt Drummond was in town and in such a hurry that Harry had cancelled his big lunch to be with him. What were they up to? Christine started surfing her way around recent news to pick up clues as to Matt Drummond's agenda.

12.35 p.m. London, The Slug and Lettuce, Docklands

'Two fifty,' Roddy said.

'No way. I want half a mil or there is no deal.'

'But we may not be able to use them. They are very close to the bone.'

'You will use them alright. You may not print them in your papers but that is your lookout.'

'OK. How about two fifty for use and three fifty if we publish them.'

'Don't be silly. You know you have been looking for this ever since your master shot off his mouth about this and you have Terry's cases pending against you. Now this lets you off the hook. Half a mil. You have his permission. I can see that in your face. So pay up. Take your cut from someone else.'

'But we must have the negatives and we must have exclusive rights.'

'Leave all that school boy stuff, Roddy. Where do I pick up the cash?'

'Come with me, lad.'

12.40 p.m. London, 10 Downing Street

There was just one more person for Sarah to find. The Archbishop was on his way to the lunch, but neither his pager nor his mobile was responding. But the brilliant ladies at the Downing Street switchboard were legendary in their ability to track people down. Finally, she got the message to him via the station announcer at Euston where he was arriving from Manchester. The Chief Rabbi and the Cambridge Professor were mildly cross at their schedule being upset but Sarah was profusely apologetic. The Very Important Persons turned out to be mortal, charming and flexible. Despite the lateness of the call, Sarah's charm and a promise to re-schedule the lunch soon finessed most of them. It was Barry Carrick (Hara Kiri as he was known to his less kind friends) who proved difficult to track down. His office thought he was at a seminar in University College London and would then come to Downing Street for lunch. But no one at UCL could help. His wife thought he was in Glasgow overnight and was not going to be at their Norwich home until late that night. He did not believe in pagers or mobiles and did not send or receive e-mails. As a moral philosopher, he said he could ply his trade with the same tools as Thomas Aquinas. All he had to do was think.

And cheat on his wife. Sarah concluded that this was a classic case of a man with a mistress sending contradic-tory messages to his wife and his secretary. The simple rule used to be that you at least did not lie to your secretary though you did not have to tell your wife the truth. Barry Carrick had gone one better. He had lied to both. The secretary, Sarah logically concluded, must be an ex-mistress.

It was five to one when Sarah gave up the hunt for Hara Kiri. Christine had said they would look after anyone who turned up for the lunch. Just having been inside 10 Downing Street would mollify their egos. She had to do something drastic to restore hers by buying some decent clothes in the 'lunch hour'. She tidied up her already tidy office, left an e-mail message for Chris-tine and dashed out the front door.

12.57 p.m. London

Harry and Oliver were going out via the back door. After some quick thinking, they decided to let the plainclothes security guard drive Oliver's car while they both slumped back behind smoked windows. They were to get into the Ritz by a side door and then up a service lift to where Matt Drummond was waiting for them.

2.00 p.m. Vienna/1.00 p.m. London

Alan was waiting for his lunch to finish. He had to be with Terence at the table where all the finance ministers were sitting with their advisers. The Austrians combined German efficiency with a French love of good food and wine. No one seemed to be bothered that they had a tough working session starting immediately after lunch. How were they going to cope with the thorny question of the budgetary implications of enlargement of the Community when they were nearly through their second bottle each, and the cheese course was only just arriving?

Alan wanted the lunch to end so he could steal a few moments alone with Jo again. Poor Jo. He had no status and so was eating in the cafeteria along with the junior officials from the Embassy, while Alan was in the closed-off posh area. Jo was a bit overwhelmed by his first European Union encounter. This, plus the suddenness of Alan's decision to leave Sarah for him, had made him giddy. Since the early morning, when they arrived at the VIP lounge in Heathrow till they got out of the car bringing them to the Imperial Palace where the meeting was, they could hardly bear not to touch each other, even for a second. Terence was quite liberal and let Alan sit with Jo, although they had to talk the policy through. Alan had promised Terence that once they got into the meeting, he would stay with Terence throughout the day. Alan knew all the highways and byways of EC/EU budgetary negotiations. Olives, he had told Terence, were going to occupy much of the afternoon. Cyprus had olives and so had Greece, Italy, France, Spain and Portugal. They wanted Cyprus in, but couldn't face the glut of olives which would result when Cyprus joined and began to enjoy the Common Agricultural Policy subsidies. They had exhausted all the jokes about extra virgin olive oil. What was in prospect was hard slog. Alan wanted the lunch over. Stuff the olives.

1.15 p.m. London, The Garrick

'So tell me now, Ian. Can you make any sense of Harry White's foreign policy?' Edward wanted Ian to sing for his lunch.

'Why? What is wrong with his foreign policy?' Andrew, ever the loyalist, asked.

'Don't start Edward on that one, please. We will be here till after dessert before he stops. In brief, Edward is upset about the impending crisis in Libya,' Ian interposed.

'Surely the crisis is not so much in Libya but somewhere in the Mid Atlantic. With our so called Special Relationship, I mean. Harry is not like Anthony Eden and likely to go on the wrong side of the Americans, though I grant you the Americans were in the right then, one of the rare occasions in post war years when they have done something right in the Middle East. But…' Robin was off on his excursus through history but Ian interrupted.

'You have to understand that Harry is a man who sees the world in black and white. There is truth, freedom and liberty on our side and out there there is nothing but darkness. His friend President Rob Roy is a cynical man and will use Harry as a shield if he can do so. So Harry thinks this is a Just War with Libya and Rob Roy wants to look after his Saudi friends and their ample oil supply.'

'No, I think you misunderstand our PM. I know he is aware of the Christian doctrine of Just War but that is beside the point. He is a man of rational analytical habits. He is immensely well read for a politician, I tell you. He was asking me the other day to give him references on history of Islam and of the schism between the Sunnis and Shia's… I am sure he knows what he is doing.'

'In my view, he is the most right wing leader the People's Party has had since Ramsay MacDonald. How he became a leader when we have a perfectly good and solid man like Terence Harcourt is beyond me. Why doesn't the party get rid of him? He just does what Matt Drummond tells him to do.'

'I think that is going a bit far, Robin. Even I, critical as I am of Harry White, would not agree with you there. I think there is something to what Ian says about a Manichean world view, all black and white, Good versus Evil,' Edward intervened.

'It is to do with his Christian beliefs…' Ian was about to explain, when suddenly Andrew said, 'Speaking of Christian beliefs, look who is here.'

The Archbishop of Canterbury was approaching their table to say hello to Andrew.

'What a rotten shower, eh? So you ended up here as well,' Andrew said.

The Archbishop shook his hand, silently nodding assent, and moved on to his table.

1.20 p.m. London, The Ritz

Harry said he would have a dry martini American style —very dry and with an olive. The waiter in Matt's suite came back with the perfect specimen of its kind. Dry with just a dash of vermouth and a fat green olive staring up at Harry from the bottom of the glass. Matt had his pint of lager, as always, and Oliver for once stuck to tomato juice. He had decided that someone had to keep his head straight.

'Cheers, welcome to London. How's tricks, Matt?'

Oliver thought it was best to start the proceedings.

'Awful. Margaret has decided to go public with our divorce and she is going to fight for control of King Korn and half of my assets.'

A split of his assets upset Matt more than the end of his 40-year marriage. He had known Margaret since their school days. They had married the day after they graduated and joined the radio station her father owned. Matt was a simple farmer's boy while Margaret was so-phisticated and urbane. Her father used to take her to Europe for their holidays while Matt had to help his dad out with the dairy cattle.

He used to miss Margaret and envy all of Europe while she was there. Someday, he had thought, I will get to Europe and show them.

And indeed he had. Working in the local radio sta-tion, he had showed a flair for business that surprised them all. He saw early on that even small towns in the American Midwest would have their own TV station. He worked out an ingenious deal with the local bank and its New York counterpart. He won a franchise from CBS for their local station at a hideously high price. But Matt knew that if he could have even two hours of local broadcasting time, the advertising revenue would make it worthwhile. He saw that it wasn't the thirteen-and-a-half minutes of programme that was the heart of TV, but the one-and-a-half minutes of commercials. So he added at first fifteen minutes of local news to the CBS news and then soon expanded that to thirty minutes. He helped Lew, Margaret's father, buy up other local TV stations or start new ones. Soon the revenues began pouring in from local business, dying to advertise on TV.

Lew Drew had no sons, only two daughters, of whom Margaret wanted to stay in Cutler City, Kansas, while her sister Cherry headed for the bright lights of St. Louis and Chicago. Margaret loved broadcasting.

She loved the arts, the music, the culture she could deliver from radio. TV bored her. She thought it was a shallow, brash medium. But she loved Matt and admired his business acumen.

Not as much as Lew did, though. In Matt, he had the son he always wanted. He treated Margaret much more like a daughter-in-law once Matt arrived on the scene. Lew was an old newspaper buff who had drifted into radio. Within five years of their marriage, Matt and Margaret had made Lew a multimedia owner—newspapers, radio, TV. It was only after Lew died that Matt ventured abroad. On their honeymoon in Paris, he had noticed how badly run the local radio and TV were. But they were state owned. So he cast about for newspapers to buy. To be on the safe side, he started buying up English newspapers—small town local newspapers, miles away from the glare of London publicity. These local sheets made money because of local advertisements. They had small staff for the local news stories, buying in a lot from the bigger services such as Reuters and AP. But there were more pages of advertisement than of news.

Then came Radio Caroline, the pirate radio broadcast from a ship anchored in the North Sea. This was the time of the Pop revolution with the Beatles and the Rolling Stones rocking the baby boomers. Radio Caroline could play non-stop pop, unlike the BBC. This broke the BBC monopoly of radio, and private commercial radio became big business. Privatisation was soon to become even more popular. On both sides of the Atlantic, the Conservative Revolution began to triumph in the Seventies. Matt took full advantage of all this. He was well known as a large donor to the Republican Party in America but also began to give secretly to the British Conservative Party. The Other Margaret came to be his sought after prize. He wanted to champion her cause and link up with her friend, Ronnie.

But Margaret, his wife and the lover of all Arts, especially music and theatre, soon came to see in the Free Market Philosophy everything that she disdained. She felt that provincial theatres and small town art galleries and museums were losing their meagre support. They had to beg for commercial sponsorship. Margaret had the money. The company was, after all, her father's and she had inherited it, though Lew had given Matt a thirty per cent share.

As Matt chased newspapers, radio and TV stations to buy, Margaret helped out small town repertories, struggling artists and writers... She put money in the Lew Drew Foundation. While Matt came across the Atlantic to buy up British media, Margaret came to admire British Theatre. She helped out young theatre companies by purchasing theatres and leasing them back at peppercorn rent. Matt made money, Margaret gave it away. Matt thought of money as one thing he never had as a farmer's boy in the Prairies. Margaret had grown up with money in every sense of the word. As she got older, her fortune got larger and larger. She did not know what to do with it.

But a shrewd instinct told her not to let her share in the Lew Drew News Corporation go. Matt begged and cajoled and finally persuaded her sister to sell him her fifteen per cent share. Matt thus owned forty five per cent of the company while Margaret, thanks to Lew, had a majority share. That was one thing Margaret would not discuss with Matt; she had no intention of letting Matt control LDNC or King Korn, as it was affectionately called in the Prairies.

Then Matt got obsessive about tax. He could not bear to pay income tax or corporation tax. He took up living on his yacht, El Dorado, shunning permanent residence in any one tax regime. Margaret did not mind visiting him, but the idea of living for the sole purpose of tax avoidance appalled her. They had no children to keep them together. They began to drift apart, meeting only when they were together on one of their many company boards.

'Why does she want your money? I thought she didn't care even for her own?' Harry asked.

'It is really sad. Margaret has cancer and knows she has only a couple of years to live. She found out about Asha. So she thinks if she dies and I get her share, it will all go to Asha and her daughter. She can't bear the thought. So she wants a divorce and half my assets. She wants to give it all away to charity.'

Asha Chan was the daughter of a Chinese father and an Indian mother from Malaysia. She was a bright young tax lawyer when Matt first met her and very much his match in her love of money. Like Matt, she came from a poor family, though much poorer than Matt could imagine. She wanted to amass a large fortune as soon as she could and strained every nerve to avoid paying tax. Tax law was not just a profession for her; it was her religion. She took up Matt's tax problems with a relish few could understand. The more complex the problem, the happier she was. She had rapidly risen in her Chambers, the first woman and the only non-English Barrister to reach the number two position. She lived in the Barbican to be near her work. Indeed, she would not have wanted anything else, not even Matt. But then her biological clock started ticking. Being an efficient, no-nonsense woman, she took the nearest man available. It just happened to be Matt, and, in any case, she was visiting him on El Dorado. Matt never had been a monk whilst living away from Margaret. When a beautiful, dark-eyed, half-Chinese, half-Indian woman hailed him near, he was more than willing. There was always the understanding that Matt would not divorce Margaret. Asha knew that; she concurred that the tax loss would be horrendous. She had her daughter Matasha and Matt stayed married.

Harry had known about Matt's pending divorce. Elisabet was a great friend of Margaret's and had told Harry how Margaret had promised her company a large endowment in her will. The prospect of Matt being left with only a couple of billion did not seem a tragedy to Harry. Still, he thought he'd better take an interest.

'So what are you going to do? Play for time and hope that Margaret goes before the divorce comes through?'

'Jesus, Harry. You are more cynical than I thought. But that is it. I have to fight it for as long as I can. I could do without the hassle. But to hell with this mess. Let's eat.'

A table had been laid for four in Matt's suite. As Harry was wondering who the fourth place was for, Asha came in punctually on the dot of one thirty. She was simply but expensively dressed in a purple Karl Lagerfield top and trousers that showed her dark skin to great advantage. She was not tall, but the long hair and the high forehead atop a compact torso gave her height. She shook hands with Harry and Oliver, pecked Matt lightly on the lips and sat down.

'To business then,' Oliver said.

'I want you to throw Scotland,' Matt said.

'What do you mean?'

'Lose the election. Let the Nats win.'

The Scottish Nationalists were beginning to irk Harry now. He had heard Gideon being grilled on the Today programme by John Humphrys. Now Matt was bringing up the same matter.

'Whatever for? That would be madness. What is more, it would cause a lot of problems among our Scottish MPs down here. If they lose up there, they will lose in the next general election. I doubt if we could keep our large majority.'

'Or any majority,' Oliver added.

'Well, it's like this. We have looked at the Scotland Act. Your mob is bound to put the tax up and go on a spending spree.'

Scotland's autonomy was rather restricted, since all the major powers were to be retained at Westminster. After much debate, the Scottish Executive was allowed to alter the basic rate of income tax by three pence in the pound up or down.

'And you think the Nats won't?'

'We know they won't. Their strategy is to cut the tax rate by three per cent. Spend the money and cause a budgetary crisis by running a deficit.'

'How does that help you?'

'Well, for one thing, your mob will also want control over the media and promote local, Scottish-owned companies. On top of that, they are still Old Labour and hate me passionately. Anything they can do to punish me for my support of the Poll Tax, they will go for.'

'But hang on. They can't just do anything they like. They are subject to Westminster.'

'Culture is a partially devolved subject and media will be covered by that. You retain the control of telecommunications down here at Westminster but that does not help me. What with a likely referral to the Monopolies and Mergers Commission down here, restrictions on cross board ownership up there and an extra three p in tax, I can't afford your mob in Scotland.'

'It is not easy to lose Scotland. In any case, my Cabinet will revolt. Terence especially. Scotland is his fiefdom. He wants his own man to be First Minister. Gideon is dying to have the job. He is all set to resign down here.'

'We calculate that a Labour victory in Scotland will cost Matt's group fifty five million pounds extra immediately and seventy five million pounds in steady state,' Asha intervened. She had listened quietly thus far. She now spoke with confidence and a clinical precision leaving little scope for argument.

'But I stand to lose my leadership to Terence, and

the next General Election to the Tories, if we lose Scotland.'

'Don't worry about Terence. We can take care of him.'

'What do you mean?' Oliver perked up.

'We have enough on him to destroy him. If we publish the stuff, he will have to resign immediately.'

'What on earth are you saying, Matt?' Harry was beginning to lose his cool.

'I will say no more. But if it is Terence you are worried about, rest easy. We can put him out of any leadership stakes overnight, as and when we choose.'

'You mean blackmail?' Oliver asked.

'No, just investigative journalism. Remember the motto of *The Herald*—Truth Holds No Terror For Us.'

'And when do you intend to do this?' Harry asked.

'As soon as we reckon you require it. Our only concern is to protect you when you throw Scotland as we would like.'

Harry was appalled and fascinated. Getting rid of Terence would make his life so much easier. He would lose a Cabinet Minsiter who was admired all across Europe but also a bitter rival who had never been a friend. Terence with his conventional marriage and his three snotty children had a lot of appeal inside the Party. He controlled Scotland and was laying careful plans to challenge Harry as and when he faltered.

Dorothy hosted a lot of parties at 11 Downing Street for MPs and their wives or partners. Dorothy made Terence send everyone a card on their birthday, even for their spouses. She remembered their children's names, and sent them birthday presents. Elisabet, bless her soul, had little time for the MPs or their partners. Her parties were full of actors, pop singers and sculptors—luvvies and druggies as *The Herald* called them. Losing Scotland would definitely lead to a challenge to Harry's leadership. If Terence were out of the way, then no one else would dare to challenge him. Harry was tempted, sorely tempted.

But then, he thought, why should he do Matt's dirty work any longer? He had received a lot of help from Matt, no doubt. It certainly would not do to have any of that easy provision of escorts for Harry to be made public. But now he was the Prime Minster with one of the largest majorities ever. Matt had no other friend in the Party and the Tories were in a shambolic state with the smarmy, oily Peter Portugal as their leader.

Harry tried to catch Oliver's eye but for some reason, Oliver was looking intently at his plate refusing to look up. Then Harry twigged. Oliver was not eating, but he had placed his knife across his fork. The message was clear—no deal.

'Sorry, Matt, I can't oblige you on that one. Winning is part of politics. Leaders have to win elections, especially big ones. This will be the first Scottish election and we owe it to the Party and Stan's memory to win this one. What I can promise to do for you is to see to it that they behave themselves. You will have observed that we have weeded out all the trouble makers from our candidates' list. We will bully them about taxation, perhaps make a promise of no extra taxation… But win we have to. The downside risks of losing Scotland are too high. Of course, we can never be sure that we will win but I have to lead from the front, whether I like it or not, and you know how I loathe Scotland and the Scots.'

Matt was disappointed, indeed, angry. He could never understand why politicians were so naïve. He had a perfect plan to get rid of Terence and shore up Harry's leadership in the Party. All for the price of a provincial election in which the turnout was bound to be under thirty per cent if the previous record was anything to go by. If the Nats were to win, they would follow an adventurous course but they would be completely ineffective. That would suit Matt; and if they got an independent Scotland, that was even better. The smaller the country, the easier it was to buy it... That was Matt's experience. So his plan could not be abandoned. He would have to bring extra pressure on Harry somehow. Perhaps the new dirt on Terence might be the trigger. For the while, Matt had to seem reasonable.

'Fair enough, Harry. Win some, lose some, that's what I say. I can see that you have to be seen to be doing your best. But I hope you won't mind if I don't wish you good luck on this one.'

'Fairly put, Matt. No hard feelings. I know how much you have helped me along the way, and within limits, I am happy to oblige as you know. I did help you on your German bid and put in a word with the President about your takeover bid for *The New York Times*,' Harry began to account for all his big pay offs.

'Don't mention it. I won't speak to you of Scotland again. There will no doubt be other fish to fry.'

There seemed to be little point in lingering. Matt was a spartan eater at lunch time and so was Harry. Oliver got on his phone and told the car to come round to the same place. They took off, leaving Matt and Asha together. Will they work out the tax consequences of the lunch at the table or on the four poster in the suite, Oliver wondered. His journalistic mind was always farming the news story.

2.00 p.m. London, Drew House, Docklands

Fleet Street had been abandoned by the print media; it was replaced by some beautiful tall buildings which had come up in the Docklands. Matt Drummond had commissioned a forty-storey steel and glass building as the principal location for the Lew Drew News Corporation (LDNC). It was designed by Norman Foster to look like a giant corn on the cob as a tribute to its Kansas roots. On the thirty-eighth floor of Drew House, Rodney Page was deep in an editorial conference with the editor of the *The Herald*, Alexis (Lex) Pritchard. Lex was Matt's friend; Matt had picked him up from a local newspaper in King's Lynn and brought him to London as his latest editor. Lex's main attribute was a total lack of taste or backbone. He was willing to do whatever Matt asked him to do. He even called up every day to check: Was Matt happy with the tabloid's front page, the nooky page and the editorial page, such as it was? Lex was proud of what he called his nipple count. He had to outclass his rivals in nude and semi-nude photographs every day; his four million readers depended on that.

But this time even Lex was taken aback. Rodney had brought in Adrian Andrew's photographs. He had cleared with Matt that they would pay the half million. The cash had been delivered early by the LDNC (UK) plc emissary in a smart leather case. Adrian had counted the contents of one pile and then the number of piles. He had worked in casinos and knew how to count cash quickly. He seemed happy and then without so much as a thank you, he swept it up and left. Lex saw to it that Rodney escorted Adrian out by the back door and that no one saw him.

Now there were just the two of them. The pictures were disgusting. How Adrian was able to shoot such intimate photos was something Lex could not figure out. Rodney seemed to be sure, Lex did not know how, that the pictures were authentic and not fakes. He kept on about the black mole visible on the hip and how he had seen that while playing rugby years ago with Terence.

'Jesus, we can't print these. We are a family newspaper.' Lex always had his hypocrisy armour on.

'The choice, as you know lad, is not thine to make. All we do is obey orders and it is the order we await. Our maker knows best and I am sure even at this moment, he is working out the answer.' Rodney was waxing biblical.

2.00 p.m. Strathclyde Police HQ, Glasgow

Chief Constable Douglas Mackie was looking forward to the evening. The Prime Minister was going to be in Glasgow and he would be there at the dinner this evening. He wanted to bend Harry White's ear about how wrong Glasgow's image was and how much it had improved in terms of crime, especially under his leadership. He had hoped he could have him tour one of the police stations but Harry White's timetable was too crowded for that. So the old Firm Game it had to be. Douglas was a rugby fan and Hampden Park was more his scene. Rugby fans were well behaved while soccer fans were animals. Hopefully today they would behave themselves though; if they didn't, his team was ready for everything. Superintendent Richard Erskine was in charge of the G district of Strathclyde Police's area and Ibrox fell in his hands. Richard was a fine officer and Douglas Mackie had nothing to worry about.

His phone rang. It was Richard Erskine himself.

'Richard, I have just been thinking how nice the evening is going to be thanks to your efficient control.' Douglas did not really wish to rub it in that it was he and not Richard who had been included in the dinner guest list, but he just could not help it.

'I am sure, Sir. I wanted to report that the RUC just called and told me that they have seen Red boarding the flight for Glasgow. You know, Redvers McGann of the Carson Irregulars.'

'Do you think he is coming to us at Ibrox?'

'Well, if he does, we will keep an eye on him. I will post his picture at every entrance to the stadium and tell our boys to be on the look out. He hasn't done anything as yet to be arrested, but we have to be vigilant. He is probably coming for the after game punch ups which will no doubt follow as night follows day. The game always attracts coachloads of supporters from Northern Ireland, as you know, Sir. But we are used to that. Leave it with me.'

'I always do Richard, I always do with full confidence.'

Now why would Red come to the game if it was not to cause trouble and what kind of trouble was he intending? Douglas prided himself on his University degree and he knew he had the superior brains of many around him. This required some serious thinking. It was not just policing.

2.15 p.m. London, The Ritz

Matt's mind was engaged on his business problems twenty four hours a day. It was no less so now, but not solely on his business problems. Within minutes of Harry and Oliver's departure, Asha had taken him over. Matt could never figure out how such a clever, brainy woman, Barrister at Law, First Class Honours from the LSE, knew so much about sex. When Margaret and he had made love in their young days many years ago, it was fast, hurried and quick. Just doing it was fun. They knew little about foreplay and knew of no positions except the only one they thought was not indecent. It was some years before Matt realised it was called the missionary position. By the late Sixties, when you could publish erotic magazines in the US, they had lost their sex urge or rather their urge to explore anything new. They were far too busy anyway and retired exhausted to bed. Matt never regretted this because sex did not interest him.

Until he met Asha. She was his junior by thirty years. He was old enough to be her father. Indeed he was older than her father would have been had he been alive. But Asha seemed to know precisely how to please older men, or at least, one old man. She knew all his hesitations, his fear of failure, and his seeming disdain for sex which arose from this fear. Matt used prostitutes when he wanted, but then he did not have to pretend with them and they did not mind nor would they talk. But Asha was different. She had this knack of love-making which seemed to last for eternity, but every time they did it in London on a normal working day afternoon, she never missed her next appointment. She would swiftly undress both of them and get him going exactly as she wanted. She played the little kitten, the lethal Lolita. Thank God Matt did not have a daughter. It came pretty close to incest the way they played their games.

Now his heartbeat had returned to normal. Asha was waiting for this moment and got herself out of his arms. As she picked up her clothes one by one and put them on, he watched her, free to think of other things.

'So what do you think, Ash?'

'Miserable sod. After all you have done for him.'

'But what about Terence and the pictures?'

'I say publish them. If Harry won't throw Scotland, let us help him lose. We publish those pictures and they can kiss Scotland goodbye. So Harry stays clear and we get Terence. Harry will come round in good time.'

'Do we publish or do we threaten Terence Harcourt?'

'Threatening Terence will only mean he will resign and the Great British Public will never know why. It will all leak out slowly and then you could hardly publish your evidence. We don't care about Terence. We want to lose Scotland and this is the best way.'

'Good thinking. I wish I could get that bastard Harry though.'

'But who else is there, if he goes as well? No one will elect Pamela now.'

'Yes, you're right. What a waste of money Pamela was. After all that we invested in her, she flopped as a Cabinet Minister.'

'I say embarrass Harry. Don't bring him down. Show him who's boss.'

Now in her full barrister gear, Asha gave Matt a deep kiss and left. Matt allowed himself a couple of minutes to recover from that sweet sense of exhaustion that comes after coitus. He had work to do. He got up.

2.30 p.m. London, Drew House, Docklands

Anthony Otto-Trevelyan was back from his lunch at the Garrick. He liked the Club and could rely on meeting other members of his profession. Thank heavens, it still excluded women or Elisabet White would be there. Today, by chance, he had a sudden and late call from the Archbishop to say he was available for that much promised, frequently arranged but cancelled lunch. Apparently Downing Street had stood him up. Some incompetent secretary had booked a lunch while Harry White was not free. The Archbishop could not stop talking about that for ages. Anthony tried to cheer him up saying the food was far better at the Garrick than at 10 Downing Street. He knew; he had tried both. But the Archbishop refused to be mollified. He was going to complain to the Cabinet Secretary.

As the Editor of the leading daily, indeed the Establishment newspaper, *The Daily Chronicle*, Anthony kept an eye on everything. He made a mental note to check on the PM's appointments. He smelt something fishy about such a sudden cancellation. But he was really interested in getting the Archbishop to write a three-part essay on Ecumenism and the Church. He wanted to know how he evaluated the Pope who had had such a long innings.

Now he was back, just getting to his thirty-sixth floor office in Drew House, the LDNC(UK) plc building, when he ran into Vera Drinkwater. Vera was an old hag, all tobacco-stained teeth, bulging eyes popping out of a horn-rimmed pair of glasses and a beaky nose to boot—but she was the nation's Agony Aunt and was paid a fortune (twice Anthony's salary) by *The Herald*. Vera, of course, insisted on kissing 'dear Tony'. Anthony could not stand such vulgar abbreviations, nor the unwanted physical contact. It was an affectation people had picked up from the French. Anthony had no time for the French. What could they talk about even on the short ride? Luckily Vera could not stop telling him about how thrilled she was to be invited to Elisabet White's opening night at the National and the party afterwards at Number 10. Vera loved Elisabet and just adored Harry and thought Anthony should stop being horrid to the PM. Anthony let out a deep sigh as he got out, leaving Vera to go up two floors more. Just then his mobile rang. It was Matt.

'O.T., I have some news for you.'

Somehow Matt could not call Anthony by his double barrelled last name and knew Anthony hated being called Tony (as did Vera, of course). So he had settled on O.T. as an abbreviation that was novel and at which Anthony had not been quick enough to take umbrage.

'Surely you are not going into journalism, Lord Drummond.' This was the one joke Matt allowed against himself.

'Listen, I want you to publish a simple factual report that the Prime Minister had lunch with me today at The Ritz. Don't make much of it, just report it.'

'So that is why the Archbishop had his lunch cancelled at such a short notice?'

'I would not know about that. You can spin that if you like.'

'What if they deny it?'

'A couple of grainy photographs of the PM getting into and out of a side entrance at The Ritz are on their way to you in a plain brown envelope.'

'Brilliant. Will do. Why are you back in London?'

'I am staying here for a couple of days, but that's not printable.'

'Understood.'

A small factual paragraph deep inside, maybe on the Parliament page and perhaps a diary item about the Archbishop's cancelled lunch. That would do the job, Anthony thought. The wise in the Westminster village would grasp the connection. Though he had better spell it out to Peter Portugal so he could use it at PM's questions. Being a Tory was hard work, Anthony sighed.

2.40 p.m. London, Drew House, 38th Floor

'Lex?' It was Matt.

'Yes, boss.'

'Go with it.'

'Do we tip them off?'

'No, let them see it in the early edition and then keep in touch.'

'Understood.'

Lex began to think he hated his job. He could see Rodney's eyes light up. That filthy gossipmonger. He thought about the front page and then a four-page spread with its sheer slab of purple prose. Then the editorial with its sanctimonious humbug about family values. Lex could do it in his sleep. He had better bring Vera into the picture or there would be hell to pay, since Vera was in charge of the nation's morals.

4.00 p.m. Vienna, The Hofburg

The subject of all this attention was bored. They had sat there for an hour now, the good lunch almost forgotten. Terence was sick of olives and all people who grew, stored, shipped or ate them in solid or liquid form. If

Cyprus was to be admitted to the European Community, the partition between Greek and Turkish Cypriots was the most intractable of their problems. In international law, only the Greek-ruled part of Cyprus had recognition as a legitimate state. The Turkish part was recognised by only Turkey. The rivalry between Greece and Turkey was age old and Cyprus was a bone of contention. If you look at a map, Cyprus is nearer to Turkey than Greece. But for many years Cyprus was a British colony and the rival Ottoman Empire had its capital in Istanbul. So the British kept the Turks out and let the Greeks flourish in Cyprus. Greece itself was a colony of the Ottoman Empire and became free only in the late 19th century. All the time Cyprus was a colony, Greece dreamed of taking over Cyprus if it could. But when it tried to do that after Cyprus became free, all hell broke loose. Turkey intervened by sending an army. When the fighting died down, Cyprus got divided into two, one Greek and the other Turkish. This problem had to be resolved before Cyprus could join, but that was so difficult that the negotiators decided to leave it for a while. As Committees are prone to do, they invented another problem which could be even more divisive issue. This was the problem of Cyprus olives.

Cyprus grew olives. Every country within the European Community received protection for its farmers from the Common Agricultural Policy. This paid farmers to grow whatever they did and bought off their surplus product. The farmers of course overproduced because the price they got was way above the world price of what they grew. So there were wheat and butter mountains and wine lakes. They were about to get an olive island. The only issue was who was going to pay. The cost of purchasing surplus Cyprus olives without taking any money away from all other olive growers of Europe was exercising their minds. Dark olives and green olives, olives on trees and olives in storage. Olive oil of various degrees of virginity.

The French and Italian delegations wanted all the adjustment to come from the Greek quota. But Greece was the poorest of the olive growers in the EC, its national income was below the incomes of Portugal and Spain. Ireland, thank God, thought Terence, was not able to grow olives. So the three poor countries wanted the two rich ones to bear the burden in a progressive way. The total output of olives—or even the unsaleable surplus—was irrelevant. The only criterion for burden-sharing had to be national income or, even better, national income per capita, since Spain had a large population.

Alan had already worked out the appropriate formula which would reduce surplus olives in the future without putting excessive burden on the EC budget. But Terence knew that the time for the correct formula had not yet arrived. Exhaustion had to set in first. After a long afternoon, with flight deadlines looming, Alan would broach that. The French and Italian ministers had to be back tonight or very early tomorrow morning at the latest. Our Man in Brussels had told Terence all this. Since they would eventually pay, the compromise had to be acceptable to them.

Terence did not mind, nor did Alan. They were staying overnight. Terence wanted to have a good excuse for being away when Harry was in his hometown of Glasgow. That way, if Harry made a gaffe, Terence could not be blamed. Harry's contempt for Scotland was badly hidden at the best of times. They had to vet his speeches, but even then, he slipped up when he ad-libbed. Such as the time when he told an Aberdeen audience how sad the whole country had been (he meant the UK, not Scotland—first fatal error) to see England not make it to the quarter final of the World Cup. Not a word about Scotland and its brave exit from the competition, so that it did not even qualify for the last sixteen. Or when he talked about Braveheart but could not remember William Wallace's name. Terence had to nudge Gideon, who stuck his elbow into Oliver's ribs to pass the message on. Harry then cleverly wove it into his speech. Honour saved all around.

So let him slip up again, Terence thought. He liked being in Vienna. It did not matter if the meeting finished late. Vienna was a twenty-four hours city. Terence knew about the open attitude of the Austrians. Their bars and their night clubs, the women out on the Gurtel in their fishnet stockings, unafraid, relaxed. It was a sexually frank society with no inhibitions and all tastes catered for. Terence looked forward to a prowl later of Vienna's night life. After all, Alan would be busy with Jo, so he was free to wander.

Alan, on the other hand, could not wait for the meeting to finish. He kept on looking behind him at Jo. Poor Jo. He had to sit at the back because that was what his position entitled him to. They could not sit together, next to each other and rub legs or touch each other, much less kiss. For Alan, it was pure torture. He hated olives, he hated Cyprus, he hated Europe.

Jo was fascinated. He had never been anywhere like this. He understood that in some irreversible sense, he had entered the inner sanctum. He himself might not be important but he was with important people. And important people had one weakness—they always wanted to be told they were important. They were afraid of being treated as ordinary, unimportant people. You had to stroke their ego as Jo had stroked Alan's ego. He could spot Alan's anxieties from early on. Alan was important, but not enough people knew that. Alan was forever worried that Sarah would treat him in some humiliating way in public. Not mimic him or anything, but just treat him like an ordinary person. Sarah had known Alan before he became important. Alan had tried to impress on Sarah how important he was by wangling the Downing Street job for her. Sarah, however, thought it was her ability that got her that job and a bit of luck. Poor Alan.

So Jo always made much of Alan, listened to his brilliant analysis of economic problems, his devastating pen portraits of the famous, his vicious gossip. And, of course, his good looks. Jo had to give that to Alan. They made a good pair. This Vienna trip was their honeymoon. He was determined to make sure that Alan would stay with him for a while. Jo needed a leg up in his career and now he knew who would give it to him. For a price.

3.15 p.m. London, on the way to the Inns of Court

As far as Asha was concerned, she had not as yet arrived where she wanted to. From the outset, every
time she had achieved something, the ground seemed
to slip away from beneath her. After a secure childhood in Kuala Lampur, she had lost her father when
she was just twelve years old. Her mother, Krishna, was
bereft, not knowing how she was going to bring up her
daughters.

Krishna was the only daughter of a respectable Tamil
Brahmin family of Kuala Lampur. Many poor Tamils
from the rural area of Madras Presidency had migrated
to Malaya, as it was known in the 19th century, to work
on rubber and coffee plantations. They came as inden-
tured workers but continued to live in Malaya, even
when they had been freed from their contracts. As they
settled and married and had children, these poor peas-
ant types needed their priests to perform the rituals of
birth, marriage and death. Krishna's great grandfather
had come for that purpose, and now after many decades,
the family had become prominent in the Indian community in Malaysia, as it was now called. She had gone
to college and acquired some proficiency in classical
Indian dance, as well. She had performed her aranget-
ram, a debut for Bharata Natyam dance, when she was
only eighteen. But soon after, she met a bright Chinese
firebrand. Chan was an eloquent speaker, a political
agitator and a very bright academic. Her family was appalled that their precious daughter Krishna had fallen
for a foreigner. Their hopes of getting her married to a

respectable boy from back home in Madras were shattered. Krishna broke off all relations with her family.

She married Chan and gave up her classical dancing and any thought of a career for herself. Chan was everything she could have wanted. They had to struggle because in a culture which punished any sort of dissent, Chan's promotion was always held back.

But their life was happy; their two daughters Seetha and Asha made up for all that they had lost.

Then suddenly Chan died. They discovered that he had cancer, and between diagnosis and death there were only three months. Krishna was left with her two daughters—Seetha who was just eight, and Asha who was fourteen. She could not possibly go back to her family. Chan's pension was meagre, and, in any case, as a widow she only got half of it. So Krishna fell back on the one skill she knew she had. She would set up classes for Indian dancing. There were enough aspiring Indian middle class families in Kuala Lampur for her to hope for something.

She went to see Natarajan, her former teacher. She remembered him as a strict but kind man, one of the new stars of Bharat Natyam in India who, for some reason, had decided to make his fortune in Malaysia. Whether Natarajan was his real name or a stage name, she never knew. Seeing him after nearly sixteen years was a shock for her. The slim and well-built man, whom she held in awe, had begun to lose hair and gain a paunch. Yet he was still her guru. He had taught her all she knew, and she had to get his blessings before she could start to teach.

Natarajan was pleased to see his former pupil. The young shy girl had now matured into a voluptuous woman. She was, of course, still in mourning for her husband, but Natarajan could not fail to be moved by her beauty. And so it started. He helped her set up her dancing class in her house. He promised to come once a week, which was a special day for Krishna and her students. They loved his teaching and, after the class was over, Krishna usually persuaded Natarajan to stay for a meal. She always cooked something she had bought specially for him. Lovely, plump, dark aubergines or tender, green beans. She would grind fresh coconut chutney and cook his favourite tamarind rice. Krishna was popular as a dance teacher but she gave all the credit to her teacher. Natarajan became a regular visitor. He got to know Asha and Seetha, as they hovered around their mother, helping her.

Asha was now a blossoming young woman at fifteen. She could sense her mother's guru eyeing her. She refused to join the dancing classes, despite his frequent invitations. Krishna was surprised by her daughter's reluctance but Asha explained that she wanted nothing to distract her from her studies. She was getting a small scholarship that paid her fees and helped her buy textbooks. Krishna was happy to agree. Asha's bit of cash often paid for their food at the end of the month when the money had run out.

And then, their quiet life erupted into chaos. Seetha fell ill and Krishna had to take her to the doctor. It was Natarajan's day to teach, so Krishna was reluctant to go. But she knew that it would take a while to get to the doctor and then wait there till Seetha was seen to. There was a bus but it was not reliable. Krishna would have to go even while Natarajan was teaching. But she prepared all the ingredients for his dinner, left it to Asha to do the final cooking so the food would be freshly made and piping hot. She had taught Asha how to cook so she was not worried. Asha had come home from school while the class was still going on. She let herself into the house quietly in order that Natarajan would not have to interrupt his teaching and come to the door. She quietly went to the room she shared with Seetha and changed out of her uniform into her usual simple dress of a blouse and a petticoat—both rather short as she was growing up fast. She went into the kitchen and did the things as her mother had taught her. The food was ready by the time the class was over. Asha heard the girls taking leave of the guru. Now was the time for his meal, and all she had to do was to prepare to serve the guru. She laid the thali, the stainless steel jug and cup of water. She took out the pickles and the precious ghee. There was the small mat on the floor on which he sat. She would serve him sitting on low stool nearby. She did everything as she had seen her mother do. Then, she went into the living room where the class was always held to call Natarajan to come and eat. Just like her mother used to.

But when she got there, he suddenly grabbed her. He had loosened his dhoti and he fumbled with her clothes. Asha pushed him away and this made the guru lose his balance and he fell hitting his head on the floor. He let out a howl. Asha was appalled seeing this large man as she had never seen him before. For one, he was naked beneath the waist and then he was lying on the floor in some pain. Her instincts were to help him and so she bent down to give him support. But as she did that, her hands brushed his body, and, to her astonishment and fear, she saw his huge stiff penis rise up from beneath a lot of hair and brown skin. He grabbed her hands and made her hold it. It was hot and throbbing and somewhat oily. His face contorted into a strange expression. Only much later she was to understand that this was pleasure and a desire for more at once. But, on that day, she fled into the kitchen, sobbing.

All this could not have taken more than three minutes. Asha was stunned, confused. Frightened. She tried to get over her sobbing by fussing with the pots and pans. She drank some water but her heart was still thumping. She could hear movement next door. Natarajan was saying something to himself. The next sound she heard was her mother coming back with Seetha.

'Why haven't you fed guruji yet, Asha?' Krishna asked.

Asha quickly wiped her face and got off the small stool she was sitting on.

'The doctor was very quick, and then Naidu auntie very kindly dropped us off. She is such a nice woman. It was so good of her to let us come home quickly in her Ambassador. Come, let me do this, you look after Seetha. She has to take these tablets,' Krishna continued.

When Asha went up to the room from which she so recently had fled, there was no sign of what had happened. Natarajan, all dressed, was now dashing into the bathroom—ostensibly to wash his hands before eating. Her mother removed her own light coat and Seetha's shoes and coat. Asha smiled at Seetha and took her into their room. She was especially solicitous of her little sister tonight and made a lot of fuss putting her to bed. Seetha was happy to be looked after.

Asha heard her mother call. 'Asha, come and give these tablets to Seetha.'

Asha was loath to leave her sister and pass through the living room into the kitchen where her mother stood, waiting. Krishna called again. So Asha tucked Seetha up once more and started towards the kitchen. Waiting just outside the bedroom was Natarajan. He had a ten ringit note in his hand and, placing his fingers on his lips, he whispered, 'Amma, don't say anything. Take this.'

Krishna was calling again. Asha quickly took the note and deftly put it inside her blouse.

3.20 p.m. London, Harvey Nicholls, Knightsbridge

Sarah did not have much time as she wandered around Harvey Nicholls, but she knew she had the money. Buying an outfit for later that day for a posh do, albeit in a director's box at a football match in Glasgow, was the main thing. She chose a sleek black dress with a halter neck which would leave her shoulders bare but be easy to slip off, if and when the moment came. That done, she bought a sober pastel pink shirt and a matching light tweed skirt for the next day in Belfast and Dublin. After all, the day would be spent with the Prime Minister rather than with Harry. Then remained the crucial night garment. It had to be sheer and seductive, if only for the short time it would stay on. Sarah found a silver grey night dress, diaphanous with a floral design which would show her cleavage to advantage. Oh yes, and a spare pair of shoes and tights, and extra make up. It was hectic, but she was in and out in a little more than an hour and a half. Fortunately, she had no problems with her size or complexion. She felt wicked purchasing a small bottle of Samsara, but what the hell. This was her first trip with Harry. She kept saying Harry to herself just to get used to it. She would have to figure out for herself when to say PM and when to get informal with him. But that was not her most urgent problem at the moment: getting a taxi was.

To hell with Alan. She felt alive and vibrant.

3.25 p.m. London, 10 Downing Street

Christine ushered the MPs delegation into the Cabinet room. That seemed the easiest way to keep them out of the way until Harry arrived back. Eric Thor was his normal immaculate self, tall and patrician with a pipe stuck in his mouth. He was always well mannered. Once he had been Christine's idol, indeed he had been everyone's idol. In those days of the Vietnam war and CND, he inspired them all. He had been a Cabinet Minister in the Harold Wilson government in the 1960s. Many thought he would succeed Harold, for Eric was always very much in the same mould. He loved technology and was always going on about the power of TV in modern day politics. He had read Natural Science at New College, Oxford, so he was also a fan of computers long before they got small and user friendly.

But Eric did not succeed Harold Wilson. Instead, he became the focus of the opposition within the Party to everything the Wilson government had stood for. He had to be given a Cabinet post, at a time when the Party was in office with no majority, because he carried fifty votes with him. Those were difficult days, and Eric's friends waited for the next election. They had laid their plans carefully, not to say conspiratorially. They would capture the Committee which would be entrusted by the Party to draft the Manifesto on which the Election would be fought. For Eric's friends, the Manifesto was a key to influence. The Party's long-held socialist principles would be reflected in the Manifesto. There was to be no compromise with the middle class softies. The Party would get back to its working class roots which Harold Wilson, in their view, had betrayed. They would move the Party decisively to the Left. They had time, Harold was good for a few more years. They concentrated on winning seats at the National Executive Committee, and building links with the rank and file of the Party.

Harold's sudden resignation had put all their plans awry. Eric had no sympathy with the new regime, and this was reciprocated. He threw a massive tantrum, and went on the back benches to fight the battle for succession the next time around. He had the parliamentary shock troops on his side, he was a darling of the Conference, a superb speaker and what was more, he was a socialist; there weren't many of them in the Cabinet even in those days.

Harry bounded into the Cabinet room. Oliver and Christine closely behind him. He asked them all to take a seat. There were six of them, all escapees from Alcatraz as far as Oliver cared. Eric spoke first.

'Prime Minister, we are a delegation from the parliamentary party, and we have come to express our concern to you about the government's stance on Libya. We believe it will be a breach of the UN Charter to bomb Libya as we believe you are planning. We think it is not only illegal, but also immoral. It will cost many innocent lives.'

'Now let me get one thing straight first, Eric. You are not an official delegation elected by the parliamentary party, are you? I am certainly not aware of any such delegation being elected.'

'No, Prime Minister, we are not. But we do represent, we believe, a strong backbench strand of opinion, and we have a lot of support in the country.'

'All the *Tribune* readers and a few *Guardian* ones as well, you mean. You know that our policy has been supported in the parliamentary party and there is all-party support in the Commons. We are liaising with our allies, and, I can assure you, if Libya behaves itself and complies with the UN Resolution conditions, there may be no need to bomb.' Harry was trying to keep calm.

'With respect, Prime Minister,' Eric started saying. Oliver looked at the ceiling and then he looked at his watch. This would have to be wrapped up soon. They had a plane to catch.

'Look Eric, I understand that some of you feel strongly about this. I will read this memorandum you have given me, and I will take up this question on Wednesday at our party meeting. If you like, we can put our policy to a vote. But, I am afraid, this afternoon I cannot give you much more than five minutes. So, let us see if other members of the delegation have anything to add.'

'Prime Minster, you know I have a large Muslim presence in my constituency,' Jimmy Cord butted in. Harry found Jimmy's accent hard to fathom but perhaps it was because he did not want to listen to him. Jimmy had one of the safest seats in Lancashire.

'My constituency has written to me in very strong terms about our Middle East policy. They think we are following the Americans blindly in their anti-Muslim policy. They may all vote Conservative if this goes on.'

Oliver quickly calculated that Jimmy's majority was larger than the Muslim population in his constituency and he was in no danger, which was a pity of course. Maybe we should bomb Libya and make his majority smaller, then he will behave himself, he thought.

'I had thought that the Muslims in your constituency were Shias, and Libya has a Sunni leader. Isn't that correct, Jimmy? I thought they sided with Iran, not Libya,' Harry said. Oliver and Christine looked at each other. How did he figure that out? Who told him that?

'Well, Prime Minister, we have to fight this imperial legacy of divide and rule, and unite the Muslims of different sects, you know,' Jimmy said.

117

'You mean unite them so they can fight us better? Are you serious?' Harry interjected.

'The point we are making is that our government should not be engaged in any armed adventure, We should not use armaments, we should not export them, we should not produce them.' Alex Little was another with a safe seat, but then in Wales they were all safe.

'Have you any idea how many jobs would be lost if we did not produce and export arms? Are you willing to argue for an extra 750,000 people on the dole? We could lose twenty Labour seats in the Midlands and the North.' Harry played his trump card. Christine was proud of him. She had forgotten her pique at his lunchtime escapade. He had the Left cornered and beaten. She sat back and touched her scarf, since she could not touch him and express how she felt.

'Thank you all, but I must go. But, as I said, I will read your memorandum, and I promise you, we will have a discussion Wednesday morning. We will put it to a vote. OK?' Harry wound up the meeting.

Eric was again a gentleman as he shook Harry's hand, and thanked him for receiving the delegation. Harry left them to gather themselves together on their way out. He had things to do.

4.30 p.m. Vienna, The Hofburg

Alan had nothing to do except wait patiently and silently, while everyone around him bored their way through the olive problem. He tried for a while to amuse himself by thinking of each delegate around the table and

how good they would be as lovers… They were not
an attractive bunch. Perhaps Benoit Fuchs, the French
Minister for Agriculture, was the best of the bunch
with his jet black hair all glistening with some oily
mousse applied that morning, his trim black moustache
and rather delicate hands; he was definitely a possibility.
Alessandro Amadeo was rather fat with pudgy hands
and small eyes. No, he would be intolerable. The young
Greek Minister Olympia Costakis was the only woman
round the table, and she was stunning. But Alan was
certain now he was beyond all that. He let his mind
drift to Jo again and thought of his body. He doodled
and tried to sketch Jo. But he could not see Jo, who was
a couple of rows behind him. He cursed his job. This
was Euro mega boredom.

Terence, on the other hand, was treating all this very
calmly. He did not have a lover waiting at the back of
the room. He was confident that, as and when the late
evening came, Alan and Jo would go their way and
he would be free to roam around the bars of Vienna.
Terence had nothing against gays, really, honestly. He
just could not see the point of it. With so many female
forms around in a variety of tantalising shapes and sizes
and ages and colours, he could not see the attraction of
his fellow male.

He had grown up in the highlands of Scotland. But
he was not truly Scottish. His father came from a long
line of Anglo Irish Protestants who served the Empire
faithfully as soldiers or engineers. They were always
the brainy sort beneath the bluff exterior. The English
hated any sign of intelligence in their officers. But the

Ulstermen got to know how to feign to be simple and yet be given the tricky jobs. His father had been a medical officer in the Army and had been posted to India during the war. That is where he met Stevie, Terence's mother. She was a nurse and they fell in love. It was when they got back to Ulster that Donald Harcourt realised that Stevie being a Catholic meant his family would not speak to him, nor would hers. They found it difficult to settle in Ulster, facing naked prejudice at each turn. It was when Terence got beaten up in his nursey school by some helpers that they decided to move. So Terence had grown up in the highlands of Scotland. Donald and Stevie chose an obscure village in the western highlands, not far from Malaig. It was a harsh place but the people were friendly. Donald's services were needed far and wide among the scattered cottages and crofts.

There was never as much money as what they had got used to in India. But it was a beautiful countryside, rugged in the hills and lush in the valleys. The sea was not far away and the islands of Mull and Skye were a short boat ride away. Terence went to a local school which was three miles walk away. There was no secondary school nearby so he had to be a day student in Fort William. This meant he spent the weekdays in school and came home each weekend. It was then in his early teens that he first became conscious of his sexual self. He was frightened. In every film or painting that he saw, women would arouse him with their sexuality. His imagination would run riot. But he was also afraid. Was he ever going to be big enough, strong enough to please such big women, whose naked flesh seemed to be so hungry for him? Would he be able to make it on the day, or would he fail? Not that there was much he could do to put his fantasies in practice. That came much later when he was at Glasgow as a university student. The pill had come, and his was the generation which believed it had discovered sex. There was sex, pot and pop music. On college campuses, there was a lot of radical protest, and an impatience to challenge all norms and taste every forbidden fruit.

But the young college women talked too much. They did not just want sex. They wanted a relationship, and it took a long night's conversation about Kafka and Existentialism and Bob Dylan before he got to the real thing. What he wanted were pliable young nubile women, girls almost. He wanted to be in control mentally and physically. Women in their twenties were too assertive, too bolshie. They were too demanding and fussy. They bored him. Anything slow and elaborate, anything where he had to think and empathise and play, tried his patience. He needed all his patience to study law as a barrister. He saw that as a perfect entry to politics. Terence wanted to be a Parliamentarian. He had a long range plan well laid out. Assiduously, he would secure his long term goal. Those early days were hard as he could not risk his reputation by being seen in the seedier parts of Glasgow. This is when he learnt the importance of a European holiday. In Europe, he could roam as he liked, and do what he wanted. The European city had few inhibitions, and practically no prohibitions. He explored Amsterdam and Paris and Berlin and Vienna.

He knew then what he liked, and how easy it was to find the source of his pleasure. Along the way, he also became a keen student of European politics.

He met Dorothy Portman by chance. Her grandfather had been a pioneer in packaging in the early years of the century. From small local shops, England was moving to big department stores in cities. The British Empire was prospering, and even working class families were able to afford the comforts of life. They liked their purchases well packaged in paper and cardboard and silver foil. They did not like dowdy brown paper or worse still, old newspapers, but something clean and pretty. Often, they liked the packaging in different colours. Julian Portman was the man who responded to the money to be made by supplying all the shops, small and large, with a variety of new packing materials. He made a fortune. His wealth multiplied twice over when the First World War broke out, and the demand for a range of the latest, durable packaging materials shot up. Julian Portman met the Army's needs for well packaged soldiers' rations, containers for water, beer, spirits and chemicals This is where he came to know the politicians. The Liberal Party had been in power by the beginning of the war for the previous nine years. Herbert Asquith was the Prime Minister. He was a fastidious lawyer who had an aristocratic air but little talent as a war leader. It was his Chancellor of Exchequer, the wily Welshman Lloyd George, who emerged as an inspiring figure that Britain needed in wartime. Early in the war, the Liberal Cabinet was reshaped into a coalition, one with Lloyd George as Munitions Minister, and later as War

Secretary. As the Allied effort floundered, the people became impatient with the government. Lloyd George conspired with his Tory colleagues to throw Asquith out, and became Prime Minister himself. The Liberal Party became bitterly divided. The Asquith faction loathed the upstart Welsh Wizard. The War was won, and Lloyd George emerged as a hero but with a divided Party. However, there would be an election soon, and Lloyd George would need financial support. Soon Julian Portman's contacts in the Liberal Party were relying on him for help in fighting the Khaki Election, as the General Election was called because of the colour of the soldiers' uniform. For this generous aid, he was rewarded with a baronetcy.

Baronetcies put the man receiving it above a Knight and below a Baron. A Knight can carry the title Sir before his first name but only during his life. Baronet can be called Sir but so can his Eldest son and forever after down the line. When the Lloyd George Liberals started selling honours there was a bit of shock. But that was just snobbery. Buying and selling honours has a solid pedigree. James the First had invented the title of Baronetcy to raise money for his ventures. That was way back in the beginning of the seventeenth century. Lloyd George was just continuing that royal practice. Henceforth Julian Portman would be called Sir Julian as would his eldest son and heir after him. He was happy with that. A Peerage would mean he would have had to give a much larger sum to the Liberals. Too costly, he thought. He would much rather invest his money in acres of land and a modest title rather than a grand title and a pretty garden. Gradually, he came to be a landlord of significance in the highlands. He built a castle for himself and entertained in a lavish style. He organised hunts and balls and parties bringing all his English and some Scottish friends to his feasts.

His son James inherited the baronetcy, the lands and the business. Plastics were revolutionising packaging, and the new Sir James Portman understood this. The fortunes kept on growing. James enjoyed his Scottish possessions, as he also did his country house in Hertfordshire and his flat in Cadogan Square. His family was large, and among his children, it was not his four sons, but his daughter, Dorothy, who was his great favourite.

Sir James was a happy, fulfilled man, though he was widowed soon after Dorothy was born. He never remarried. He had his business in England and his acres in the highlands. Life was perfect, or rather nearly perfect except for one irritant. Sir James did not like the ramblers and walkers who invaded his hundreds of acres in the highlands. He did not want any intrusion on his property. The ramblers argued that they had ancient rights of way through his lands, and James was determined that they would be challenged. He hired Terence, who was recommended to him as a rising young barrister in the Edinburgh legal circles. It was a tricky brief. As a highlander, his instincts were with the ordinary people who wanted to roam about in their own countryside. But as a young barrister, he was lucky to get the case. What he did not know that his whole life was to change, because that was when he met Dorothy.

As the only daughter in a family with four sons and a widower father, Dorothy had a lonely childhood. She was teased and bullied by her brothers. Her father whom she adored had much love, but little time for her. She treasured the few moments he spent with her, when he would come and snuggle next to her, cuddle her and kiss her good night. In every other matter, Dorothy was very privileged. She had been brought up to be a lady of leisure. Sir James Portman had envisaged a titled husband for his daughter, and he was willing to pay her troth. She had grown up beautiful, with a large round babyface, a flawless skin and a slim figure. Her golden blonde hair crowned her pale green eyes. Dorothy had been educated in England, and had been to a finishing school in Switzerland. She could ski and sketch and sing. She had a simplicity of nature, as if she did not want to grow up. The more Terence saw of Dorothy in Scotland, the more he realised that here was the perfect answer to his problems. She was like a young budding girl, with innocent looks, indeed his ideal sexual type. Marrying Dorothy would give him happiness as well as the cushion of money he would need to reach his goal. He now saw that with a bit of luck he could aim higher. He could be a Cabinet Minister in a future Labour Government and, who knows, even Prime Minister. The question was, how was he to win Dorothy?

Luckily for him, Terence had the gift of gab. The Scots talk more than the English, though perhaps less than the Welsh or the Irish. Terence combined the inheritance of the Ulster Irish with the storytelling lo- quacity of the Scots. But the lilt in a highland accent was clearly attractive for Dorothy. She met Terence at one of the dinners her father gave at the family castle. Terence began to tell Dorothy about his dreams for the future. He told her about his father and his days in India and how the Ulster Irish had done so much for the Empire. He told her how his parents had come to Scotland to escape the sectarian prejudices of Ulster and how he had grown up in the Highlands. He also told her the history of the Highland Clearances, of the cruelty of the English as they evicted thousands of crofters and the cottagers out to make room for large holdings for English interlopers. Dorothy was fascinated. All her social life had been in London, where she met highly eligible public school types who were always 'something in the City'. They were supercilious and immature. They had no hinterland. Here was Terence who could talk to her about things she had never been aware of. She felt a bit guilty as an English interloper in the Scottish highlands. She was ready to pay her dues to right ancient wrongs.

Thus it was that Terence met and married Dorothy, the daughter of an English baronet and a lord of thousands of acres in Scotland. James was pleased that he had found a young and clever barrister for his daughter. He knew Terence's career plans, and he was willing to bankroll him. He gave his daughter off in splendid style, and set the happy couple up with a large house in Edinburgh in the New Town. It was in Venice on their honeymoon that Terence found out, to his delight and amazement, that Dorothy was more than he could have wished for as a partner in pleasure. Dorothy loved sex. For her, it fulfilled the emotional needs which had been starved in a family of five men and no other woman. Terence guided her through myriad acts of game playing. He was her sexual mentor and a father substitute. With him, she could remain the little girl that she always wished to remain. In his wanderings in Europe, he had always searched for the younger girls, the immature ones. Now, he had married his ideal type. It was a union made in heaven. He dominated her. He asked, and she gave.

But then, the girls came one after another, Rowena and Susanna, four years apart. Dorothy's interest in sex began to fade. Her looks matured, as did her body. She no longer looked, or felt, like a young girl. She was now worldly wise. She wanted Terence as much as ever before. Her emotional needs were seeking fulfilment through physical pleasures. But she was no longer the woman Terence fancied.

Dorothy realised that Terence's eye was wandering. Now he was an MP and had been promoted early to a junior minister. He was an expert on Europe and his role became prominent in the big debate that was taking place in the country on Britain's place in the European Common Market. This meant that he was away a lot, and Dorothy did not have to know what he got up to. But she knew what he wanted. She had nannies to look after her when she was growing up. Now the world had moved on, and there were au pairs. These young girls came from Scandinavia or Germany in their teens. They were blonde and pretty and young, and they were just perfect for keeping Terence coming home for the weekend.

Dorothy understood that Terence had to have his bit on the side. It was quite cosy, really. She let him have a free range at home and outside. Even when he stopped being a Minister and began to spend more time in Edinburgh at the Bar, she was happy to turn a blind eye. If the au pairs complained, they were replaced with other ones. Dorothy always chose the type she knew Terence would fancy. They never spoke about it. How and when he got around to his peccadilloes she did not wish to know. Dorothy was happy that her girls were growing up to be beautiful lasses. She was proud of them, but also feared lest her little lambkins be set upon by horrid boys. She felt uneasy when workmen or servants came into the house.

Soon Susanna got to an age when an au pair was no longer necessary. Terence was now spending more time in London. His career was going well, although the Party could not win elections. He was more prominent in the public eye, and Dorothy knew that he would not want to be caught in any compromising situations. Then, he began fussing a lot with the girls, bathing them and taking them off to swim. Rowena and Susanna were getting just to the same age as the au pairs were. They had their mother's good looks. She knew the danger signs, and had to tell him that if he misbehaved with his daughters even an inch she would divorce him and tell the world. Terence vehemently denied that he would ever lust after his own daughters. He accused Dorothy of having a dirty mind. He said she was no longer in love with him. If she wanted to leave him, he would go away though he would miss her and their daughters. They quarrelled a lot but eventually made up. Each needed the other more than they could admit.

Like in all such reconciliations, there was the inevitable aftermath. Catriona was born twelve years after Susanna and when Rowena was going through her teenage angst. Dorothy was happy at this sign of Terence's abiding love for her. She was now emotionally even more dependent on him than before. Terence took her more under his control, and soon Dorothy realised she could not stop him. She reckoned this way at least the girls were protected from those horrid boys who were their school fellows. All the newspapers were full of teenage pregnancies and assaults and rapes. She wanted the family to stay together and not break down. Terence had been good to her. He was a good father, and he would bring the girls along gently. In due time, they would get married, and leave the home so what harm was there if their father loved them as well.

Still, she made sure that she was around in London as in Edinburgh, when the whole family was together. She had to fend off curious journalists and gossip mongers who were always looking for dirt.

For Terence, having Dorothy around all the time was a small price to pay. He was very careful in his way with the girls. He started ever so gently to initiate them. His years of experience with young women across Europe had taught him a lot about the psychology of young girls. They needed reassurance and a lot of tenderness. There was to be no fear and no consequences. The act had to be safe and unhurried. Terence had his den at the top of the Edinburgh house. The attic was above anyone's else's window level. He had it soundproofed and fitted with luxurious furniture suitable for pleasure. No one would see him, and no sound would escape outside.

Rowena led the way. She adored her dad. What she gathered from her magazines and her girl friends was disheartening. There seemed to be a lot of fumbling and a risk of failure with raw young lads, who were often needlessly hurtful. With her father, she felt no guilt. There was ample time; she was at home and she knew he would not hurt her. When she went to university, however, she chose to go to Durham University rather than Edinburgh or any other Scottish University. This way she was away, but not too far. Susanna slipped into her place, and there was no fuss. Rowena had told her how wonderful Dad had been for her as a first man. Now older and with experience, her relationship with her boyfriend was fantastic. Dorothy told herself that Rowena was completely happy and normal. They married her off to Malcolm who was also a barrister, and Terence was the perfect father of the bride. At Rowezna's wedding, Susanna and Catriona were bridesmaids. Susanna was now an undergraduate and with a boyfriend in tow, while Catriona was just growing up pretty like her big sisters. Looking at them, Dorothy saw that Terence was a good man in every sense of the word, a good husband and now a good caring father.

All he now lacked was political success. He was hoping for an election victory and a rapid rise to the top. Dorothy began to help him by coming to London more often. She took interest in his colleagues and invited them for dinners and parties. Her training in

Switzerland had equipped her to be the wife of a busy corporate or political leader. She brought that into play. She used her money to engage a secretary. But Dorothy did not want a young woman anywhere near Terence. That way lay trouble.

She preferred young men from good families like that nice Adrian, son of Viscount Summerfield. He worked for her in the London office. He kept Terence's diary and was willing to help out at dinners and parties. He also regularly photographed MPs and their families. Dorothy diligently sent the photos on. Adrian had no attachments. He told her he was gay, though he had been married once. Dorothy was surprised, but such revelations were no longer shocking. At least, this meant that her daughters were safe with him. He was as happy to come to Edinburgh as work in London. Thus, he became a part of the family. She could leave things to him when she went out, and all would be well. But then, that is good breeding for you.

3.35 p.m. London, Hilton Hotel, Heathrow, Terminal 4.

Adrian was starting the best holiday of his life. He had the case with the cash. It had been hard work but worth it. He had chosen his target carefully. He had made himself useful to Dorothy. She had placed a small advertisement in *The Spectator*, for a helpful person to look after a complex diary of a prominent politician. Adrian's friends in the Tory weekly had tipped him off who it was. He knew that, beneath the demeanour of an

MP's wife, Dorothy was an English snob. As expected, she hired him. He regaled her with stories of what the aristocracy were up to, and who was getting off with whom. In turn, he picked up useful hints about skeletons in other MP's cupboards, which would come in handy sometime in the future. He had free run of the houses in London and Edinburgh, especially during the holidays when Terence, Dorothy and all the girls were in their favourite Tuscany. He figured out that Terence preferred the Edinburgh house to the London one for his assignations. He soon discovered Terence's den in the attic, and fitted hidden cameras in it. Adrian could sense that Terence was impatient. He had been restless since he lost the leadership contest to Harry, and very frustrated that Harry showed no sign of weakening. Susanna had gone to college, leaving a gap before Catriona would be ready. Adrian got some pictures with Rowena on her visits back home, but she was now a grown up girl. Adrian waited patiently for Terence to move on to Catriona. She was only nine but was a very pretty girl with curly blonde hair and eyes like her mother's. She was big for her age, and nearly as tall as Susanna. Adrian could see Terence eyeing his daughter, fussing over her when they were together, and trying to shove Dorothy out of his way, when the three were together.

Adrian was invisible as far as Terence cared. He hovered around, waiting for his chance. He knew Terence would slip up. Sure enough, last weekend, he had. Dorothy had to be in London to attend a centenary celebration of her old school. It was to be a giant hen party of friends who had not met for long time. Terence was excused as long as he promised to be in Edinburgh, and look after Catriona. Terence had the field clear with the older daughters away, and Dorothy in London. He could not hold back any longer. The hidden cameras did the rest. Adrian's ship had come home.

4.40 p.m. Vienna, The Hofburg

When abroad, Terence had his routine, depending on which country and which city he was in. Vienna was the least problematic. So what if he had to wade through a lot of boring stuff about olives, he did not mind. Terence had a keen interest in matters European all his political life. Europe offered another career path for the enterprising politician, if national politics was frustrating. Roy Jenkins had gone off to be President of the European Commission, when he could see that he would never lead the Labour Party, and become Prime Minister. Terence was not giving up hope yet, and keeping good relations with European colleagues never did any harm. He had learned to wait until he got the perfect version of whatever it was that he wanted be it food, sex or power. He could handle minor frustrations along the way, but he did not want to settle for second best. He never believed in being so hungry that he could not wait for a gourmet meal. Vienna guaranteed a sexual feast.

Idly, he started listing all the MPs he was sure would back him in a leadership challenge, if Harry was ever to falter. Harry was not invincible. He was about to take a very unpopular decision about Libya. The Party would not stand for such slavish following of America. The hard left had voted for Terence in the leadership elections, and Terence kept in touch with them. He made a mental note to speak to Adrian, and set up a meeting with Eric Thor tomorrow, when he was back in London. A little bit of Party trouble would add spice to his life. And, who knows, the Glasgow trip might not be the day when the world would do ill to Harry White.

3.45 p.m. London, Drew House, 38th Floor

Normally, Lex felt elated with a scoop. His blood raced, and the adrenalin pumped in his veins. The whisky bottle, opened by lunchtime on those days, was never put away. But this was different. He had to choose among the rather disgusting pictures Rodney had bought. He thought it best to take the less explicit, and more sugges-tive ones, but hated that he had to do it. This was a mega scandal. In his scabrous, sanctimonious way, Lex regret-ted that by the time he got into this profession, scandals were hard to come by. The reading public had become unshockable. Extra marital affairs were small beer. Gays were out into the open, and those who were privately gay could not be attacked—not unless you were a gay rights weirdo like that sanctimonious git who went around outing bishops and MPs. But children were a different matter. There was a national outrage ready to be tapped on the issue of paedophiles. That was the last barrier. The Great British Public, four million of whom bought his newspaper every day, bless all their souls and their wallets, would not stand for tolerance of paedophiles.

However, this was even trickier stuff than that. It breached barriers which were beyond scandal. He had to consult Vera. It was urgent, he told her. Unfortunately, as soon she walked in, he knew she was pissed. He couldn't abide the filthy cheroots she smoked. Where she found them, he did not know. Probably hand made from Turkey. He strode across and threw open a window. Vera tried not to notice.

'What is the problem, Alexander?'

Lex hated this elongation of his name. Vera had taken it upon herself that Lex was short hand for Alexander, when it was actually for Alexis. His parents had a weird taste in names. Why had he not been born an ordinary mortal, doing an ordinary nine to five job and making 25k as all average people did and been called Tom or Bob? Why did he have to be called Alexis, make 200k and be talked to like this by a batty old fruit?

Lex explained the situation to Vera and showed her the pictures. Rodney had discreetly skulked away. His presence, he knew, would have inflamed Vera. Vera was horrified by the pictures, as Lex had been. But she could see that Lex would not have called her if he had a choice.

She looked at them for a few minutes, really hard, really professionally. Then she said,

'Do the decent thing, love. Do this one with lots of blacking out and keep the rest.'

Lex saw that she had chosen the one picture where Terence was clearly recognisable but not the other party—though they had all the information on the other pictures. This photograph hid her face but not Terence's. Vera was protecting the victim. She had sound instincts about the tolerance of the public.

'You think...'

'Don't worry, love. This will bring him down. We don't need to bring more filth into the public eye, even though we have it. This will tell him what we know, and it will keep that poor thing from being hounded all her life.'

'Will you do a front page edit piece?'

'You bet. You do the full page editorial on the politics. Leave the morals to me.'

'You are the works, VD.'

'I wouldn't say it is a pleasure, but I know such problems don't come our way all that often. Extra print run of a million. Not less in any case. Let's get going.'

Lex knew that he had to be careful about letting the first print run out. BBC2's hard hitting programme *Newsnight*, which went on the air at 10.30, showed the headlines of the next day's editions just before going off the air at 11.15. Should he release his first edition in time for that, or just tip off a few insiders? He would have to alert Peter Portugal's office, but what about Terence Harcourt? Should he tell Chris Mott, his press secretary? Lex knew Chris as a fellow journalist since way back, when as two juniors, they used to get pissed on cheap booze. Harry White was in Glasgow that evening watching the Old Firm game, so Oliver would be with him. What about Oliver, could he be kept out of the loop? Lex had many things to do and not enough time to do them in.

3.50 p.m. London, 10 Downing Street

Nor did Oliver. Harry had just gone upstairs to do his packing. Elisabet had left already, so there was no one to say farewell to. Oliver was happy to see Sarah was back, a bit flushed but all set with her newly-acquired suitcase packed and ready to go. She had put on fresh lipstick, tidied her hair and smelt of Samsara. They did not exchange a word, since Sarah didn't want to talk about the cancelled lunch and Oliver wanted to avoid any mention of the lunch that had taken place. Oliver silently thanked Sarah for her discretion. Let us hope she won't make a fuss when she is thrown over like the many others before her, he thought.

Harry came down, all spruced up, contact lenses in place and some fresh aftershave on. So, obviously, Oliver sat in the front of the car, leaving Harry with Sarah in the back as they sped off to Northolt. Harry sat well back to escape attention. Sarah took note and did the same. Harry patted her hand.

'Don't worry, Sarah, you will enjoy this.'

'I am sure I will Prime... Harry. But I will be glad when the day is over.'

'And, I hope, you will look back on it with fond memories.'

Those blue eyes are devastating, Sarah thought. How will the day end?

3.55 p.m. London

It was her large brown eyes that men found most attractive about Asha. But back in Kuala Lumpur, she had also understood the lure of other parts of her anatomy, and she kept them well guarded from the roving hands of Natarajan. When he offered to move in with Krishna as her paramour, Asha knew why. Her mother was so happy, Asha thought it best not to spoil things. Asha had sensed her power over the older man. He was marrying her mother, but wanted Asha. She had heard enough through school gossip and magazines to sense that there were barriers she should not cross too early. She had realised that she had the ability to please men with some simple and delicate gestures. Only Natarajan had a rare chance to get her alone, but then, after that first incident, she knew how she could make him pant for more.

She varied her single theme. She could be coquettish, but he liked it more if she was cool and detached, doing him as if her mind was on something else entirely. For some obscure reason, this gave him a more powerful erection. She never let him touch her and she only touched him where she was most effective. And he always rewarded her for that.

Asha figured she would have to leave home as soon as she could. She had decided to win a scholarship to some British university—LSE would be the best. The money he gave her was helpful in getting better books, and of course she was very bright. Even Krishna did not question that Asha had spare cash. Krishna had told herself that it was Asha's scholarship money. She did not want to know more. Asha was determined to get out and get to LSE before this all came to a head.

And she had her way. She got a scholarship to study at the LSE when she was seventeen. She had learnt a bit about men, older men that is. She knew how to master them with a little deft turn of her supple fingers. When she entered the legal world, she started with at least this advantage to offset being of non-European origin and a woman. In a profession dominated by old white men, she had the secret of what tickled older men. She did not languish at the bottom for long; her legal acumen made a significant but small contribution to her advance.

'Good afternoon, Miss Chan, nice lunch?' her secretary asked. Linda was very useful in arranging Asha's busy and complex schedule and she was totally loyal. Asha could trust her.

'Good food, lousy company. Most of it anyway,' said Asha as she went into her rooms at the Chambers. There was, as usual, a mountain of stuff to do, but her brain also had to work out a solution to the one problem that was proving difficult—Harry White.

Asha had to find some sort of solution to the tax problem Matt was facing, if Harry refused to co-operate. She wasn't sure whether he was bluffing or just playing for time. It had not escaped Asha's watchful eyes that Oliver seemed to be Harry's guide in these matters. This meant they had to get something on Oliver, but another prong of attack on Harry was also needed. As Asha worked through the papers on her desk, at the back of her mind, various wheels were turning to find the answer.

Linda knocked and brought her tea. Asha indulged herself when she was in the office, around four o'clock, with a large pot of freshly brewed Darjeeling tea.

'Thanks ever so much, Linda. Just what I needed. Could you do me a couple of favours, please? Could you run a check on what we know about Oliver Knight, the PM's press secretary, and could you please find out whether our friend in Glasgow is available for a word? Thanks.'

Linda knew that when Asha demanded something like this ever so politely, it was urgent. Often, Asha preferred Linda to access information, so that her name would be kept out of any fallout. Linda had a way with accents, and often made phone calls pretending to be an old lady from Shropshire or a housewife from Cumbria. People were so gullible. There was no risk that any one would find out.

4.00 p.m. London, Lyttleton Theatre, Waterloo

It was always going to be a risky proposition to stage Ubu Roi. It was a controversial play when it was first staged, and remained so even after a century. It was a godsend for columnists and cartoonists. Here was the Prime Minister's wife staging a play about an arrogant, boorish and stupid man usurping power, ruining his kingdom and getting thrown out by a people's revolt. And with a wife who is a perfect shrew! What was Elisabet doing? But then, as Harry knew, that was always her style. To make matters even more controversial, Lisa had decided to do an all-women production. Then she had chosen the glamorous and well known French star, Anne de la Manche, to act the Ubu part.

Lisa had met Anne at one of those summits she had to go to with Harry. This one was in Rambouiellet, and Anne was part of the 'culture' for the summit. Lisa and Anne hit it off immediately that evening. After that, it was only a matter of time before they did something together. They were very much alike. If the Great British Public had problems understanding Harry's wife, the French were dismayed that such a beautiful, sexy woman as Anne should be a lesbian. The tabloids had great fun when the cast of Ubu was announced. Anne was over in London, and there were pictures of her and Lisa hugging on many front pages. *The Herald* lived up to its reputation with the headline LISA LESBO LOVE LARK.

But time had passed quickly, and now Lisa was sitting in the darkness of the Lyttleton Theatre, watching the dress rehearsal of Ubu. She was particularly happy, because her good friend Margaret had come specially for the occasion. Margaret was going to be there for the first night tomorrow, but this was an extra treat. Margaret and Lisa had become great friends despite, rather than because of, their husbands. Harry disliked the arts slightly less than Scotland or football. But of course, before the election, the artistic community had been thrilled that Lisa was a professional theatre director. Luvvies had fallen over each other trying to get to know Harry. They had hopes of largesse after decades of Tory meanness and Labour's economic incompetence. What is more, in Kim Carpenter they had a trendy Heritage shadow minister. Kim had been a don briefly at Oxford, having written an obscure and swiftly remaindered study of Robert Herrick. But at least he could read and write, unlike many MPs of the People's Party—or so the Luvvies reckoned.

Alas, in office, Harry had dashed their hopes. The Government had come into power in the wake of a financial crisis. Battens were hatched down, and, if anything, Harry had proved to be an even greater philistine than his predecessor, whose tastes did not reach beyond Trollope and tripe. Kim Carpenter had great ambitions of moving on from his Heritage portfolio, which he felt was a dead end. So he played along. After being feted and flattered for months, he had slunk from one media event to another with his (once) perfectly shaped boyfriend. Being dunked in champagne by the lions of theatre was not his idea of fun or duty. At the first opportunity of a Cabinet reshuffle, he begged to move on and was now in the arid deserts of Transport and Regions. Pamela had replaced him. She, too, flattered the trendy crowd of artists and actors for a while, but then she found she was ignored completely by Harry and Terence. If there was one thing they agreed about, it was the neglect of the Arts. So Pamela was left to struggle with the portfolio, and now she was in her final days.

And this is where Margaret came in. Unbeknown to their husbands, Margaret and Lisa had hatched their own plot. Margaret was to set up one of the largest endowments for the Arts the country had ever seen. She was to leave a billion dollars to the Lew Drew Arts Fund but it was to be set up in Britain. And just to put the boot (or an elegant stiletto) in, it was to be located in

Glasgow. Lisa had helped Margaret with the plans. She knew about her friend's cancer, and while she always prayed for Margaret, she knew that time was short. She had, of course, hinted to Harry that Margaret may leave her an endowment. She had not spelled any more out, but Harry being Harry she was never sure as to what he knew and didn't... Margaret did not tell Matt, nor did she care if he knew. It was her money and she was determined to blow it, rather than give a red cent to him or his Malaysian mistress.

The play was going well. Lisa could hear the select guests invited for the dress rehearsal laughing and cheering. She had had the novel idea of flashing words like BLAST and POW electronically at crucial stages, so the play looked like a comic strip come alive. Everyone had been encouraged to camp it up outrageously. There was no point in playing Ubu as if it was serious or deep. It was a scatological political cartoon.

Annie was brilliant. Margaret passed a note to Lisa, 'He is a pompous fool just like Matt.' Lisa read it in the semi-darkness, leaned over and whispered, 'I modelled him after my Harry, not your Matt.' They both started giggling. The stage manager demanded, 'Silence.' This hushed them both but their giggles continued quietly.

Soon the laughter got very loud. There was the scene where the Bear attacks Ubu and his straggling followers. In another brilliant move, Lisa had asked the ultra thin, almost anorexic model Kath Ross to play the Bear. Kath had agreed, knowing that it would lead to some weird publicity. She had to be swaddled in a heavy padded costume making her fat and ugly. ROSS GROSS was one of the many headlines as a result. But Kath enjoyed acting as it gave her a break from modelling. She hoped it would be her big break into Hollywood if the play did well. Lisa wasn't sure there were many parts of fat ugly women which Kath could hope to get on evidence of her acting, but then Hollywood was a strange place.

Now everyone was laughing and hooting and getting into the spirit of the play. Lisa was relieved. She had worked hard on her Ubu. This was her first production at the National, oops, the Royal National. Lisa had to be careful about such trivial matters of protocol. She was, after all, the PM's wife. But she could now prove that she was there on merit and not because of Harry. Tomorrow the world would know that Lisa was someone to reckon with.

4.20 p.m. Glasgow, on the way to Robertson Estate

Deirdre was weighed down by her shopping bags. This was her routine. Not having a car, it was difficult. She could take a cab from the supermarket and did so occasionally. But today she felt mean. It was, after all, not far from the supermarket to her council flat. The bus took her most of the way. The walk at the end was not all that long, and mercifully the lift was working again. Sam would not be home yet. Her college did not finish till half six. Then, after college, she went to the pub to earn a bit of pocket money. Deirdre wished her daughter did not have to work, but it had always been this way. She had had to grab for a penny when she was Sam's age, and it was not pleasant in those days in Glasgow.

At least, now Samantha was getting a college education in Culinary Science and Food Therapy—making chips and telling people it was bad for them, as Roger described it. He was funny, was Roger. He had a way with words. He was also so good with her and with Sam. So gentle. After a violent husband and a criminal lover, Deirdre did not mind that Roger was, let us say, not very demanding. But he was sweet and gentle and cuddly. He would do the deed, if Deirdre felt the urge, but even then she had to bring him on. Bring him along, if you know what I mean. He never messed with Sam. He made her laugh and taught her things.

That is how they had met. Sam was having ever so many problems with her maths. The teachers were hopeless. Mind you, Sam, being a girl, did not need maths anyway. Then, there was that afternoon Deirdre would never forget. She went to the public library to see if she could get any help finding books for Sam. Roger was there, and he was ever so helpful. He was a temporary Assistant Librarian, and so different from the regular ones. He was willing to spend a lot of time with Deirdre and Sam, talking about mathematics and making it interesting by telling Sam stories and puzzles. He found a lot of books for her. Soon she began to pick up maths. Roger went on helping her. He even offered to come around on weekends and tutor her. Well, what could you expect with Deirdre feeling lonely, having had no man for three years? She cooked him a lovely roast one day. That was before she found out he could do wonders with pasta and sauces and steak and even stews and vegetables.

So Roger had become a part of the ménage for three years now. He was unlike anyone else Deirdre had known. He could be stroppy and put his foot down. He knew ever so much about everything. He had smooth skin and hands. He taught Sam and helped her pass her exams. He could even fix the windows. Actually, Dierdre could do that herself. She was good at DIY, was Dierdre. It was the classical music he had on with Radio 3 that intrigued her most. He knew all about these composers and conductors. He hated pop music but he adored jazz, and he knew just the kind to turn her on.

No, Dierdre couldn't complain really. She had no idea where he had come from and how long he would stay. He was good about money, and did not beat her up. That, for Dierdre, was the works. Occasionally, he cooked her a fabulous meal with herbs and spices, and bought fancy wine. She suspected he had known better days, but as far as she cared he was there and was available. So what if he was not a randy, hard drinking bastard like the rest of them?

When she got home, Roger had heard her coming. The door was ajar, and there was the aroma of a pot of tea and toast with butter. She was expecting that. But Roger was up and about and all dressed up.

'What's with you then?' she asked.

'Got a job tonight. A good one at that.'

'Where?'

'At the club.'

'Are they playing?'

'Och, aye.' Roger had picked up the lingo.

'So how long will you be?'

'They want me to serve drinks at the bar. So I reckon I will be done by midnight, like. They pay well, Ibrox do.'

'Midnight? That must be something special.'

'Och, aye. It's Harry White, the Prime Minister, coming down to watch the big game. The Directors have a big do for him, drinks and food and all. All the biggies will be there, I reckon.'

'Oh, I hate that Harry White. You can keep him. Wish he would drop down dead.'

'Whatever for?'

'He is a Tory bastard, he is. Not a penny for us workers and millions for his rich friends.'

'Oh, come on.'

'Don't you come on me, remember that nuclear deal which got him a million?'

'Not him, his Party.'

'Who cares? It's all the same. It is the rich who talk to the rich when the money is good. If it's the poor, the money is always tight.'

'Well, he is coming for the election.'

'I hope he loses.'

'Well, all I have to do is to mix his drinks.'

'Poison him for me, will you?' Dierdre was not going to hide her anger.

Roger was startled. He had never seen Dierdre express such a strong opinion before. He had his own reason for hoping that she did not mean it. But now was not the time to explain why. So he turned away to go to the kitchen, saying only, 'Easier said than done, Dee.'

Roger got her a cup of tea. He put his own cup down and began to put away the groceries. He was like that. Considerate. Yet, it did not make any sense. He made Dierdre uneasy if he was good. She was not used to men being gentle or good. He was not normal, not natural like.

'You know, Dee, only one British Prime Minister has ever been assassinated. It is not like the Americans, who are forever shooting their Presidents. Spencer Perceval was Prime Minster in the days of the war with Napoleon. He was shot by a bankrupt businessman, John Bellingham, who blamed him for his troubles. From Liverpool. Right inside the Houses of Parliament. Not the present building. That was before it burnt down, and they had to build a new one. But you know something strange? Ever since, they don't let anyone die there— not in the Palace of Westminster. Even if you die, they say you died in the St Thomas's, which is across the river. They have a thing about Palaces. As if the people inside were immortal.'

That is typical, Dierdre thought. He was ever so keen to educate her. Ask a question and you got a lecture, but not boring, mind you. And, all the while putting the things she had bought in their place.

'Drink your tea. I will do the stacking in a minute.'

'It's nearly done. Anyway, I must gulp and go.'

4.30 p.m. London, Lyttleton Theatre, Waterloo

Lisa's mobile signalled a message. She was annoyed, as she had put it on silent mode. The Stage Manager shouted, 'Mobiles off!' She looked at the message and smiled. She saw that it was Harry saying he was off to Glasgow, and that he would call her later. That meant he was feeling guilty about something. Lisa wondered what it could be, or rather who? Christine was not travelling with Harry. Lisa knew that, because she had a long chat with her that morning. So a new affair, but who with? Her thoughts were interrupted by a great roar and applause. The run-through was over. Lisa was happy, but she had a few changes to make yet...

Margaret had to go. She gave Lisa a fond hug and whispered, 'Great. See you tomorrow. I am sure you will wow them.' She gave her hands a squeeze and was gone in a trice. Lisa realised once more how her tall, big-boned friend was getting even more beautiful as age and the dreaded disease were taking their toll. She said a silent prayer for Margaret. May she have a long life and much happiness.

4.35 p.m. London, Bell Yard, off Fleet Street

Not if Asha had anything to do with it. She wanted Margaret gone and soon. It was not even the money that she was sure Matasha would inherit. It was the sheer irrationality of Margaret's attitude about money which infuriated Asha. Not to have it, to have to struggle for it, to save and skimp and even to blow it on personal luxuries. That, she could understand. But to give it away to the tax authorities, when you could avoid doing so, and to throw it away on some namby-pamby charity was more than Asha could stomach. Ever since Matt found out that Margaret intended to give her money away to an Arts Foundation, Asha had wished fervently that Nature would do her job on Margaret faster than ever. She had looked up articles on the rate at which cancer spread, but then there was no agreement among specialists. Margaret could live for a month or for years. Asha had to do something—but the question was what?

She buzzed Linda.

'Can you come in for a mo?'

'Yes, Miss Chan.'

'Can you find out where Margaret Drummond is today? I know she was in London earlier today but I want to know if she is still in town. Ask Matt's office, but don't let them know who you are.'

'Understood, Miss Chan.'

Asha was determined to get her hands on that money, even if it meant doing drastic things. Nothing illegal like taking out a contract on Margaret—just hastening her along to her end. But how?

4.45 p.m. London, Central Lobby, Houses of Parliament, Westminster

That was Eric's problem. How was he to get rid of Harry? He and his group had come back empty handed from their meeting with Harry. He had challenged them openly to defy him at the Party meeting the day after next. How were they going to organise their numbers? The Libya issue was bubbling, but had not yet come to a boil. There were rumours flying around of an Anglo-

American stitch up, which was about to start unilateral bombing. Could Eric and his group somehow stop this likely carnage?

'Hello Eric, you look worried. What is the matter?'

It was Ian who had drifted, out of habit, into Central Lobby of Parliament. His lunch had been soaked in booze, and, apart from that, eating from a haunch of venison with all the trimmings and following that up with a summer pudding soaked in double cream was hardly health food. So he had decided to walk down from the Garrick. He got on to Charing Cross Road, and went past Trafalgar Square and Whitehall to the Palace of Westminster. Along the way he had been tempted by the bookshops and the antique shops. He dawdled a while, but failed to buy even a good first edition of Geoffrey Boycott's autobiography. He was sorely tempted, as the Yorkshire batsman was one of his English heroes. Now, after a hot day out walking, he appreciated the coolness of James Barry's lovely construction. He had come in from St. Stephens Entrance. The attendants knew him, and his pass was still valid. He loved the splendid high dome of the Central Lobby from which a large chandelier hung down. There on the four ends were four arches, and above them were the likenesses of the four patron saints of the United Kingdom. There was St George for England above the arch leading off towards the House of Lords, St Patrick of Ireland on the door to St Stephens where he had come in. There was St Andrew above the door leading off to the dining rooms and the Terrace below and St David above the arch leading to the House of Commons chamber. In between the arches, there were four marble statues in the classical style of prominent politicians of the nineteenth century. There was Gladstone and Lord John Russell, both Liberal Prime Ministers. The now forgotten George Gower, the Earl of Granville and Stafford Northcote, who had been a Foreign Secretary under the Tories, but had a heart attack when Salisbury took over his portfolio for himself without warning him. With the obituary still on his mind, Ian wondered how important sudden death had been in wrecking and launching political careers. Looking at the MPs strutting around busily in the Central Lobby, Ian wondered how many had thought of sudden death as a possibility.

This was the place that gave lobbying its original meaning, for this was where citizens could come and ask to meet their Member of Parliament. All they had to do was to request the attendants by writing the name of their MP down and off the attendant would go in search of the quarry. Hence the number of MPs lingering to meet the groups of their voters who had made previous appointments. It was also the place for aspiring researchers and eager political anoraks to hang out. There was always a buzz, with people passing through on urgent errands from and to the Chamber.

This was old hunting ground for Ian. With his pass, he was free to wander through the arch under St David towards the corridor just outside the Commons chamber. He nodded to the policeman on duty and said a cheery hello to the attendant and passed into that inner sanctum. There was an aggressive-looking statue of

Lloyd George and a bull dog like one of Churchill.
Few would recall the glory of Anthony Eden who also
somehow rated a statue here. He had started full of
promise as the successor to Winston Churchill, but led
the disastrous Suez expedition and came to grief. Will
they honour Harry White as one equal to Lloyd George
or will he end in ignominy like Eden did? These idle
thoughts were occupying Ian, though he was still
hoping for an anecdote or two about Harry, when who
should he meet but Eric Thor.

Ian had known Eric since their university days. They
had been close once, but had fallen out over Vietnam.
Eric was a minister then, and pro-US policy, while Ian,
still a journalist even then, had been against. But they
had made their peace in the long years Eric had spent
in opposition, getting farther and farther to the fringes
of his own Party. For a man who was once thought to
be a likely leader, this was a long way down and out. Of
course, there were still some out there who wished for
Eric's return. The People's Party was incorrigible.

'Have you heard any news about Libya, Ian?'

Eric did the usual thing of answering a question by
asking one in return. He didn't really want to let Ian
into his plans, but then if news got out that a rebellion
was brewing that wouldn't hurt either.

'I know no more than you Eric. Even less perhaps. I
don't, as you know, labour in the vineyards of the print
medium anymore. Rumour has it that Harry and the
President are thinking of bombing Libya.'

'Has it now? Don't you think the country will rise
up in revolt if that happened? Shouldn't we stop him?'

'No, to both questions. The country doesn't have any love for Gadhafi or Libya or for anyone who supports them. And, you couldn't stop Harry even if you wanted because he would crush you.'

'He will have to seek the approval of the Party, or at least of the Cabinet surely?'

'Since when has Harry given a fig for either the Party or the Cabinet? He will do what he likes, Oliver will tell you all what to think, and the sheep will dutifully jump over the cliff.'

'You are too cynical. I am sure if we started now, by Wednesday's Party meeting we could build up a momentum for a challenge.'

'Well, that's news, Eric.'

'But, Ian, you are not to tell anyone. This is strictly off the record.'

'As I told you, I am no longer an active journalist. All I do is to write obituaries. Now what can you tell me about Harry White that I can use for the juicy bits of the obituary?'

'You have come to the wrong man for that, Ian, as surely you must know.'

'Well, thanks anyway, and good luck.'

Ian knew he was on the scent of a story. Even after all these years, the excitement of a news story never diminished. He would have to ferret out bits and pieces. It was too early to go to Annie's for Ian, not even five o'clock yet. But he thought the terrace on the river might provide some willing talkers. What an item would this make for the obituary, if it blew up.

2

4.45 p.m. En route to Glasgow

Sarah had never been in a private jet. This one was not private but it was the Prime Minister's personal jet for priority use. There had been no checking in, no waiting, no long walk to the boarding gate. They had been driven on to the tarmac. Gideon Crawford and his Scottish office entourage were already there. When Sarah hesitated, Harry took her arm, and led her to the steps. Her bags were carried in by the crew, and before she could think about it, they were airborne.

She sat by herself. She wanted to gather her thoughts. Harry and Oliver were deep in discussions a few rows in front. Gideon's crowd were noisily drinking and chatting at the back. They had carried their beer cans up with them. Sarah felt very self conscious. What would the day bring? What was expected of her? Christine had asked her to buy things to wear, and she had done that. But when was she going to change and where?

A nice middle-aged stewardess walked up to where Harry and Oliver were sitting.

'Prime Minister, your dry martini, just as you like it, with an olive, and Mr Knight, your whisky.'

'Thanks, Maria.'

'A pleasure, Prime Minister.'

It actually did give Maria pleasure merely to be able to mouth those words, 'Prime Minister'. She had said them many times and to several Prime Ministers and yet it always gave her a thrill. She saw Sarah sitting by herself and could see she wasn't used to travelling VIP class.

'What would you like, Madam? Can I get you a drink, a tea or a cup of coffee perhaps?'

'Just a cup of tea, please.'

'And how do you take it? India or China and milk or lemon?'

'China please, with lemon, Thanks. Oh, and sugar, if that is alright.'

'No problem at all, Madam.'

Maria took her time serving her guests up front because she knew that the Scottish contingent at the back were going to be odious and demanding. She brought Sarah her tea. It was in a pot with the full works. Sarah felt overwhelmed, and thanked her profusely.

'What sort of trouble do you think Matt has in mind?' Harry asked Oliver.

'Difficult to say. He has been gunning for Terence ever since Terence sued *The Herald*. I can't see what he has. Terence is squeaky clean about money. He is happily married with three lovely daughters. They may have found something from his past, long before he became a minister. I will make inquiries'.

'Do. And what about this evening?'

'There is a meeting of party activists that Gideon has organised. Like a fool, he has chosen a University campus location. Our security people will be there, so we will keep the Trots out, but our own members up here are pretty loony.'

'The usual—taxation, nurses, pensions?'

'Yes, more money, more redistribution. No tuition fees. Oh, and Libya.'

'You reckon?'

'Sure. Foreign matters always attract nutters. The farther away and more exotic the country, the nuttier the support. So, you will have to do yet again what you did to Eric and the brothers.'

'OK. And then the game.'

'That's a dawdle. It should be a good game, so even you may not find it too boring. It is the season's final game. It is not often that these two teams have a fixture this late, but what with other competitions they have been in—the European Cup, the Scottish FA cup, this match is the last. It is also crucial for them both. They are on the same overall number of points, but Rangers are ahead on goal difference. Celtic have to win outright. If they draw, then Rangers are champions in the Scottish League. Of course, if Rangers win, they are clear champions.'

'I hope I am not expected to understand the subtleties of all this,' Harry said.

'Don't worry. They will tell you themselves several times. I am just warning you. But it is not only football. It is also, as you know, tribal warfare. In Northern Ireland, they fight with guns and bombs; in Glasgow, they do it with football. Two teams with fiercely loyal sectarian support. You have to be careful not to be seen to be supporting either side during the game. Your hosts are the Rangers bosses, but, even if they goad you, stay neutral.'

'As I don't know much about the teams and care even less about football, that should be easy.'

'You are not to admit ignorance under any circumstance. But no one will know as much as they do. So they will keep telling you really obscure stuff, just keep smiling.'

'So these are Protestants?'

'Thank God, you know that much. Things have relaxed a bit. They hired Graeme Souness as manager a while ago, and this despite him being a Liverpool player, rather than Everton.'

'So what?'

'Oh God. Liverpool is a Catholic team right. So they are like Celtic. Everton are like Rangers—Protestants.'

'They can't still be taking all that seriously.'

'They do in Ulster after all, and Glasgow is just a large suburb of Ulster. Or, maybe the other way around. They fly the Irish Republican flag on Celtic roof tops.'

'Is that allowed?'

'Who is to stop them? Do you want riots in Glasgow as well as troubles in Belfast? They tried once in the 1930s. Celtic said they would rather get thrown out of the Scottish Football Association than take the flag down; so the flag flies.'

'Will there be trouble at the match?'

'Nah, it's all under control now. It used to be bad in the old days. They once had a game more than a hundred years ago, in 1887, as a matter of fact, which had to be abandoned after seventy minutes. The match was oversubscribed, and the crowd spilled over on to the pitch. Mind you, Rangers were trailing Preston North End by eight goals to one so the fans may have just sabotaged the game. But nowadays, things are much easier. The football stadiums are all refurbished, and no one has to stand on the terraces any more. It is an all-seating stadium like everywhere else. The fans may fight later on, in the course of their pub crawls. But it should be alright. As I said, Catholics now play for the Rangers. Of course, it helps if they are foreigners.'

'How long will all this last?'

'Kick off is at seven forty-five. It is an unusual fixture, being on a Monday, but Matt's Rainbow TV has a tie in with the Scottish FA, and he insists on some big games being scheduled on days other than Saturdays.'

'Not Matt again.'

'He's everywhere. Anyway, the match should finish at about quarter to ten and then there will be a reception and dinner in your honour.'

'Do I have to?'

'Well, you promised Calum Kennedy that you would come and be Chief Guest. He is very keen.'

'He is a strange creature. What drives him? Why does he keep on funding these moronic football clubs?'

'He is a docker's son and was a docker himself. Then he did a grand tour of the Revolutionary Left. He was a Stalinist, then became a Trot and had a go at being a

Maoist in the heyday of the Vietnam War. But then he dropped it all, went into selling advertising space. Some say he was disgusted by the Cambodian dictator Pol Pot, who managed to murder a sixth of the population of his country, others say it was his marriage falling apart that did it. He needed money for alimony, and had to quit agitation. So advertising it was, and his bullying manners made him a great success. Now he owns a TV station or two, and gives the Party a lot of money.'

'What's his game?'

'He wants to be Lord Kennedy of the Gorbals.'

'Can I skip the dinner, if I promise that?'

'No, come on. You'll enjoy it. All the business leaders of Glasgow will be there as well as a lot of political types of all Parties, I should add. Prime ministers don't often come to Scotland, and when they do, they go to Edinburgh and not Glasgow. So this is a big event, and you will get a lot of kudos for it.'

'As long as I don't cheer half way into the game, if Celtic score.'

'That's about it.'

6.00 p.m. Vienna, The Hofburg

That, Terence thought, was that. Cyprus olives were sorted out. As usual, Alan had been brilliant. He had waited till the moment he knew the French and Italian delegations began to think of their flights home. Then, he produced one of those classic European Community solutions. It solved nothing, but gave everyone the chance to go home, and live to fight another day.

Eighty per cent of Cyprus olives were to be covered by the scheme immediately, and twenty per cent absorbed within five years of Cyprus's entry. France and Italy were to lose twenty per cent of their quota, but this was suspended until the date of entry. They could exceed their quotas (i.e. cheat), if they paid an excess charge. But, this excess was to be calculated in present prices, not future prices, unless the price of olives had fallen. Every other country was to agree not to import olives from anywhere else except in bottled form. No one could calculate what any of this would eventually cost, but no money was required up front. And, by the time Cyprus entered the European Community, the ministers would be different, and it could all be argued again. A good day's work was done, and now time for the fun to begin.

Fond farewells had to be said all around, but Alan quickly rejoined Jo. This being Europe, he could hug him and kiss him lightly as well. In the meantime, hands had to be shaken with all the various ministers and officials, double kisses on the cheeks for the closer colleagues and the few women. Briefcases were snapped shut, little mounds of paper left behind for recycling, half-filled water glasses and bottles of Evian now looking stale and forlorn. Terence did the farewell bit superbly. He was in no hurry. He was staying over. His pleasures were to come later and they were not to be hurried. He could be gracious and effusive to ministers and officials. He remembered their wives' names and sent his compliments unfailingly, asked after their children, bantered knowingly about their local gossip.

He was happy to be in Vienna. Anywhere but Glasgow, where Harry was left to face the mob. No doubt, Chris would call him later, and tell him any news. He would normally be with Terence, but they thought he should keep an eye on Harry, the excuse being Chris could help out if Harry needed someone to assist Oliver. They both knew that Oliver would rather die than ask Chris for help.

The boys were impatient, so Terence swept them along. Terence had never liked the posh hotels near the Opera. He knew of a decent four-star place near the Schotten Ring. As a Scotsman, he had gravitated there long ago and now kept up the connection. Hotel Franz Joseph was comfortable, easy to get to and more intimate than the posh ones.

As they squeezed into the car, Terence graciously sat in the front with the chauffeur, leaving the love birds to get on with it. He knew the answer he would get, but still he asked for form's sake.

'I reckon you lads won't want to join me at the Ambassador's house for dinner? I can make excuses on your behalf.'

'Thanks, Terence, that is very considerate of you. Do give my most sincere apologies to Sir Clive and Lady Olds.'

'Done. Remember, it is an early departure tomorrow morning. You will have to be down in reception by six thirty.'

'Oh, I hate these early morning flights. Can't we take a later one?'

'There are two flights leaving almost simultaneously

in the early morning, and then nothing until after lunch when again two flights take off.'

'That is airline competition for you. Do we have a busy day tomorrow?'

'Aye. Harry is in Glasgow tonight and goes to Belfast for an early meeting tomorrow morning. I better be in London in case the Libya thing blows up. We can't rely on Frank Thompson, now can we?'

Frank Thompson was Deputy Prime Minister, but was for ever being made the butt of jokes. 'Yes FT, no comment' was the least rude thing people said about him. Frank was loyal, Frank was solid. He had deep roots in the Party, and in his own unaffected way, attracted fierce loyalty. He was like a frayed old shirt, once fashionable. You wore it for comfort and nostalgia, not for style. And you were faintly embarrassed for keeping it around in your wardrobe. But Frank was Harry's battering ram if the Party misbehaved. Frank was so grateful that Harry had chosen him as his Deputy on the leadership ticket and then kept faith by making him Deputy PM, that he was ready to kill for Harry.

'OK, you win. Six thirty in the morning it will be. But don't expect us to be awake.'

'Would I ever? Here we are. Franz Joseph, here we come.'

5.15 p.m. London, Lyttleton Theatre, Waterloo

'So, are we all set?' Lisa asked. The cast had gathered in a huddle on the stage. There had been hugs and kisses and congratulations. Everything had gone according to plan. Lisa had to sort out a few things with the lighting. Annie needed a more directed focus in all the funny bits; people had to be able to see that lovely face, even though she was playing a stupid man.

'What's the plan?' Annie asked.

'There's a pub cum restaurant at the National Film Theatre, which is just next door. We can sit outside, and get pissed. Then we have a short walk, no road crossing, to our restaurant The Archduke. We eat there, and as long as we clear off before midnight, the owners won't mind.'

'Do you want us to act tomorrow after this?' Kath groaned.

'You don't have to be here until half past four in the afternoon. Anyway, hangovers improve concentration.'

'The butterflies in my stomach before the performance will be more than enough,' Annie said.

'The bus will take you back home or to the hotel, as you like. So, you don't have to hold back. No driving, just lots of drinks.'

Lisa didn't like cars, nor driving. She went, if she could, by public transport everywhere. Sometimes, the Security men worried about this, but Lisa was adamant. By herself, she would not get into a car, but if necessary, take a taxi. As Prime Minister's wife, she would do as she had to, but she did not hide her hatred of cars or the pollution they caused. She disliked, even more, the political discussions about voter preferences of the Mondeo man or the Sierra woman. Harry was much taken by those images, but Lisa thought it was criminal to glamourise cars and their owners.

So the motley looking group of fifteen women set off. Even before they were out of the door of the Royal National, they were attracting a lot of attention and even some wolf whistles. A crowd was gathering in time for the evening performance. A quartet was playing soothing, harmless music. Even the short walk from the Royal National to the National Film Theatre took a longish time, as they stopped to look at things inside the Theatre. Several went into the bookshop, while others spilled out on to the South Bank and stood by the river. There was an open market with many stalls of second hand books which absorbed Annie and Lisa.

'There will be several gossip items in the papers tomorrow, Annie,' Lisa said.

'What about? We have hardly done anything yet. I could, if you wanted some publicity,' Annie said.

'No, thanks. The British journalist finds the most trivial acts of people in the news fascinating. It is just name dropping. We are a nation of snobs. When they read tomorrow about us carousing noisily, they will feel like they almost know us. Anyway, it sells papers.'

'You are pretty relaxed about this constant pressure, Lisa. How do you cope?'

'Well, I know that they think I am a bit crazy, so as long as I fulfil their expectations and shock them, they don't probe too deep.'

'And what will they find if they do?' Annie asked, clearly trying to provoke Lisa.

'Let me get the drinks orders, and then I will fill you in.'

They were at the NFT. There were wooden benches

with tables like on some campsite picnic area. They were lucky to find enough empty tables, and off went Lisa inside to get the drinks.

5.45 p.m. Glasgow, The King and the Spider

Even two hours before the start of the game, the Spider was choc a bloc with Rangers fans. There was noisy singing and many had already got drunk, though Kenny could not imagine how. They had arrived at the airport about two hours ago and had been catching up with the people who had come by coach and ferry. Their own group was fifty strong and they were all in the same stand, so Kenny knew whatever happened he would be among friends. Red had already told them they were to take no weapons in the stadium and leave the rucksack with him. He knew the publican and could safely put things behind the bar until he needed them. He, of course, would not be at the game. What his movements were to be was mysterious. He had told them to be at the airport in time for the return flight. That was all.

Ritchie was taking over the leadership task. The most essential of which was, of course, to buy the drinks. So he turned to Kenny and said,

'So what will it be Kenny? Are you old enough for a pint of the best or will it be diet coke?'

'What are you having?' Kenny asked just to have some time to think.

'Well I will have my pint of Guinness with a chaser of a double malt, Lagavullin. But I won't advise you to try that. It will kill you.'

'Let me have a pint of bitter. You choose whatever you think will be good for me.'

'Aye lad. That's wise. Your mam will kill me if you went home sick. Ok lads, what will it be for you? The usual?' Ritchie knew, of course, what the rest were having. Without even waiting for an answer he marched off to the bar.

6.00 p.m. Glasgow, walking the streets

Red was far away from all this. He had to keep his head clear and do nothing foolish which could lead to the Glasgow police coming after him. He had been in trouble in Glasgow before, though not as often as in Belfast. Glasgow was, after all, home away from home for him and his own people. Glasgow had its own Orange Order building and its own parades, though they had them the weekend before the Golorious Twelfth of July, when the Glasgow boys could join the big march down Garvaghy Road to annoy the papists. But Red had to concentrate. He had already checked that the rucksack contained the ingredients he needed, the mercury and the small sandwich box and the timer. He had read up about bomb making and got himself the smallest bomb which he hoped would do the trick. After all, it was based on the simple notion that it was the movement of the car itself which triggered the bomb. You could hardly call it murder; it was almost a suicide. Just another couple of hours and Harry White would be fitted up. After the big event, the game would also be over and then he would have a proper drink with the lads.

6.15 p.m. Glasgow, en route to Ibrox

Drinks were on Roger's mind as well. He had looked up his book of cuttings on recipes for cocktails. Of course, there will be the usual beer and Guinness drinkers, and those who would not let anything but a Highland malt touch their lips. But once the game was over and they had their first thirst quencher, some of the guests were sure to get fancy. To be invited by the Directors of Rangers for an Old Firm game went to their heads. Free booze and that at the expense of the Rangers, and people started muttering Chartreuse and demanding an Armadillo or a Negroni. You had to be prepared and quick, of course, because there were five others banging on.

But it was a simple cocktail that occupied Roger— an American style Martini. Gin and vermouth in any combination you like as long as it was dry. Gin in a large measure, a multiple of the amount of vermouth, ideally chilled with some crushed ice, though some preferred ice cubes. Americans liked crushed ice and some Glasgow types went that way. The English from down south liked theirs with ice cubes. Not that they often came to Glasgow, nor, if they did, were likely to come to the Ibrox.

But the Englishman coming tonight wasn't just anybody. It was Harry White, Prime Minister to everyone else, but as far as Roger was concerned, a warped and evil man. Not because Roger was left wing, which he was. His wilder days on the extreme left in Glasgow were well forgotten. Calum Kennedy, his old mate, knew of course. They were even comrades once. Roger shuddered as he thought of those days. Not so much about himself as about Calum, and how far he had betrayed his past. From two young agitators for the Communist Party selling *The Morning Star* on cold wet mornings to the shipbuilders and fighting the Trots at public meetings, they had ended up miles apart. Calum was a millionaire and Roger was just about alright. He had the dole, or rather the Jobseekers Allowance as it was called nowadays, and then he had casual jobs for cash as a bartender. In fact, it was Calum who used to find him such jobs in the old days, when they first went their separate ways. Now he got the job through his own contacts. He was careful not to be greedy. He did the odd job, now and then, for big companies. They could pay good wages and lose a large wad of cash in their accounts, and no one was any wiser. There would be five hundred quid at the end of the evening. But that was only the half of it. Less than half. Maybe only one per cent.

This was an evening Roger had been waiting for since that fateful morning when he was summoned to the Bursar's office twenty five years ago. It was early for Cambridge undergraduates to be out of bed, especially since he, like many others, had been up till three the night before. Yet the summons was peremptory, the porter banged hard and long on the door to make sure Roger woke up. As Roger staggered up to his door, muttering and cursing, he was told to dress quickly and come to the Bursar's office. Roger could not recall what he had done the previous evening. As he splashed cold water on his face, he tried hard to remember. He had gone to a Union meeting where they had debated the legalisation of drugs. Roger had spoken in favour of course, but the religious societies had packed the Union and the motion lost He had then come back and drifted into Mill Lane and gone to the pub on the river... He had seen Melissa early on. Meeting Melissa like that had been a shock in itself. They had not spoken for nearly a year. In their first year, they had been friends. Melissa was a vision when he first saw her at the Freshers' Party. She had a luminous white skin, tumbling auburn hair, long legs and the most innocent smile. She was ferociously intelligent, reading for the Maths Tripos. She was also a violinist of talent and sang in her college choir. And yet she was fragile in a way that Roger found hard to define. She was a trusting soul, having been brought up in a happy family. For someone brought up in these modern times, she was remarkably naïve.

When they met a second time after the Freshers' Party, Roger fell head over heels in love. Yet he found it very difficult to be able to be physically intimate with her. Melissa did not seem to mind that they did not get beyond kissing. Very soon, everyone thought they were a couple. She was his girl. Many were envious, even jealous. Roger was happy and he was popular. Everyone invited him to their parties in the hope that he would bring the sylph-like Melissa along. She was a prize, and it was Roger who had the prize.

When Roger got to the Bursar's office, he saw immediately that something was seriously wrong. There were five police officers around and the mood was deeply sombre.

'Birch, thank you for coming. May I introduce Detective Superintendent Atkinson. He wishes to ask you some questions.'

Roger was really frightened now.

'What is the matter? What have I done?'

'That remains to be seen Mr. Birch.'

Roger was tall, just under six feet, but he was hunched up that morning and the policemen seemed big and burly next to him. Roger felt a chill going down his spine as Atkinson produced a photograph of Melissa.

'Do you know this person?'

'Yes, of course, it's Melissa.'

'When did you last see her?'

'I haven't seen Melissa for months. We quarrelled. We were friends last year. What has happened?'

'Are you sure you did not see her last night?'

'Only from a distance at the bar. We did not speak.'

'Think carefully sir. This is very important. You are not under oath but it would be in your interest to co-operate with us.' Atkinson had to get tough with this callow youth.

'Is Melissa hurt? Has she had an accident?'

'Birch, Miss Musson is dead.'

It was the Bursar. Atkinson looked very unhappy that this vital piece of evidence had been revealed. Roger went numb. He had to sit down and then he broke down. Atkinson waited patiently for a while.

'I talked to her at the bar last night but not for long. We quarrelled a few months back and were not really close. Then suddenly seeing her last night... Oh God...'

Roger broke out in sobs again.

'Go on.' Atkinson had not much sympathy for such dramatics.

'I said hello, and then something sarcastic about her looking pale like a princess. She smiled, but she was looking tired and sad. All that she said was it was nice to meet like this, because she may not come to the bar again. I thought she meant this being the final year, she had to get serious. So I asked her if she would come to the final May Ball with me. She didn't say anything but just turned away, and went out. I thought she had tears in her eyes, but I cannot be sure.'

'What time would this be, sir?'

'About half ten. They were still serving drinks at the bar.'

'How do you know?'

'Because I was so gutted by her walking away like that that I decided to get totally pissed. I went up to the bar, and bought a triple brandy for myself with a double whisky chaser. I already had several beers earlier in the evening. Excuse me, can I go to the toilet. I feel sick.'

The Bursar took Roger firmly by the shoulder and sped him to the rather elegant toilet attached to his office. He left Roger to come to terms with his insides. It didn't get easier after that. Melissa had committed suicide by taking sleeping tablets. Her next door neighbour Christine Brown had gone to borrow some milk and found her limp on the floor. There was a note to Roger. It said: *I am sorry I couldn't explain Roger. I meant goodbye.*

No one knew what it was about except Roger. It was at the end of term the previous May that he had taken

Melissa to a party given by Harry White. Roger had come to know Harry in the Union. Harry was a very good speaker, and everyone thought he must get to the top some day. Roger was a poor speaker, but he was very well read despite being a science student, a chemistry one in fact. He read widely and discussed things with Harry, and was always chuffed when he could find echoes of his ideas in Harry's speeches. Harry would never forget to acknowledge him afterwards, and they became good friends. Roger could see Harry was ambitious and cunning, and yet he felt that Harry was straight. At least, with him.

And then Harry stole Melissa from him at that party. They had gone together and Harry was very charming. He had made a punch which he recommended. Melissa was a non-drinker. She would stick to juice and coke. As soon as they got there, Harry gave Roger a glass of punch. He asked Melissa what she would like. She said, 'Oh anything. Even water is fine'. So Harry led her into an inner room where the drinks were. Roger didn't remember much else from that evening. The punch had been spiked by Harry, perhaps specially so Roger's glass. He talked to some people for a while, but then he had to sit down. Melissa was a long time away. The next day, he woke up with a hangover in Harry's flat. Even in his dreadful state through hazy eyes and a thumping head, he saw Harry and Melissa entwined in another corner. Melissa had little on, but she was blissfully asleep in Harry's arms.

Roger tiptoed out of the room. He was shattered. He could have killed Melissa, but then maybe it was

Harry's fault. He tried later to contact Melissa to have it out with her. Why had she kept him away for all these months, saying she was not ready for the full thing. She couldn't take the risk and then suddenly at the end of the year, she did not seem so scrupulous anymore. Couldn't she have been a little more…cautious? Roger was in love with her, and she was sleeping with a man she had just met.

But Melissa wasn't in the mood for explanation or even a simple meeting. She refused to see him. In any case, it was holidays soon after the party. When they came back, he lost touch with her completely. Harry acted as if nothing had happened, and never mentioned the party or Melissa. It was their final year and Roger was less active in the Union. Harry was reading eco-nomics which was an easy going subject compared to chemistry. He never saw Harry with Melissa at any party. He thought best not to be nosy.

'Can you tell me, Mr. Birch, when did you see Me-lissa before last night? Can you recall? Try.'

Roger didn't have to think.

'We went to a party at the end of last term. But that was when our friendship ended.'

'Can you tell me why?'

'I got drunk and passed out. She became friendly with someone else.'

'I am sorry to have to ask you this. Did you and Miss Musson have a physical relationship?'

'No, of course not. She wasn't that sort of girl.'

Atkinson smiled. The Bursar looked away.

'Can you be available for the rest of the day if we

need you?'

'Yes, of course. I will see to it.' This was the Bursar taking over.

It was some days before Roger found out. Melissa was pregnant when she had taken the sleeping pills. It had to be Harry. Roger tried to confront Harry over this. Harry laughed it off.

'Don't be daft Roger. People sleep around these days. Who knows who else she had in her thrall? Just because she fooled you about her innocence, she didn't fool me. Anyway, if she didn't want the baby, she knew what to do. Mind you, she was an easy lay. It took me only a small amount of vodka in her second glass of orange juice to get her going. Fine body though.'

Roger lunged at Harry but Harry was too quick. Tall though Roger was, he was not nimble. Harry landed a punch on him and then casually remarked,

'Grow up Roger. You will meet a lot more of them in your life. Lay them, don't love them.'

Roger was humiliated and horrified. He talked to Melissa's girlfriends and then pieced together the whole story. Melissa had told no one about Harry. She had gone back to her parents after the party. They always went camping for their holidays. She sent Harry post-cards, but had received nothing from him. When term started, she had thought they would resume that lovely tryst they had on that summer evening. But Harry was cold and aloof. He showed no interest in Melissa. He had, as it were, had her and that was that. It was all over. She was a conquest, another trophy notched up. Melissa began to find out about other women he had seduced.

Her next door neighbour Christine Brown was one such. Christine told Melissa he was a one night stand man. Charming, seductive and swearing love when he needed to, but cold and withdrawn the morning after. Christine did not seem to care; she was still friendly with Harry. Melissa was different.

Melissa was destroyed. She had always thought that everyone was nice and trustworthy and loving like her parents. Like Roger, who stuck by her and never breached the barriers. She planned her suicide carefully. She went to the College health officer and complained about her inability to sleep. This allowed her to stock up on sleeping pills. As a last fling, she went to the bar that night and ran into Roger. When he asked her out after all she had done to him, she could not bear it. She ran back to her room. But she felt she had to say something to Roger and left him a brief note. If she did leave a note for Harry, the police never found it.

Roger never finished his degree at Cambridge. He became ill and had to drop out completely. He took up temporary jobs, as and when he needed the money. He couldn't face his parents, who were disconsolate about their son's failure and could find no explanation for it. And now, after years of wandering, he was to come across Harry White in person. This was his chance to serve Harry a drink, and there was no way he was going to miss it.

Roger had thought long and hard about how he would take his revenge on Harry. He had thought he would go one day to Parliament and confront him and perhaps beat him up. But when he went to London and to the Central Lobby of the House of Commons, he found the atmosphere too intimidating. There were too many people and policemen and attendants. He did fill in the slip to summon Harry White from the Chamber, but then lost his nerve and ran away before Harry arrived. As Harry rose in the public esteem, Roger found it more difficult to plot his revenge. He could have approached some tabloid for a kiss and tell story, but then he had no proof and he did not want to hurt Melissa's parents or her memory. The only way was to kill Harry.

How does one kill a Prime Minister? It was not like the USA where everyone could own a gun, and people took potshots at Presidents. Roger read up everything he could about Kennedy's assassination. Was it Lee Harvey Oswald, or, some other people behind the grassy knoll? Either way bullets had been fired... But here, you could not own a gun without a lot of fuss and bother.

Political violence was much more an Irish thing. The Irish Republican movement routinely used violence as a weapon once it got started. There was a constant battle between the Loyalists and the IRA in Ulster. Occasionally it came over to the mainland. The IRA managed to bomb the Grand Hotel in Brighton where the Conservative Party leadership was staying during the Conference in 1984. They may have planned to kill Margaret Thatcher, but did not succeed. Two minutes earlier she was in the bathroom of her hotel suite which was destroyed by the bomb. They killed some other people instead. But then Roger was hardly going to join the IRA and be entrusted with such a task, even if the IRA did plan to kill Harry. Now, with ceasefire in place in Northern Ireland, an assassination of Harry White was not going to be delivered by someone else. Roger had to think of a way of killing Harry himself.

The idea of poisoning Harry came gradually. Among the many odd jobs Roger picked up, there was bar tending and the odd job of catering for small parties at private functions, Roger began to educate himself in the arts of cooking and cocktail making. He soon learned about how food poisoning can occur if one is careless and mixes the wrong ingredients... His chemistry education was useful, since he could understand the chemical composition of the ingredients, which did or did not mix. He could poison Harry's food, if he got the catering contract some day What held him back was the risk of killing more than just one person. But drinks were personal, and cocktails were made to order for each person. So his fantasy moved on to poisoning Harry with a drink. As Harry became prominent in public life, articles about him began appearing, and Roger took a keen interest in them. He got a job as Library Assistant occasionally and read up past newspaper files to look for details on Harry's habits...

It was then that he discovered Harry's favourite drink—an American-style, very dry Martini with an olive in it. It was the olive that was to be Roger's weapon for his revenge on Harry. Hurting Harry would not be enough, because he would not connect his food poisoning with his past misdemeanour. Melissa's death had to be avenged with Harry's death; nothing less would do.

So Roger began his study of poisons. After all, even in fairy tales, there were always stories of princesses being poisoned by wicked step mothers.They were usually fed some berries which, though dipped in poison, still tasted sweet. But would an olive retain its flavour after being rendered poisonous?

Roger knew from his studies that certain metals and materials are more prone to be poisonous than others. Indeed, the human body regularly carries many poisonous elements, but in such modest amounts that they help rather than hurt. Poisonous elements like mercury, arsenic, lead, antimony exist in small amounts; as do metals such as cobalt and iron and tin. So do iodine and sulphur and nickel and molybdenum. Even silicon exists but in a small measure, except for implants. The key was to inject a dose that was not modest but lethal. It was all possible provided the body absorbed it and did not reject it immediately. Harry would have to swallow the poison and it should reach into his gut.

The death had to be quick, but not instantaneous. The way Roger had fantasised the event was that Roger would administer the poison hidden in a drink, but then make his getaway before Harry died, and before people began an autopsy. Nowadays, with forensic sciences being so advanced, the poison would be traced to the olive soon enough. Roger had to rely on the shock of a Prime Minister's sudden death creating confusion. It would be some time before anyone would make a clinical examination, say at least one hour or maybe two. So Roger saw himself leaving town and country as quickly as possible. This meant it had to be Ireland, where he could go without anyone examining his passport. Once there he could run away to some obscure South American region, perhaps the Amazon jungles of Brazil.

All this planning had been done while Roger had been drifting around Glasgow, on his own, consumed by his hatred for Harry. He had tried getting into a relationship many times, but every time he had ended up back on his own. Melissa's memory haunted him to such an extent that he had even lost his capacity for loving. He had tried counselling, but did not want to let anyone into his secret. He learned enough from his counselling that there was a big obstacle at the back of his mind which had crippled him emotionally and concluded that only by taking his revenge on Harry could he become whole again.

He had not counted on meeting Dierdre and Samantha. He had not thought of Dierdre as a person he could have a relationship with. She was so different from anyone else he had been with. He was used to middle class professional women. She was working class, and not at all his type. That is perhaps why he dropped his guard. He had now become quite fond of them. With his parents now dead, they were the only family he could claim. They did not know much about his past. He had kept his Cambridge days well hidden. He told Dierdre he came from Cornwall, which sounded far enough away to her. But once Harry was dead, the police would trace him back to her home address, and she and Sam would face many inquiries. He wished he could avoid that or tip them off. Perhaps he should leave a long note. He was so surprised when earlier that afternoon, Dee said he should poison Harry's drink. Roger almost thought he must have been talking in his sleep. But he soon realised that it was just her simple and direct way of expressing her political views.

Anyway, Roger found out that mercury could kill but required a very large dose, and indeed may not kill immediately. It could take as long as a week. Harry would have the best medical care if he was found to be poisoned, and so they would empty out his insides and frustrate any effects. Arsenic was in some ways a better bet, but the art lay in the precision of the dose... In its mineral state, arsenic is solid and does not dissolve. But, if Roger could get hold of arsenic trioxide, he would have better luck. It was soluble and colourless as well as tasteless. He could dissolve it into water and then soak the olive in the solution. Hopefully, the arsenic would transfer itself to the olive. But he had to be sure. He had read about too many cases of abortive attempts at murder through arsenic where the culprit was punished though he had only succeeded in making the victim violently ill. He had to be sure. It was time to bring back his Cambridge scientific training into some practical use.

Roger needed to mix his poisons and experiment a bit before he was sure. Luckily for him, Glasgow had a number of higher education institutions. The old University of Glasgow, Strathclyde University and the Poly, though it had now upped itself to a University called Glasgow Caledonian—all had Chemistry Departments. There were also hospitals with medical research divisions which hired assistants as well. Students did not like to take Science options nowadays, so Chemistry Departments ran low on teaching work. Some survived by their research reputation and got funds from research grants to carry on work. But Scottish Universities had not suffered the severe cuts that English Universities had and so there was still a bit of fat to employ occasional research assistants, like Roger, to help out in the laboratories.

So Roger had his locker in the Uni and though he did not have a permanent job, they never took his locker away. He could go in and out and have access to the ample supplies of chemicals the Department kept. He got his mixtures made, and then tried them out on hamsters he bought in pet shops. This was before he had moved in with Dierdre. Samantha loved little creatures, and would have scratched his eyes out if she knew what he had done. But during his drifting years, Roger had worked out that he needed to soak his olives in an arsenic trioxide solution. It was only a fortnight ago he had learnt about Harry White's visit to Glasgow. Calum had sent a word to him that he would fix Roger a big job at the Ibrox for that evening, as he was hosting the dinner afterwards. Now Roger had to get to work. He had bought his olives, fat and dark green, in a small jar. That jar was for pickling. He kept it in his locker soaked in his favourite solution. But he also got a larger jar of olives so he could keep the clean ones separate from the pickled one. He knew someone else would ask for a dry Martini, once they heard Harry asking for it. There were always toadies where a Prime Minister was around. Roger did not want anyone else killed just by accident. That way he was squeamish.

When he reached the gates of the University, he saw there was something afoot. There were young men and women thrusting leaflets in people's hands. They were political leaflets. He didn't take one, but saw some on the ground. They had HARRY SHITE! prominently printed, and no doubt further abused since Roger could see that this was one of his old Trotskyist factions. They would no doubt go on about imperialism and bloated capitalists and poverty in the Third World and blame it all on Harry White and his pusillanimous Party for selling out the cause of Socialism. He saw people were steadily drifting in, no doubt headed to the Hall where Harry would be speaking.

Roger quickly slipped past them and found his way to the Chemistry Building.

He was surprised that, even at this late hour, there were still people working away in the Department. That is how he ran into Ken MacIntosh. Dr MacIntosh was Senior Lecturer in Chemistry and had been in the Department for some twenty five years. He was active in the teachers' union and in the local Labour Party, but not very much in Chemistry.

'Kenneth, I never thought you worked after lunch. What has happened to you? Mandy not talking to you?' Roger thought it best to put Ken on the defensive so that he would not probe too deep into what he was doing in the Chemistry Building this late himself.

'Don't you go on as well. It is diabolical nowadays what they expect. We have Research Assessments every

four years, and we are supposed to submit four published papers for judgment by our peers, which means
outside and unknown snoopers. It is slavery now working in higher education, not fun.' Kenneth was ready
with his tale of woe.

'Doesn't sound bad to me—one piece of work per
year. Not like what we have to do at the coal face in the
outside world.' Roger wanted to keep him talking and
seem relaxed; it would help his alibi later.

'How can you say that? We don't just do research,
after all. It is not even our main job. We have teaching
assessments, tutorials, marking continuous assessments,
Departmental and University meetings to go to and we
have to mentor junior staff. Then someone evaluates
us every two years to see if we have met our targets
and whether we have any problems. I would say I have
plenty. How can one get any research work done with
a work load like that?'

'But I thought you were active in the Staff Union.
Why don't you go on strike?' Roger knew what Ken
really spent his time on.

'You must be joking. Those days are gone, lad. It
is worse than in the days of Thatcher's cuts. It is the
new lot who we all thought might give us some respite.
But no way, thank you. Students have choice, and we
have to deliver. And you should see some of the new
recruits to the staff. Every one has his head down and
eyes firmly on the greasy pole of promotion. They are
apolitical, the lot of them Anyway, what brings you to
this slave ship?'

'Oh I was passing by on my way to Ibrox so I thought

that was as good a time as any to make sure I cleared my locker. It has been sometime since I looked at it and I reckoned I should collect my things before they start smelling, and they throw them out.' Roger had been there just a fortnight ago but he thought he had better get a cover for what he was about to do.

'What are you doing at Ibrox then? Got a ticket for the game?'

'No, I cant afford a ticket, not with my money. I got a job to mix the drinks in the Directors' Box as the PM is coming tonight.'

'That bastard Harry Shite? Oh my God. He is every-where. Why don't you poison him while you are at it? I can give you a few tips if you wish.'

Roger went cold with fright but only for a second. It was macabre how the whole world seemed to have the same idea.

'No thanks. I am not political anymore. I just want the wad of dosh at the end of the evening. Poisoning Harry White may make it difficult for me to get paid, especially if he was to drop dead at my feet, thanks to one of your lethal recipes.' Roger was skating on dangerously thin ice now, but enjoying the delicious irony.

'Well, he is coming to the campus in a few minutes, and I am off to barrack him. You may be apolitical. I am not. I want to teach him a lesson which will make him stay away from Glasgow for ever. See you.' Ken was keen to sign off.

Roger heaved a sigh of relief. He was running out of time and Ken could have talked for ever. He wanted to avoid any chance of Harry seeing him. He did not think Harry would recognise him after all these years but then politicians have long memories of faces and names. If he saw Harry suddenly before he had carried out his plot, his resolution might weaken. So Roger had to get out of the place fast.

6.25 p.m. London, outside the National Film Theatre, South Bank

It took some time but Lisa came staggering out with a large tray loaded with everyone's favourite drink. It was difficult to get Pernod, but not impossible. The bartender had to look around the stocks at the back for a spare bottle. The sherry and bitters and vodka tonics were easy. Shouts of joy and applause greeted her. They were determined to make every gossip column the next morning. No such thing as bad publicity, Lisa always said.

'So tell me Lisa, what is it that you get away with?' Annie was still curious.

'You know, the odd escapade, just to keep one's ego intact.'

'Like who?'

'Well, since you don't know anyone, and are not likely to meet them...'

'Or, remember their names, if you told me,' Annie was egging her friend on now.

'There was a nice Tory once. Man called Roscoe Hartley. Tories are ever so polite with women. They are chauvinist bastards, of course, but then so are Harry's lot, except that Tories have manners. They also have the dosh so you can meet in posh places, very safe.'

'Sounds alright to me. But what was Harry doing at this time?'

'Well, he was in opposition, and I am afraid he was working hard to make a fool of Roscoe in Parliament.'

'Did he succeed?'

'He had to. That was the least Roscoe could do for me. Though mind you, I never asked. He had given me enough to be happy as it was.'

'Do you still see him?'

'Occasionally. He is in the House of Lords now, and he is on the Board of the Royal National.'

'So will he be there tomorrow?'

'I hope so, but so will Harry.'

'You must introduce me. I am dying to meet the gallant Lord.'

'But you wouldn't fancy him. You are not into les garcons in any case.'

'Well it's always fun, how did you put it, to keep my ego intact. I don't want to be typecast you know, chin chin,' Annie winked and raised her glass.

'Down the hatch and long live liberation.'

6.30 p.m. London, The Bell Yard, off Fleet Street

Linda knocked and came in.

'She is on her way to Glasgow on the shuttle and they expect her there by seven forty-five. She will be at the Meridien. I gather the office car will pick her up at the airport.'

Linda knew the score. No names mentioned. She

handed the flight details to Asha on a piece of paper;
can't trust email to be confidential.

'Thanks Linda.'

'Shall I get our friend in Glasgow for you?'

'Please, Linda. Thanks.'

Asha knew that Linda could read her mind a couple
of steps ahead, but would never say the words, just in
case she had to answer any queries in the future. Asha
could happily leave Linda in charge, and know she
would be equal to anything.

6.30 p.m. Glasgow, Ibrox Stadium

David Byrne held on tightly to the hands of his twin
sons Robbie and Alistair. Although it was still an hour
and a bit to go, the stadium was filling up. He had chosen
the tickets in a somewhat expensive range thinking this
would keep the crowds down. Sophie had been unsure
whether taking the twins to the game was a good idea,
given the reputation of the fans on both sides. So David
had called the Rangers ticket office and said he wanted
to bring his eight-year-old twins to the Old Firm game
and asked whether there was any problem, any risk of
violence? A polite, soft-spoken woman at the other
end of the phone assured him that Rangers had a strict
stewarding policy nowadays. They wanted families to
come and enjoy good football. When David said this
was the boys' birthday treat, the woman said she would
give him a good price for the seats. She also gave them
seats near the bottom so the boys could see the game
without people blocking their view. Still, David took

the precaution to arrive early.

David was an ex-marine. After giving up his job as a marine, he had taken up security jobs. They had a lovely house in Ayr, from where David and the boys had driven down at ten in the morning. Sophie thought it best to be at home with Nicola. She was six and very cross that she was not included in the party, but Sophie promised to take her to Glasgow on her birthday, just the two of them, girls together. So that did the trick. The day had passed in going to the Haggs Castle where the kids were delighted by all the children's things down the centuries, but they had little patience for the People's Palace. The history of Glasgow city was boring for them, though David always enjoyed it, having grown up there. They had their treat of sausages and chips and ice cream in between the two Museums. The People's Park was a good place to rest as they could just sit and look at the river and relax. They ate the sandwiches Sophie had packed for them. The boys were tired, otherwise David would have taken them across to St. Mungo's as well. He was, after all, the founder saint of Glasgow or rather Gleschow—Green Place—way back in the sixth century. But all his descriptions of the lovely thirteenth century Cathedral were of no avail.

Now they were in the Stadium.

'Dad, this is so big, isn't it?' Robbie's eyes were popping out.

'Dad, how old is this place? Is it very old?' Alistair asked.

'Dad when will the match start?' Robbie again

'You know it is at a quarter to eight Robbie. Dad has

already told us that.' Alistair knew and he had to tell.

'OK. We have plenty of time. So let me tell you. Rangers started way back in 1872. But they moved here about a hundred years ago.'

'Is that older than you are, Dad?' Alistair again.

'It is older than your mum and me put together. If you add Grandpa's age and mine that comes to just over a hundred. So you can see.'

'Dad who will win today? Rangers or Celtic?' Robbie asked

'I want Rangers to win.' Alistair said.

'Why Alistair?' David asked.

'Cos this is their ground.'

'I want Celtic to win then.' Robbie had to choose the other side.

'Who do you think will score first? Rangers or Celtic?' David asked.

'Rangers. Numan will score first.' Alistair had read about the match.

'I think Larsson is the best,' Robbie said.

'Well, let us see which of you two is right.'

The stadium was filling up on all sides. There was already a lot of singing and shouting. Looking around, David Byrne was not reassured that this was a family-friendly gathering. Many displayed tattoos and clean shaven heads, bare arms and knuckle dusters at the ready. Their dress was an odd mixture of T-shirts and torn trousers and some kilts, funny hats and earrings and even some wrist bands which were more like steel bangles. There were not many women but those who were there were at one with the men, with faces painted in the colours of their favourite teams and garish make up and, yes, tattoos and various degrees of under-dressing. But there was music playing on the PA system and the overhead TV was showing clips from previous Rangers matches. The boys, at least, were fascinated. David Byrne carefully noted the various exit signs. You never know.

6.35 p.m. London, House of Commons

Frank Thompson hated it when Harry was away, and he had to be in charge. One would have thought, and indeed many hoped, that he would be itching to take over, and give the Party its old heritage back. But Frank knew he had come to the peak of his career. A coal miner's son from Barnsley, he had escaped his fate of going down the mines like his father and his grand-father, but only by running away from home. It was after one of those nights when his father had come home more drunk than normal and taken the strap to his mother. Frank had intervened and was beaten to within an inch of his life. He had staggered out the very next day. He ran away to the sea, but got only as far as Grimsby. He joined the fishing fraternity, but they soon found out that he was only fourteen, and so Social Services took him in. He was sent to a technical school. When they noted his ability at reading and writing, they taught him the printing trade.

By the time he was eighteen, Frank had a job in Leeds in the newspaper printing business. These were the days of hot metallic press, and printing unions were rough and powerful. Frank learnt his revolutionary economics in the trade union branch. Soon he was a delegate, and before he was forty on the Executive Committee and an alternate delegate to the Trades Union Congress. He could attend the annual Conference of the TUC and vote if the main delegate was absent for some reason.

He kept up his studies, following courses with the Open University. Being a Union official gave him the chance to do evening courses in Leeds Polytechnic. He loved his courses and argued the backs off his teachers. They all fancied themselves as Marxists or whatever, but they had never been near a lathe. Frank kept on haranguing them, as they subtly taught him the ways of winning an argument. They made Frank into a well-read, patient persuader. He was extremely proud of his B.A. Political Economy and did not mind that it was only an Ordinary, not an Honours degree.

There was a knock at the door, and the Chief Whip, Austin Mills, came in without waiting for an invitation.

'What's up Austin?'

'Have you heard anything about Libya? What is Harry planning?'

'Haven't the faintest. Ask Nick Davies.'

'Can't after lunch, as you know. He is too pissed to talk to. He will sober up about seven for half an hour.'

'Isn't that soon enough?'

'It's just that I have a feeling in my bones Eric and the idle boys are up to something. Jimmy would not come with me to Annie's for a pint.'

'Well, that is pretty serious. What's up?' Frank came

back to his favourite conversational gambit.

'Eric and Alex and Jimmy will probably table a motion on our Libya policy for Wednesday's party meeting.'

'Let them. They will get ten votes.'

'Harry would take that as a serious revolt, and my job would be on the line.' Austin knew the score with Harry.

'I wish our leader had lived through the days when we had no majority to speak of. Two lads down with flu, and we were on tenterhooks. In those days, you expected a revolt every afternoon and thanked your stars it had not happened by division bell time at ten. He now has four hundred MPs and freaks out at a revolt of ten.'

'He was still learning his knives and forks at Cambridge in those days.'

'Oh no. Harry knew that in his kindergarten. They don't let you into those posh public schools with coal in your bathtub. No, he was learning his economics, which helped him to make a lot of money at that fancy foreign bank.'

'Which is why he can speak in German in Bonn and French in Paris. He is not one of us, is he now?'

'He is our leader, and that is good enough for me. I have been here longer than him, but it makes me nervous to stand at the Dispatch Box. Look at him, the way he slaughters Peter Portugal every week.'

That was it. Frank had found that all his education did not measure up to a tenth of what Harry had. He was not fluent in any foreign language. He could harangue the Conference, but in the cut and thrust of the House of Commons, he usually lost. As the new intake came in the 1980s, Frank began to feel the difference. In the earlier days, the new MPs would be trade unionists or teachers or just maybe an odd old barrister. But the new lot were all fresh University graduates with Doctorates and the like. They spoke posh and used long words that threw Frank. But, while the others patronised him, Harry had made friends. He had asked him about the lore of the Party—the myths and the legends, the hoary old disputes and the alphabet soup of the initials of the many sectarian formations. Harry never said what his opinion was about anyone or any issue. He always listened with attention, and thanked Frank for all he had told him with enthusiasm. Previous leaders had not forgiven Frank for one or other quarrel of the 1970s. But Harry was innocent of all that, or wished to be.

In befriending Frank, Harry was buying into the Party's past. In a myriad subtle ways, Harry won Frank over to his side. He wielded the scalpel, using Frank as a battering ram when necessary. The more he got to know Harry, the more Frank was convinced that he was not cut out to be a leader. He was a Deputy, and a faithful one at that. Harry was the works as far as Frank was concerned. And anyway, he loathed Terence and the Scottish Mafia.

'Listen, I will send my spies out. Can you do a stint in the Chamber?'

Frank looked at the House of Commons Annunciator and groaned. On the TV screen, it said the subject being discussed had to do with the Department of Culture. They were debating the Arts Council grant, a right load of waste if you asked Frank.

6.40 p.m. Glasgow, in the Prime Minister's car

Sarah was pleasantly squashed in the car. Harry and Oliver sat next to each other with the Inspector in the front seat. When it came to getting in the car, Harry saw to it that Sarah was at his side. It was something Sarah had not even dreamed of the previous weekend. Here she was, thigh to thigh (with layers of fabric in between, of course) with Harry. He smelt nice as well.

'Why don't we drop Sarah off at the hotel before we get out to the meeting? Someone can bring her to the game, Oliver.'

'No problem. It is on our way anyway, since the University is downtown as well. But we will have to be quick.' Oliver did not want Harry to linger too long with his new conquest.

It would have been much more sensible to send Sarah off with one of the local cars but Harry would have none of it. So, a detour had to be made to drop Sarah off at the Meridien. She would have an hour to change. Sarah thanked her stars she did not have time to dither in choosing what to wear. Her lunchtime expedition had fixed her choice. It'd better work, she thought. But work at what?

Oliver's pager buzzed. It was Christine.

'Expect a call from DC.'

It soon came. It was the President.

Harry was suddenly very serious. All around him in the car knew they were not supposed to listen.

'Hi, Rob. What can I do for you?'

'Harry, glad we can talk. We are about to go on Operation Rosa. It should happen by 5 p.m. Eastern, O.K?'

'Sure Rob. No problem. It will be ten o'clock our time. We will handle it at our end. I will tell Mary Duggan to liaise with your guys. Our chaps are eager to go.'

'You're a pal, mate. We will go public five minutes before zero hour.'

Operation Rosa was the codename for the US bombing of Libya. It had been under consideration for some time, but the precise date and time had to be the Pentagon's decision. Harry had won a small role for the RAF as support team in the operation. The American bombers were to take off from Fakenham in Norfolk, so there were bound to be questions in Parliament. Mary Duggan was Harry's unorthodox choice as Defence Secretary. She had been on the left of the Party, but was not a pacifist. With her Irish Catholic background, she had always regarded force as necessary for achieving a United Ireland. In her student days, she had associated with IRA front organisations. But, over the years since, she had steadily drifted away. She realised that a sectarian movement can easily turn intolerant; there was a huge distance between sectarianism and socialism. Mary was a socialist, first and last.

Now, she was in Harry's cabinet. She had shadowed defence very successfully. They liked her immensely in the armed forces. She could swear like a trooper, never fussed about going anywhere, no matter how risky and how inconvenient. She wore no make-up, and her clothes were jumble sale stuff. Mary had become one of the boys, a true success story of Harry's cabinet.

'What about Nick Davies?' Oliver asked.

'If we keep the news from him past his wakeful hour, he will never complain. Tell Christine to get Frank ready for questions in the Commons. It should be a Prime Ministerial Statement, read out by Frank. That way, neither Mary nor Nick can complain. Where will we be at ten o'clock?'

'The game finishes at around quarter to ten, so you will be at the dinner in the Director's room at the Ibrox.'

'I'd rather be in the air on my way to Belfast. That way the reptiles won't get to me.' Harry's first concern was to avoid the media at this juncture.

'I can keep them away, if I have to. But we can always claim urgent business.'

'If bombing starts at ten, they will want a spokesman on *Newsnight*… Get Mary Duggan to cover that. Frank can schedule his statement after Division, say around ten fifteen. They can carry that live on late news. Ask Christine to send over the draft statement, I left it with her, and while I am speaking at the Party rally, you revise it. I will give the final run over on our way to the game. Can we get it across before the game starts?'

'Depending on how soon we can get out of the Rally, we may just make that deadline. If not, I will do it while you are watching your least favourite sport.

Don't worry. We have all the stuff necessary to set up a mobile communications centre.'

'Can I be of any help?' Sarah asked hesitantly

'Thanks Sarah, but not really necessary. You will be reached at your hotel by Christine if she wants to pass something on. We have cleared the Hotel for security. You can then bring it over to the match.'

Oliver was businesslike as usual, but he didn't really want Sarah to see a top secret statement. Harry turned to her, fixed her with his blue eyes.

'You haven't come here to work, Sarah. Christine said you had to enjoy your trip here.'

As he said that he threw his arm around her shoulders, and drew her a fraction of an inch nearer. Sarah was happy to be squeezed by the Prime Ministerial fingers. Things can only get better, she thought.

'I intend to enjoy myself. If I don't, Christine will kill me.'

Harry caught the mischief in her eyes.

'Oh, no. It's me who she will blame. So I have to see to it that you have a good time.'

Oliver busied himself with his mobile. Harry's hand was now travelling up and down Sarah's bare arm, so Oliver too moved away an inch from Harry. Sarah let her hand rest on Harry's thigh. Then, very easily, she found herself stroking it.

'Could you tell Gordon's people to go straight to the meeting? Tell them we will stop at the hotel for a few minutes while we settle Sarah in, OK, Barney?'

'Yes, Sir.' Inspector Barney Jones started on his mobile.

How many minutes would that be? Sarah was asking loudly, but only inside her head. Whatever time it would be, she knew she had to be ready for whatever it was Harry had in his mind. It was only eight hours since Christine had broached the subject of her going to Glasgow, and here she was already panting for...for what?

They were at the hotel in the George Square. Gideon had connections so all the big visits ended up at this location. Rooms had been booked for the PM's party, though everyone knew he would hardly be there for long. But an office had to be set up, and Harry preferred it away from the usual Party bureaucracy or the Scottish Office.

They stopped just off the Square, and got out swiftly. There was no crowd but Sarah could hear some people shouting, 'Hey, Harry! How are you?' The Harry in question was gently detaching himself from her, and once again being Prime Minister. The Manager had come out with all his staff to welcome the Prime Minister, and made a little speech welcoming him to Glasgow and the hospitality of his hotel. Sarah wished he would shut up, and get out of the way.

Harry thanked him very graciously, introduced Sarah and Oliver, but his manner was urgent without being hurried. The Manager offered to show them to their room, but Harry signalled that they had to rush. Oliver had to view the equipment set up in the Prime Min-isterial suite. Harry took the keys from the Manager's hand, and got into the lift with Oliver and Sarah.

Not a word said, but Oliver went on to the big suite,

and Sarah was led by Harry to her room. It was a large room overlooking the Square but dominated by a large bed. There were two sofa chairs by the window with a table beside it. Sarah threw her jacket over one of them, as she heard the door click shut behind her. It was Harry, right behind her, holding her. He was no slouch as his hands roamed all over her. She sighed, and leant back towards him. She took his hands and put them where she knew Harry was headed. He had to see that she had a superb pair of breasts.

Soon, he was kissing her with passion and power. She was with him all the way, returning his tongue with her tongue, laughing and murmuring his name. He was fantastic, cupping her breasts in his hands one second, nuzzling her neck, sliding his hand down her back and grabbing her firm buttocks and round again.

Sarah was amazed to see how strong and taut Harry's body was. His jacket was off, and he had loosened his tie, so all she had to get on to was his belt. But he seized her busy hand, and took it further down so she could feel how stiff he was. And impatient, Sarah thought.

Her dress had slipped off on to the floor and Harry had expertly unhooked her bra at the back. A man of experience, to be sure. He gently nudged her towards the bed. Her feet were still on the floor but there she was drawing Harry's mouth to her nipples. He yanked off her—Oh MY GOD what colour were they, were they decent?—underpants. No time to think. The man wanted her and Sarah welcomed him. Harry was half standing, his mouth now exploring her belly and venturing further down. She suddenly had a thought.

'Harry?'

'What?'

'Can I have a…?'

Harry looked surprised, thrilled and immediately knew what she meant. She slid down and crouched taking his throbbing cock in her mouth. She licked it, stroked it with the tip of her tongue and then just for a quick second put her mouth round it. He gasped.

'OK, all yours.'

She was back on the bed spreadeagled, welcoming Harry inside her. He had been enormously aroused by her gesture. His first hard thrust meant it was her turn to gasp. He was unstoppable as he came in and out, all the while telling her how fabulous she was, kissing her, biting her, as she tried not to dig her nails into him.

It seemed like ages, but then he exploded inside her. She hadn't even thought about it but there they were practising unsafe sex. More unsafe the better, she thought. By the time he got a condom, the Division bells would ring in London.

Harry reached out for a box of tissues by the bedside table and ever so gently withdrew, kissing her yet again on her hard nipples. He gave her some tissues and started carefully wiping himself. Sarah drew the bedsheet over her, suddenly shy. She had not been so aroused for ages and her orgasm left her serene and floating, savouring the moment, thinking of all that fire and that frenzy.

Harry was in and out of the bathroom in no time, looking immaculate. His tie back on, hair in place, not a smudge of lipstick or something worse. He leaned over her, gently pecked her nipples and then kissed her full and long.

'It will be slower next time, I promise you.'

'If I let you be slow that is. Sprinters do more laps than marathon runners, Prime Minister.'

'Yes, Miss Disney.'

'See you at the match.' And then he was gone.

And soon after, she thought. She looked at her watch. It was not yet seven. He had plenty of time to get to his meeting. They had after all taken only five minutes.

Sarah luxuriated in a state of half sleep for some time. Then she ran a hot bath for herself. The hotel had thoughtfully provided aromatic bath salts and gels. As she lay there in a heat-induced torpor, she wondered what Alan would think, if he could have seen her in the last half hour. But there was more to come. She had to be at the game. There was so little time, now that her life was in the fast lane.

8.00 p.m. Vienna, Hotel Franz Joseph, Room 305

Alan was too amazed and astonished at how smooth, white and fragrant Jo's body was to think of anything else, much less of Sarah. This was the first time he had been with Jo with absolute privacy and acres of room to play in. In London, Jo shared a flat with three others, and the few times they had been at his place, the flat-mates were for ever going in and out of each other's rooms as if it was some BBC sitcom. They had had to rush everything; it was almost like teenage sex in the backseat of a car. Now, there was this large double room in the Franz Joseph with a large DO NOT DIS-

TURB sign in four languages outside. The drinks had been ordered, along with enough sausages and chips to keep room service out of their way. And then there was Jo. He was almost as tall as Alan but younger and thinner. His attraction had been his look of vulnerability with his eagerness to please. Alan had watched him at work, and on the football pitch. It was when they were in the shower together that he had been smitten by Jo. But then, there were eight other raucous men in the showers after a hard game of five-a-side soccer. Thus it was that Alan began to make excuses to Sarah. He was exhausted, or worried, and would come very late to bed. He had realised his true passion.

As Alan drooled over Jo, he also began to thrill to the discovery that young as he was, Jo was no novice. He knew all the arts of flirting, coaxing and seducing those he wanted to fancy him. A nibble here and a bite there, some amazing deep-throated kisses directing Alan to where he wanted to be caressed. He teased Alan as much as he could in the confines of their room, escaping and then getting caught. Alan was in the seventh heaven as he impatiently pushed himself inside Jo.

'Thank Heavens for Vienna.'

8.02 p.m. Vienna, Hotel Franz Joseph, Room 402

Terence Harcourt could have echoed those sentiments word for word. Not that he was engaged in any carnal pursuits. Not yet anyway. Terence's style was to take it slowly, prepare carefully and then have his pleasure in a leisurely way. He believed that making love was like committing a murder. However passionate the act, you had to be cool headed about it before and after. You had to plan every move to get your quarry. Then, after the deed, you had to make sure that no clues would be found. Clear away all the smudges and the stains. Wipe off every tell tale sign. Change the sheets, dump the towels in the laundry basket, flush the biodegradable bits down the loo. The point of having pleasure, especially of the illicit variety, was to be able to enjoy its afterglow. For that, you had to take the worrying out of the thought that someone, somewhere may find out what you were up to. This is why he preferred inside to outside and home to hotels, and younger to older girls. They tended not to complain or tell tales. Even when one was having adult consensual sex, a politician could not be careful enough. Journalists do not judge politicians by their own moral standards, and even young and innocent-looking volunteer researchers keep diaries for that future newspaper exclusive.

So Terence did a lot of his pleasure-seeking abroad, and he kept it to towns, where there was a culture of tolerance. Vienna was his favourite city for that reason. Brothels were legal, as was soliciting in the city centre. He had made this discovery thirty years previously walking in the Kohlmarkt after a good dinner. Taking a short cut to his hotel, he was surprised to be approached by a tall blonde. She could not have been as old as she claimed to be. She was obviously dressed for a purpose, and her matter of fact manner had taken him aback. But he had really enjoyed this first encounter in a large bedroom in a hotel nearby that seemed to be furnished for pleasure. Indeed, the hotel was owned by an Italian woman who had a stable full of young girls around in various kinds of dress and make up. Rosa Giulia was a kindly large lady, who seemed to be a kind of universal mother whore.

There was no fuss, no worry. Rosa Giulia provided all her girls with condoms and health care. Terence took some time getting used to condom sex, but he had no other complaint,. The girls knew how to please him, and got up to all sorts of tricks once Terence conveyed his desires in sign language. The money was reasonable, the Pound was strong in those days. Half an hour later Terence had discovered his El Dorado.

Tonight, Terence was looking forward to visiting his old haunts, now of course away from the Stefanplatz and the Kohlmarkt, and along the Gurtel where there were other nightclubs and houses and women soliciting the cars speeding past. What with the Balkan wars and Eastern European immigration, young Slav and Hungarian and Polish women had flooded Vienna. The choice was just fantastic. Soon, he would be making a beeline for Rosa Giulia's. But before that, he had to have dinner with the Ambassador. He needed a stiff drink or two to endure that.

7.05 p.m. London, House of Commons Terrace

'Cheers,' Frank said as he raised his pint of John Smith. 'So what's up Ian?'

Ian was looking for stories, not about to provide any. He had been hanging around the House of Commons

Terrace, hoping to catch some minister, even of a lowly variety, to find out more about the revolt brewing up. But he had had no luck. The old practice of MPs hanging around Annie's Bar and the Terrace or the Pugin Room had waned. They all had halfway decent offices now but outside the Westminster Palace and a short walk away on the other side of the street. They were all young snots, sitting at their computers, e-mailing their constituents. They came into the Palace only when asked by their pagers to do so. As for the rest, the whips had to make sure that enough bodies were in the Chamber to keep track of the business, but not too many as they might start caucusing. That way lay trouble. Only the old hands, the unreconstructed reprobates, still behaved like independent, free-thinking adults. But Ian knew their stories anyway. So, it was to avoid them that he had wandered past the library. As he was walking down the long corridor behind the Speaker's Chair, who should come out of the Chamber but Frank. Ian had never before seen Frank so pleased to see him. Frank had been bored out of his mind listening to the Arts Council debate. He was getting angry, and could have shouted 'Bollocks' at more than one speaker as they went on about the good things the Arts Council did. He had done his time, and Austin should be content with that.

'Nothing very much, Frank. You know I am retired so I am hardly the person to ask.'

'So, if you are retired like, what are you doing in this den of iniquity?'

'To tell you the truth, I was hoping to pick up a

few stories about Harry White that I could use in the obituary I am writing. No, don't panic. Nothing has happened to him.'

Ian had to add that quickly, because he saw Frank was about to spew his beer all over him, as he gasped at the word obituary.

'Well, it's not as if there aren't a few people who wish he was dead. And they are in his own party as well, even here.'

'You are not getting paranoid are you now, Frank?'

'No, it is the ingratitude of the human race which gets me. Especially in this Party that I dearly love. They don't remember any longer that we were crushed flat till Harry came along and added two hundred seats. Now they have found their old religion again, and it's Tolpuddle martyrs time all of a sudden.'

'But, surely, that is a healthy sign. The Party is back to its bad old ways, because it is no longer scared of losing the next election.'

'You've been around long enough, Ian. We behaved like that when we had a negative majority, remember. Harry is innocent of all that. I had to tell him the stories of those long nights, when we had comrades in wheel chairs and ambulance beds arriving to vote. Now we have a rota to keep them off the premises in case idle hands turn to mischief.'

'How can you keep Eric off from this place? It is his home.'

'His kennel, more like.'

'You are in a foul mood today, Frank.'

'Aye, I always am, when Harry is not around. And, I

suspect that gang is up to no good, but don't quote me on that.'

'Promise. But what are they up to?'

'The usual. Motion before the Party meeting on Libya. What else?'

'But that would get them ten votes. Why bother?'

'Just what I said to Austin. But he's afraid Harry will cut up badly.'

'Even with that small a revolt?'

'Harry is the only Stalinist I know, who wins elections with an Opposition not in jail.'

'Can I quote you on that?'

'Don't you dare.'

7.10 p.m. Glasgow, Ibrox Stadium

Daring is what Roger decided he had to be. Daring and discreet. He knew Harry wouldn't recognise him, not in the middle of a crowd of sycophants, all jostling to get the Prime Ministerial ear. All he had to do was to get his drink ready. He was sure Harry had not changed his habits about drinking. But there were still tricky issues ahead. He guessed Harry would not arrive in time to have a drink before the game. So, it was either in the half-time break, or if not, then after the final whistle, that he would want a drink. Roger had to be careful, since he did not want to be around when Harry was sinking. His experiments had only been on hamsters, and the rest was based on his extensive reading of cases of death as a result of poisoning. So, he had to give Harry his lethal drink sometime during the dinner after the game, say about ten o'clock. Harry was bound to get away quickly after dinner, and so Roger could safely leave as well.

'Roger, nice to see you. Didn't know you were on today.'

It was Alex. He always greeted people at the Ibrox. Alex had been there for decades, and knew all about the Club. Bored Roger stiff since he had heard those stories a hundred times. But today, Alex was looking spruce and smart.

'So Alex, what are you all dressed up for then? Not for the Papists, surely?'

'Now, now, lad. We don't talk like that anymore, do we? It is the Prime Minister himself, that I put my finery on for. You know something Roger, in all the years I have been here, let us say fifty-three years man and boy, no Prime Minister has ever come to the Ibrox, not even for the Old Firm Game.'

'You wait all these years, and all you get is Harry White, eh?'

'Don't be cheeky now. We have to give him a welcome he will remember the rest of his days, Roger. Take it you will be dishing out everyone's favourite poison as usual. Let Harry White have the best of whatever he wants.'

'Will do Alex, as you say.'

'Did you know, Roger, Rangers are still ahead on the score since the first fixture in 1888. Guess how far ahead?'

'Tell me, Alex,' Roger said with a resigned tone.

'We are three ahead, thirty five to thirty two, the

rest being draws. And, you know what, they have not had a win since before…'

'Must go, Alex. Have loads of work to do preparing for the big event. Cheers.'

'I should say… We are going to have the biggest crowd tonight for a long time. Did you know Roger, when was the largest crowd we have had?'

'No, tell me Alex.' Roger started climbing the stairs but Alex was right behind

'January 2nd, 1939. It was an Old Firm game as well and there were 118,567 in the crowd and you know what? There has never been a larger crowd anywhere in a League level match, not in Scotland, not in England. Not anywhere. Tonight may compare with it, though.'

'Well, I hope they all behave themselves. It is such a crucial game I hope nothing bad happens,' Roger said, more in hope than anticipation.

'Don't worry lad. We have not had that sort of trouble here for ages. I can tell you, Scotland is a new country since we got this Parliament promised to us. People know the eyes of the world are on them.'

'Well, if it is not the new Parliament, the fact that there is no major League game anywhere on a Monday night will ensure that Rainbow TV gets a global audience. Matt Drummond will make a killing tonight.' Roger did not know how long Alex would have detained him but luckily he saw someone else coming towards him, so he took his leave.

'Hello, uncle Alex,' Red said.

Alex was very surprised to see his new visitor. Guests invited to the match with seats in the top seats were arriving and he did not wish to be seen with his new arrival.

'What on earth brings you here, McGann? Hope you are not looking for tickets because there aren't any, and, even if there were, you are not welcome.' Alex was firm.

'Is this any way to speak to your own nephew, uncle Alex? Don't worry. I don't want any tickets and I am not here to embarrass you.' Red was unusually emollient.

'So, why are you here? I have work to do. Tell me quick.'

'I just wanted a glimpse of our Prime Minister. I thought you could let me stand here somewhere so I can see him arriving in his snazzy car. I thought I could take a photo. You know. For my mam. She would love it.' Red showed Alex his digital camera as proof of his intentions.

'I don't believe a word of any of that. But seeing you are my sister's only son, though I dare say you will go the way your father did—but I do hope that happens before you entice some lass to marry you. Stand in that corner under that awning and don't attract any one's attention. If you get caught, I don't know you.' Saying that, Alex turned away from Red.

'But tell me, uncle Alex, are you going to be standing outside all evening and not to get to see the great game?' Red had to know something more.

'Don't you fear, son. I shall be watching it on Rainbow sitting in my office down here where I can keep an eye on the comings and goings. It is not just me, you know. I have to look after all the drivers who don't want to miss out either. So we have set up some nice entertainment facilities down here. But don't go around getting any ideas of trouble making. There will be police presence through the evening. It is not every day the Prime Minister comes to Ibrox.' Alex knew his nephew was up to no good.

'Why should I make trouble, and that too at Ibrox? I just thought I could relieve you of looking out so you could watch the game.'

'No thank you. Now get going.' Alex had other guests to welcome.

Red got to his spot and he was happy because this was the front of the main entrance and VIP cars would be parked there. He saw various painted signs for the Chairman and the Vice Chairman. There was even one for the manager. Reserved car parking space, real posh. So Harry White's car was bound to be parked here. That was all Red needed to know. Now he just had to wait. He knew that watching the game would be too strong a temptation for any policeman. They would get complacent after a while and drift in to watch and he just had to be prepared for the moment.

After he had taken his leave of Alex, Roger bounded up the stairs to the Directors' Dining Room. It was by no means a big room, nor even very luxuriously furnished. Roger had once been at the Oval, when Cambridge were playing Surrey. The Oval lunch room had been prodigiously large compared to this. The walls here were covered with Rangers Trophies with the pride of place for the European Cup Winners Cup of 1972 displayed prominently. That was the memorable game in

Barcelona when Rangers beat Moscow Dynamo 3-2, with Willie Waddell as the manager, and the moment was captured in his photograph with the winning team. Even more prominent was Bill Struth who had been Manager in the '20s. Bill would play the piano to soothe his nerves and, in those days, the piano used to be kept in a separate room for him, the Blue Room. Roger thought Waddell was the greater manager though he had stayed only three years. He had been a player for the Rangers but came back to manage. Once Jock Stein had won the European Cup with Celtics in 1967, it was agony for the Rangers to be taunted by their arch enemy that they had been only runners up at best, not winners. So, 1972 was the most memorable Cup victory in the annals of the club. Waddell quit after having got the Cup to Ibrox. There were lots of other trophies and memorabilia—Scottish FA Cups, Scottish League Cups, including the racing bicycle that the St Etienne football team had presented to the Rangers team when they played in the European Cup together in 1975. But the predominant impression was of a lot of solid wooden furniture. On the left hand side, there was a smaller office for the really important guests, and on the right was an anteroom where the preparations had to be made for the half-time drinks. They would have to re-arrange the rooms for dinner. Roger had to set up his bar in the right hand side corner, next to the windows.

7.15 p.m. London, The Bell Yard, off Fleet Street

Asha had to set up her long distance gig. She had to be

careful and hope that Willie, her mate in the Transport unit of LDNC Glasgow office, understood her. Willie was from Singapore but had to leave the place, since he was a radical in those days. Asha's father was his mentor. Once he got to Britain, Willie lost his politics but he also found it very difficult to get any job that would use his education. They could not quite understand his accent and so he was hopeless as a tutor. He started doing odd jobs. He got a job in the newspaper industry to arrange delivery. This was high pressure work as a lot of lorries had to be galvanised in a short span of time to deliver the new print run late at night across Glasgow and the rest of Scotland. Some bundles had to be put on trains so they got to London and Manchester and Birmingham. Willie soon became an expert, since he had the mathematical skills for scheduling such transport runs. He had met Asha soon after she had arrived in London and helped her settle in. Asha had always taken Willie into her confidence. He was now quite a well paid manager in Matt Drummond's Scottish newspaper offices. When Asha wanted something done that she could not trust anyone else with, it was Willie she turned to. He was her Chinese cousin.

She had taken care to go to a public telephone outside the Temple. It was her favourite red telephone box, a rarity nowadays but at least she could use it to contact Willie as he knew the number... The noise was awful on the Strand, and she had to shout.

'Just a brush, not more. All we want are scars, which need hospitalisation. Take great care. I expect she does not use seat belts.'

'I hear you, loud and clear. Over and out.' Willie had also taken care to go to a public telephone in Glasgow. He had many delivery vans as well as drivers on a casual contract at his disposal, and driving at an insane speed was their speciality. If one of them drives a limousine off the road in a crash, so what?

7.18 p.m. Glasgow, a meeting room on the Campus

'So, what if the Scot Nats win, you say? I will tell you what is at stake. All that the Scottish Labour Party has built up here in Glasgow and all over Scotland, all that the Labour Party in the country has built up—the schools, the hospitals, the benefits...'

Harry had spoken for five minutes and could sense that there was going to be a lot of heckling. So, he swiftly moved into a question–answer mode. That way, the heat would go out of the meeting.

'Bullshit. Who cut the single mothers benefits?' Ken MacIntosh was first off the mark.

'We did not cut them, as you say. We have radically restructured them, so the single mothers have opportunities to work, to get out of the poverty trap, to have better life chances.' Harry had to shout in the crowded hall of hundreds of angry men and women. There were banners: 'No War with Libya', 'Raise the Minimum Wage to £5', 'Nationalise ScotRail'.

'Call that Socialism, do you?' Ken persisted.

'I will tell you what. Which country do you think has the same single mothers benefit system as us?'

'Bantustan,' someone shouted, and there was laughter and loud applause.

'Not really. It is Sweden, Socialist Sweden which has the same policy as we do. And so do Norway and also Denmark. Life has changed. I tell you, we don't live in Clement Attlee's Britain any longer. There is a big revolution out there, called Globalisation. If we don't prepare to compete with the world, it will be the Chinese workers and the Korean bosses who will dominate world trade. We need to reskill our workers. Even single mothers will need a proper job some day, when their babies grow up. They need education to do that. As do the long term unemployed. They should be in further education institutes getting a diploma, not hanging about in despair because they are on the dole. We need to invest in our people; not dream about Scotland's oil as the Nats do. They will just spend all the taxpayers' money, and crash the economy and then who will bail Scotland out?'

'Scotland's oil for Scotland,' someone shouted.

'Shouting slogans is easy. But who will pay, if the oil is nationalised? Are you willing to take on a debt of 75 billion pounds? And what for? So that the oil companies who are at present taking risks of profit and loss, sleep happily at peace with our money, and our grandchildren are still paying off the interest on that debt? Is that what you want? Because that is what the Scot Nats are offering you, dreams and delusions of spend now, pay tomorrow and the day after and for a century more. Is that what we want?'

There was applause, albeit signalled from the platform by Gideon's claque. Harry White appreciated the pause.

'What about Libya? Are we going to be America's poodle and bomb Libya?'

'I am proud of our special relationship with America. Every Labour Prime Minister has cherished that special…'

'Except Ramsay MacDonald,' someone shouted. More applause and laughter.

Harry needed this.

'Well, I am sorry, but I have never thought of Ramsay MacDonald as a Labour Prime Minister. If you think he was, you are in the wrong party, mate.'

There was thunderous applause. Harry had touched the oldest raw nerve in the Party's collective psyche. A cliché yes, bashing Ramsay MacDonald, but it worked, especially in Scotland. Go to any Labour meeting and you only had to say 'Ramsay MacDonald' to know that your audience was at one with you. He had betrayed the Labour Party in the midst of the Depression and got into a cosy coalition with the Tories and split the Party. Ramsay MacDonald was the one Scottish leader who became Prime Minister and then he blotted his record. Scotland never forgave its son.

'And not just every Labour Prime Minister. Even Stan Davies, our dear departed leader, and how I wish he was standing here in front of you as a Labour Prime Minister…' The rest of Harry's sentence was drowned in applause.

'Yes, and it is for Stan who promised Scotland its own Parliament that we must win the election. Don't let the Scot Nats steal our clothes and pretend that they did anything to bring this about. It is our Party and our Party alone with the able leadership of Gideon Crawford—where is Gideon?—come up here. Gideon Crawford, my friends, who will lead the Party to victory in the coming elections. Thank you, but as you know, I must now go to a genteel tea party at the Ibrox.'

More laughter and applause, but also boos and shouts of 'No War for American Oil Barons' followed as Harry and Oliver made for the door. Gideon Crawford had the unenviable task of closing the meeting and seeing the rabble off. But he, too, wanted to be at the Game. So he took the gavel.

'Alright?' Harry asked.

'Brilliant. I liked the way you managed to say nothing about Libya. Honour saved.' Oliver was relieved.

'Of all the crowds, the radical hotheads are the easiest to manipulate. They are sentimental and unthinking. Now, if this was a meeting of City brokers or the Women's Institute, I would be unable to get away with that kind of bullshit. But then, that's our Great Party for you.'

7.30 p.m. London, House of Commons

'The Party will be in turmoil, I am afraid, when this gets out,' Austin said.

'That will come later, and may be not till Wednesday, when Harry will be back. What we now need to sort out is the rest of today and who is going to which news programme,' Frank said.

They had all gathered in his office in the House of Commons. Austin, Christine, Mary Duggan and Nick

Davies, surprisingly awake and coherent.

'Harry's message is that Mary should go to *Newsnight* as soon as they request someone. But we need someone urgently for Channel 4. I have promised Jon Snow someone will get there before the end. But whoever goes is to say nothing about the American announcement, and nothing at all about us.'

'Shall I go?' Nick suddenly perked up.

'Are you sure you can cope?' Christine asked bluntly.

'Well darling, as you know, this is my lucid half hour. And, what is more, if I say I know nothing, I will mean it.'

'OK, there is no time to lose. Off you go to London Television Centre. Don't drive. Take the pool car, won't you?' Christine was solicitous as ever. Nick Davies left quickly.

'So, Nick to Channel 4 and Mary for *Newsnight*. What else?' Frank asked.

'There is a Prime Ministerial Statement which Frank, you will have to read. Austin, will you clear it with the Opposition Chief Whips? Has someone told the Speaker's Office yet?' Christine had to make sure proper courtesies had been observed. A Statement made by any Minister in the House of Commons required that the appropriate Shadow Minister from the two main opposition parties should be present to respond. It was the job of the Chief Whip to sort out such details to make the flow of business smooth. This would all take place behind the scenes, through the usual channels, as the Whips were called.

'I have already tipped off the Opposition whips office that some statement could be made. I will confirm that and let you know if they have got John Altrincham ready. I have also told the Speaker's Office. I reckon the Division should take about twelve minutes in all. So we can schedule the Statement at 10.15 p.m.' John Altrincham was the Deputy to Peter Portugal and he was the appropriate person to respond to Frank when the Statement was made.

'That will be good, since it will be the lead story on *Newsnight*. Do we know who it is tonight?' Mary wanted to know.

'Jeremy', Christine said. 'Don't let him bite you; go on the attack immediately.'

'Don't worry. I will sort him out.' Mary had sparred with Jeremy Paxman on *Newsnight* on many occasions.

'How soon can I have the Statement, Christine?' Frank was anxious.

'Oliver says once the game starts, he will have time to finalise. They must now be finished with the Rally and so on the way over Oliver was to let Harry make the final corrections. Oliver would then dictate it over the phone to the secure office in the hotel and we should have it by eight o'clock at the latest. Will that be alright, Frank?'

'Yes, of course. I just need a couple of reads before I am at the Dispatch box. But I also need a full briefing from the FO and your lot for any questions that may come up. The Tories wont create any problems, but you've got to watch the Lib Dems. You can never trust them.'

'And Eric from our backbenches. Don't forget.'

Austin had had Eric on his mind all day.

'Aye, but then I know almost word for word what he will say, and since he will take his own sweet time to say it, I can always answer Eric as even I can think faster than he speaks.' Frank resented Eric's education and his patronising attitude.

'Fine then. I will see to it that you have the full briefing. I will coordinate with our beautiful friend the Baroness about the FO,' Christine said.

Letitia (Letty) Brighton was the Foreign Office Minister in the House of Lords, where they said the Opposition benches were always packed whenever she had to answer a starred question or make a Statement. They came not to listen but to gawp at her. She used to be a model before she went on stage. Now, to the regret of her hundreds of theatre fans and the delight of the Noble Lords, she had taken up her perch on the Government front bench. She doubled as Leader of the House so she would be reading the statement in the Lords. So, no problem there.

7.40 p.m. London, Drew House, 38th Floor

The front page had just one word in large red type: FILTH. Above it, next to the masthead, the first sentence of Vera's piece said:

Children are God's tears on Earth...

There was no Page Three, no nipples, no talk of nooky. This was the hard version of *The Herald*. Vera's piece occupied all of page Three. The one photograph with the girl's face blacked out, the tattoo showing

MUM with a heart pierced with an arrow was spread across pages four and five. Terence's back was shown, as was a part of his hip with the black mole. Roddy had considered that mole the crucial feature in accepting Andrew's claim that this was authentic.

Lex had been staring at it for nearly five minutes now. He had gone over the design with great care, camou-flaging anything that would identify the young girl. He felt sorry for Terence for the first time in his life. This will hound him not just out of politics, but out of the country as well. It was the nuclear option. Not what he would have launched, if he had anything to do with it. He would have tipped off Terence, given a hint of what was to come. He could then have resigned quietly making the standard excuses—to spend more time with the family, seek new challenges, hang up ye old boots or whatever. That could have settled the matter. Even now, he was tempted to call up Chris and give him a hint of what was coming. Where was Chris? He dialled his number.

'Chris?'

'Yes, hi Lex, how's tricks?' There was a lot of noise wherever Chris was.

'Where are you?'

'In Glasgow with Gideon Crawford and at the Great-est Game in town. What's up?'

'I need a few minutes. Very important. Can you talk in confidence?'

'Not now. Maybe later. Tell you what, can I call you at half-time? Can it wait that long?'

'Sure. There's no hurry. But do call me at half-time.

And don't tell me the score when you do. OK?'

'Done.'

So, that gave Lex just about fifty minutes to agonise as to how much to tell Chris. If he messed up and Terence escaped, Lex knew Matt would kill him before firing him. There was half a mil on this one, and if carried in tomorrow's *Herald*, an expected sale of five and a half million. He had to get it absolutely perfect in his timing.

7.45 p.m. London, The Bell Yard, off Fleet Street

Asha calculated that the event in Glasgow should happen sometime before eight o'clock. Before, that is, she had to join Matt and the ten largest institutional shareholders in LDNC plc in a private dining room at The Ritz. She did not want her mobile to go off in the middle of the dinner. Allowing for a preliminary chat before dinner for ten minutes, she had to know latest by ten past eight. She was hoping Willie would call while she was on her way to The Ritz. It was to be a wrong number signal if everything had gone right. A text message saying Miss You otherwise. It was not often that Asha was stressed out.

7.47 p.m. On board the London-Glasgow shuttle

The Stewardess cleared away Margaret's half-drunk glass of Chardonnay. This was the sign that they were preparing to land at Glasgow. She looked at her watch. The flight was on time and she looked forward to being in her hotel by eight-thirty. Traffic permitting.

'Tell me,' she asked the Stewardess, 'what will traffic be like at this time in Glasgow?'

'Whereabouts are you headed Madam?'

'George's Square.'

'Normally on a weekday, it should not take more than half an hour from the Airport. But there is a football game tonight at the Ibrox. The Prime Minister is coming for that, so traffic could be bad. But the game starts at seven forty five, so everyone going to the game should be off the roads by then. Shouldn't be a problem, I reckon.'

'Thanks ever so much.'

'Not at all. You're welcome.'

These Americanisms were everywhere now, Margaret thought. She wanted Britain to be different from America, to keep the old charm and not become like a shopping mall. She had to try her best to help preserve the difference. Tomorrow, she had to see the lawyers, who had drawn up the deeds for the Trust under Scottish Law, which was better than English Law in this regard. Now that culture was a devolved subject, she could also be sure that her plan to spend the money on culture would not be subject to a challenge by Matt after her death. The Scottish Parliament would not change the Law just to suit Matt, as she was sure Harry White would gladly do.

7.55 p.m. Glasgow, Ibrox Stadium

Sarah was looking forward gladly to whatever it was

that Harry would do. There was a wait, an agonising two hours at least before she would be able to be close enough to touch him, let alone be alone with him. And when would that be? On the way to the airport? On the flight to Belfast? Or later still? She had a lot of time to think now that she had arrived at the Ibrox ground and was sitting down... Sarah was trying to be as calm as she could manage.

Her luxury bath had refreshed her and she was glad about the dress she had chosen. It was simple but the halter neck showed off her shoulders with just a hint of cleavage and a lot of bare back. She had chosen light purple sheer tights which she thought showed her legs off better. She was preparing carefully for her adventure. She sprayed herself generously with the Samsara that she had bought as long as five hours ago in Harvey Nick's, just to remind Harry of the joys to come. Arriving at the stadium entrance, she had been greeted by a young man whom she had seen earlier on the plane with Gideon's party.

'Hello. I am Jamie, Jamie Hencke. Gideon Crawford told me I had to make sure you were well looked after.'

'Thank you very much Mr Hencke. How kind of you. And how nice of Mr Crawford.'

'It is nothing really. Except Gideon would be very cross with me, if something went wrong. And, if that got as far as Terence Harcourt, I am a dead duck in Scotland.'

'Would that matter?' Sarah was just trying to make polite conversation while climbing interminable stairs to where they were going.

'Yes, if I want to make my way in Scottish politics, maybe even British politics. I am hoping Gideon will help me to, maybe, have Terence take me on in his office in some capacity or another. That will do for a start. Then, who knows how far I can go?'

'So, how far would you like to go? To where Harry White is?' Sarah was trying to provoke a response.

'Well, hardly. That would be too far up and what is more, the Prime Minister is quite a young man. He will be there for twenty, maybe twenty-five years yet. I would be happy if I ended up in the Scottish Executive or maybe even in the Cabinet.'

'What interests you then, Sports and Culture?'

'No, it is health really. I am a medical doctor, so I would like to stay with that. But I have to pick up some Economics and stuff like that. I am doing a Masters in Health Economics at the Uni here. How to pay for the NHS is something I worry about. Maybe, I can help Terence think about how European experience in financing health services can tackle the NHS's problems with that.'

Sarah was seriously impressed. She had not met many men who could bear to hide their light under a bushel. Here was a man who was a Doctor just about Alan's age, but so modest. She looked at him properly for the first time. Not bad-looking either, she concluded.

It was a couple of floors climb before they arrived. After the dark stairs, they suddenly emerged in the open. There was still much daylight though it was already after half-past seven in May. But the ground was floodlit and there were bright lights in all the stands. The noise was deafening. Even five minutes ago, when she arrived at the gates, she had not registered the commotion. The Directors' Box had about a hundred seats, but wooden ones. She presumed that elsewhere, the sitting must be Spartan at this rate.

When she got to her seat, the Public Address system had announced:

We welcome today the Right Honourable Harry White, Prime Minister of the United Kingdom. Welcome to the Old Firm fixture, Prime Minister. Have an unforgettable experience.

There was scattered applause but mainly from where Sarah was sitting. From the crowd on her left came a chant:

Harry Harry Harry. Out Out Out.

There was general laughter and catcalls. Not to be outdone, the stand on her right shouted,

Harry White Total Shite.

There was a sea of people singing, shouting and waving banners. On her left hand side, the stand was full of green coloured shirts.

'Those are Celtic supporters. Across are the home side—the Rangers,' Jamie said helpfully.

'I am told this is real sectarian warfare.'

'Used to be much worse than it is now. Now they have players who are from the other sect, or even not Christians at all.'

'Like what? Muslims?'

'No, Jews like me,' Jamie said.

Sarah remembered the joke Alan had told her about this.

'Yes, but are you a Catholic Jew or a Protestant one?'

'I see, you know all about us in Glasgow.'

'Not really. I once had a boyfriend who was a football fan so I picked up a few of the myths.'

As against my current boyfriend, she thought, who hates football and can't wait to get away from here. Nor can I. She looked around. Behind her, right at the top of the Directors' stand where she was, the Prime Ministerial welcoming group had gathered. Harry was surrounded by the Chairmen of the two clubs and many besuited middle-aged white men. There was Gideon, of course, in the same row of seats. Oliver was there and gave her a wave. Harry looked in her direction and flashed that lovely smile. She waved back at both of them.

'You know, this is one of the great fixtures of Scottish football. These two have been rivals for over a hundred years and have been at the top of Scottish League all that time.' Jamie thought Sarah should be duly impressed by the occasion she was at. He was about to go on but then a roar erupted.

'Oh my God,' Jamie shouted. 'They have scored.'

Celtic had scored. There was an explosion on the Green stand. The two big TV screens atop opposite stands across were showing the goal in slow motion. The Public Address system announced:

Hendrik Larsson scored that goal.

There was another outburst of applause from the

Greens. Sarah wondered who that announcement was for, since everyone there must have known who had scored. Even she had read the information on the replay on the large TV screen.

'Why do they do that? Surely, we all know,' Sarah said.

'Well, yes, but there are some blind spectators here.'

'Seriously?'

'Yes, of course. Both clubs have special facilities for disabled spectators. There are some partially sighted, and one or two blind fans. They come regularly and just love the atmosphere. They are also encouraging families with small children to come and watch so that football becomes everyone's game, not just that of the fanatics. It is a real community here.' Jamie was glowing with pride.

8.00 p.m. Glasgow, in the Ibrox stands

'Did you see that Robbie? Wasn't that what you wanted?' David asked.

The boys had to strain themselves to see everything properly. They were pretty much at ground level but people still kept passing in front or jumping up in front of them. David had told them to look at the TV screen just to make sure.

'I saw it on replay, Dad. It came too quick to see the first time,' Robbie said.

'I want Rangers to score now, quick.' Alistair was still hoping.

8.02 p.m. Glasgow, en route from the airport

There was a screech and a thump.

'Fucking blind are you? Watch where you are going.'

Margaret was jolted from her newspaper. Her chauffeur just narrowly missed a motorcyclist, who had come on the wrong side.

'Sorry Madam. Are you alright?' the chauffeur said.

'Yessssssssssssss…'

Margaret was thrown that very instant to the side windows of her car, and that was the last thing she remembered. The car in which she was travelling was flung to the side as it was hit by a large delivery van. They had just come off the M8, passing the Ibrox ground and had got on to Paisley Road. This was always a tricky junction and the light had just begun to fade moments ago. There was chaos all around. Cars behind had to screech to a halt and there was a pile-up. A crowd gathered; the car was too smashed up for anyone to help the bodies out. The delivery van driver was Chinese and knew just a few words of English. He was close to tears. Then they heard an ambulance as well as a police car approaching.

8.05 p.m. Glasgow, Ibrox Stadium, Directors' Dining Room

Oliver was trying to concentrate. He had come away from the Directors' box and was down in the dining room. He had to speak softly so that the person standing there, polishing the glasses, would not hear. Roger indicated that there was an inner sanctum where Oliver would be alone. Oliver, still on his mobile, waved a thanks to Roger and moved into the inner office on the left, and shut the door behind him. He had to let Christine have the text of the Statement. He got a safe line via the unit they had set up at the hotel. He heard an ambulance going by and wondered what that was all about. Maybe someone too drunk to make it to the match but ill enough to need attention. Old Firm games were excuses for drunken orgies among other things.

8.10 p.m. London, Pall Mall

Asha's taxi was just turning into St James's off Pall Mall when her mobile rang. Thank heavens, she muttered. There were only minutes to go before she arrived at the Ritz. She looked at the number and said, 'Hello.'

'Sorry, wrong number,' a voice said.

Now all Asha had to do was show surprise when Matt was called to be told about Margaret's accident. Asha sincerely hoped it would be only a few bruises and nothing more serious. They had arrived at The Ritz.

'Thanks. I will call you later to collect me.'

'Yes, Miss Chan.' Asha was a valued customer of the City Cab agency. She took cabs everywhere as it was more tax efficient.

'Good Evening, Miss Chan.' The welcome at The Ritz was warm as usual

9.10 p.m. Vienna, British Ambassador's residence

'How nice to see you again, Secretary of State.' Lady Olds gave Terence a peck on his cheek. Sir Clive was standing right beside and shook his hand.

'Welcome to our humble abode.'

'I like that, a humble abode indeed. What beautiful surroundings you have here in the nineteenth, or is it the seventeenth, district, Ambassador. It must be lovely later in the summer to go sit in those wineries and wander about in the woods.'

Terence was showing off that he knew Vienna. The Ambassador's House was near Wienerwald, the woods at the edge of Vienna. He had visited some hostelries where vineyards sold their latest vintage. Sitting out in the open in the rustic outskirts of a big city was a special pleasure that visitors to Vienna would have.

'Well, yes, it certainly is. Some day you must come for a longer visit in the summer.' Sir Clive was warming to Terence.

'And you must bring your wife and daughters along with you. You shouldn't be the only one having all the fun,' Katharine, Lady Olds, added.

'If you think talking shop about boring old olives of Cyprus for a whole day is fun, I will gladly let you do my job. Thank heavens for Alan Carling, who sorted it all out finally. I don't know what I would do without him. Incidentally, he was too exhausted after that marathon negotiation to come here. He went straight to bed. He asked me to send his most sincere apologies.' Terence was secretly proud of how close to the truth he could be about Alan's whereabouts.

'What a shame. But then we have you all to ourselves. Jolly nice.'

Terence almost expected Katharine Olds to say 'Tally Ho' any second. The FO attracted these horsey-type wives of public school men. When will the old culture change? Who will dare change it? Not Nick Davies, surely...

8.10 p.m. London, Channel 4

Nick had done well. He had survived the Channel 4 News ordeal. Jon Snow had tried to get some truth out of him about Libya policy. He held on to a diplomatic answer.

'I have myself had no conversation with Washington. I have also not spoken to the Prime Minister today. We have to wait and see how soon Libya is ready to comply with its UN obligations. What the future will bring, who can tell?'

Having said that, he tried every variation on this answer. Jon Snow was quite frustrated. He could see that Nick was lying, or at least not telling the whole truth. As the News ended, Jon asked,

'Now tell me, Nick. Just off the record. What the hell is happening?'

'You know me, Jon. I am only in the Cabinet because of Wales. Since my dear darling wife Val died eighteen months ago, I have not been any good at my job. They carry me kindly, but come the next reshuffle I would be glad to go. Harry is his own Foreign Secretary. He is happy with me because I don't bother him. But I'll tell you this. I smell trouble ahead.'

'Really, Nick? Tell me more.' The journalist in Jon was curious.

'Trouble on the backbenches. Expect rumblings by mid-week. I wouldn't be surprised if we had a revolt.'

Jon realised he was being soft-soaped. This was hardly news. What was Nick hiding?

'But if nothing has happened on the Libya front, why should there be trouble?'

'Did I say nothing would have happened? It all depends on Harry. He would love to bomb Libya if only to rub Eric's nose in the dirt. He is a vindictive bastard like that, is our Harry.'

'So you expect Libya being bombed before mid-week?'

'I neither say yea nor nay. Good night, Jon. It's getting past my bedtime.'

'Good night, Nick. Take care how you go.'

8.12 p.m. Glasgow, Ibrox Stadium, Directors' Box

Sarah kept on glancing back at Harry. He was being introduced to people who were leaving their seats and walking up to the top, being introduced to him, shaking his hand. A good thing too, Sarah thought. This way at least he won't get to watch much.

Suddenly there was a howl from the crowd. There was a Rangers player on the ground writhing in agony and what looked to Sarah like a Celtic player waving his arms and asking him to get up. The referee blew his whistle and walked over to the Celtic player. He then ran over to the linesman and ran back in just a second or two. He blew his whistle again and pointed towards the Celtic goal. It was a penalty. There were shouts from the crowd and what looked like a melee on the pitch.

'I am afraid Giovanni was fouled by Rafael. It is a penalty. There is trouble here. If Rangers score now and hold the match to a draw, they have won the League.' Jamie was being helpful again.

On the pitch, the two teams were at each other's throats. Someone, it looked like the man who had scored the goal—Larsson, she remembered—was pulling a player away. The referee's head could be just seen. He was waving his hand clutching a piece of paper. He was about to give a card to someone. There was shoving and punching. The referee had picked up the ball when someone from the Celtic side behind him tried to knock it out of his hand. The referee turned around and waved a red card. There was a huge howl. The man being sent off had number 30 shirt.

'Oh, my God. He has sent Riseth off. This is so amazing. It is not like Peter Houston. He is normally a mild referee.' Jamie looked shocked.

'Why?'

'I think Riseth must have argued the penalty with the ref, or maybe just swore at him. This is bad news for Celtic. Oh no.'

Jamie's shout was caused by what happened before their eyes. Some object was thrown at the referee and hit him. The whole stadium exploded. Everyone was standing up and shouting and hurling abuse at each other. The missile had come from the Celtic stand, or that at least was the presumption. Police began to gather around the bottom of the stand where the Celtic fans were. Some of the Stewards began to get inside the stand and their colleagues on the ground pointed to places where they thought the likely culprit was. One fan jumped over the barrier and started running towards the referee. A policeman ran after him and tackled him. More policemen converged on that man and took him away. Some fans still inside their stand started fisticuffs with the Stewards who had climbed in to catch the person who had hurled the coin.

'I think the referee was hit by something sharp and hard, may be a metal key or a sharp coin. It could be a two-pound piece, that would do it.' Jamie was not a doctor for nothing.

The referee was sitting down on the ground. The players were still arguing with each other but at least not fighting. Meanwhile the referee had to be seen to by the Rangers' physio who ran on to the pitch. There was blood spurting from his head. The PA system was vying for attention from the crowd.

Please sit down. Please sit down. Order must be maintained. There will be arrests if missiles are thrown at the players. Please comply with the police orders.

And on and on. But it was hard to hear. Even in the Directors' Box many were standing up. Sarah could see that the rival Chairmen were gesticulating and shouting at each other. No one quite knew what would happen next.

8.15 p.m. Glasgow, Ibrox Stadium, the stands

'What's happened, Dad? Why has the game stopped, Dad?' Robbie was asking.

'Is the referee hurt, Dad?' Alistair said.

David was himself trying to figure out what had happened. He could sense the danger level rising. The TV screen was not showing any clear picture. Its camera was wandering around among the players.

'Wait for a bit. It will all be clear. I can tell you in a minute.' It was the best David himself could manage.

The referee blew his whistle and that attracted some attention. He was wearing a bandage. His bandaged brow was red and the blood was still oozing out. With a determination Sarah had to admire, the referee marched to the penalty spot outside the Celtic goal and pointed at a Rangers player.

8.18 p.m. Glasgow, Ibrox Stadium, the Directors' Box

'That is Numan. He is brilliant'. Jamie was obviously a home side fan. Sarah had decided as a person from the Deep South, she better stay neutral.

There was a relative quiet for a minute, and then, as Arthur Numan scored the penalty, another explosion of noise and banner-waving from the opposite stand showed the joy of Rangers fans. There were boos and shouts from the Celtic fans, and more things were thrown on the pitch. The Referee pointed towards the centre again, and asked the two teams to come to order.

Everyone was now standing up. Two players from the two sides who looked to Sarah like they would be captains were walking towards the middle holding the ball. But elsewhere, the players had still not calmed down and there were scuffles among them. One appeared to be punching another. The referee's back had been turned but he soon saw what was happening. He blew his whistle and stopped the game from resuming. He walked over to the scuffling players.

8.20 p.m. Glasgow, Ibrox Stadium, the stands

'Did you see that goal Alistair?' David asked.

'Yes. What a super penalty kick.' Alistair was happy.

The referee pointed a red card at two more players. They were Celtic players. Sarah could see that man Larsson again, the only one she could identify, pleading with the referee but being pulled away by another player. Suddenly the Celtic stand erupted and dozens of fans jumped out on to the pitch. This proved to be a signal to the Rangers fans and they poured down from their stand. The Belfast boys were keen to prove they were no slouches when it came to a fight. So the Carson's Irregulars got to work. Kenny was astonished as Ritchie lifted him up so he could get over the barriers and before he knew it he had landed on the pitch. Soon the others followed. Ritchie was shouting himself hoarse. But he was not alone by any means. It was as if a trained army had got its orders to charge over the hill.

The players and the referee were bewildered by this. The referee blew again and indicated he had stopped the game. Soon the players and the referee were fighting their way back to the tunnel. The police waded in trying to separate the fans but to little avail. There were fisticuffs and blows and kicks. Some heads had blood streaming out. The noise was incredible now. The PA system seemed to have given up. Loud pop music was being played now instead of appeals. But if anyone thought that would distract the fans, they were wrong. There were firecrackers set off, and soon enough one was hurled at the Directors' Box.

8.22 p.m. Glasgow, Ibrox Stadium, the Director's Box

Jamie and Sarah stood up.

Barney Jones was quickly at their side.

'Miss Disney, the Prime Minister says you better get out of here and meet us in the Directors' Dining Room and Bar.'

The entire mass of besuited men and the few women but with heavy fur coats (in May at that) were rushing out in a jostle. Sarah looked about for where Harry was. He was standing calmly, letting the two Chairmen behave much like their fans. Sarah had no choice but to follow Jamie as Barney had indicated. He was hurrying back to be at Harry's side. The stairs which were just mildly uncomfortable earlier in the day were now full of people pushing and shoving, some almost slipping and falling. There was loud raucous singing coming from the ground.

'What is that?' Sarah asked Jamie.

'More trouble, I am afraid. Each side has sectarian songs, mainly to hurl abuse at the other side.'

'Such as?'

'Rangers fans are singing *Billy Boys*. I can't possibly tell you all the words, but the words *We are up to our knees in Fenian Blood* are in it. You can imagine the rest.'

'Oh, how horrible. Why are Rangers fans like that?'

'The other side are no better, but I won't get into their song. Let me assure you this is not at all usual.' Jamie was angry and apologetic at the same time. He was embarrassed for Rangers and for Scotland. Perhaps a bit for himself as well, as he had wanted to make a nice impression on this good-looking woman. He couldn't stop talking.

'We have had accidents, like when the stand collapsed during an Old Firm game killing sixty-six people. But that was nearly thirty years ago and the ground has had a lot of rebuilding since. They don't allow any bottles to be brought into the ground. That usually keeps the crowd violence down. We thought we had gone past all this sectarianism. But in a game like this, because the League championship is at stake, every goal counts. You see, Celtic needed to win outright and, being a goal ahead, they were on to a winner. A draw favours Rangers. So the Celtic players are angry. A penalty decision is bad enough, but a red card as well and then two more. Three Celtic players sent off and there is no telling where it would end. I do hope the Police can restore order and we can resume play. After all, we still have the second half to come. It would look terrible for Scotland, if the game caused the wrong kind of head-lines when the Prime Minister of the United Kingdom is here for the first time.'

The Prime Minister could not care less, if you only knew, Sarah thought, but Jamie was so nice, so gauche, that she decided not to shock him. An Old Firm game was a great treat for him, but, for Sarah, the only con-cern was, when would it end?

8.23 p.m. Glasgow, Ibrox Stadium, the Stands

David stood up and grabbed his two boys in each hand and said, 'Hold fast to me. Don't let go. We are getting out of here.' From where they were sitting, they had to go up half-way before they could get to an exit. There were people rushing down to the bottom to scale the barrier so they could jump onto the ground. He was fighting his way up, making sure the boys would be alright. Robbie and Alistair did not say a word. They were scared but were sure Dad would take care of them. They knew their Dad had been in the Marines. They had seen pictures of him in uniform and heard stories about his adventures. But the push down was terribly heavy.

Behind them there were people trying to get out. Someone had let off some fireworks and smoke was bil-lowing around. David managed to reach midway up to the exit. The push from behind meant he had to try his best not to fall.

8.25 p.m. Glasgow, outside the Ibrox Stadium

The noise inside finally got the policeman on duty running in to help out. Red saw his chance. He had about ten minutes before more police would arrive. So he opened his rucksack and got to work.

Meanwhile, Chris Mott decided that he had better return the call from Lex. He had spent many years in public relations and had been friends with Lex for even longer, but he sensed that, when Lex asked him to call back, there something big afoot. He would not normally rush in the middle of a good story unfolding in front of his eyes at Ibrox that evening. But something told him he had better get hold of Lex.

He had difficulty rushing down but his experience as a bouncer came in handy. Various people cursed him but he was down and out into the open before anyone else. He was now in the carpark where there was relative quiet. He only saw one person lurking under an awning on his knees. Maybe looking for his lost car keys, he thought, so he kept away from him. Red was also happy that he was not disturbed while planting his device under the VIP car in which he had seen Harry White arrive.

Chris was out of breath from all that rushing down. But he got through to Lex immediately.

'Lex, you must watch this on the box. There is a superb front page for you in the punch up going on here. Penalty, a red card and the ref hit by a coin and then two more red cards. Fucking incredible it is.'

'Chris, are you alone?'

'Yes what is it, Lex?'

'I have a front page already and it is very different. I was going to keep it a surprise but I thought I had better warn you.' Lex was still struggling about how much to tell. It was nearly eight-thirty. The time to order the print run was fast approaching.

'What are you talking about? Is it to do with Terence? Is he alright? He was in Vienna earlier today, coming back tomorrow.' Chris could feel fear rising inside himself.

'Listen carefully. We have now got solid evidence— authentic photos of Terence. Devastating stuff.'

'You filthy bastards. That shit Matt Drummond. I hate him. I will get him.'

'Don't lose your cool, Chris. Concentrate. If you want to see the evidence, get to our Glasgow office and I will send over the stuff on the computer, but only on our secure one. This is mega. When this hits the streets, Terence is dead.'

'Is it that bad? What is it, floozies? Boys?'

'It's much worse. Let us say a female relation, underage.'

'Oh my God, my God. So, what do you want? We can buy the pictures off you. Terence has money. How much?'

'Whatever else Matt Drummond may lack, it is not money. We are not talking blackmail here. The nation's morals are our concern.'

'You filthy hypocrite. What are you asking for? His resignation?'

'That's a promising start. But I must warn you, when

this gets out, Terence will be unable to live freely in this country. He is finished. He had better disappear.'

'You are joking.'

'Well, the police will want to take interest in these pictures. It's not just paedophilia. It's incest. The British people do not take kindly to that sort of thing. I can show you if you wish.'

Chris was as sick as he had not been since when, as a child, he had tried to empty his dad's brandy bottle in one go. His head was spinning.

'Listen, I will call Terence. How long have I got?'

'You know the newspaper business as well as I know it, mate. We are printing a million extra, so I would like an answer soon. Don't tell him to call me or Matt Drummond. This is between you and me. Matt will kill me, if he finds out I told you. This is for old times' sake.'

'Thanks, I guess. I will call you back.'

Chris looked around. The man on his knees was no longer there. But even so, he could not be sure. He had to have absolute privacy. He had to locate his car and call Terence.

8.35 p.m. Glasgow, inside an ambulance

'Is there anyone you would like to call, Madam?'

Margaret had just opened her eyes. There was a big piece of cotton wool across her left eye, and a young man in some kind of uniform was bandaging her wrist. She slowly came to.

'Where am I? What happened?'

'You are in an ambulance Madam, in Glasgow… Your car was involved in a crash with another vehicle. Luckily, you are not hurt very much.'

'What about Paul? The chauffeur?'

'I am afraid we had to take him to emergency. He was badly cut, and lost a lot of blood.'

'Can I go to my hotel? It's in George Square.'

'Don't you have relatives here or friends?'

'No, I just came from London and must fly back to-morrow. I have some important work in the morning. I am Margaret Drummond. The LDNC office here can look after me, I am sure.'

The paramedic looked puzzled.

'Oh, *The Glasgow Times* people.'

'Would you like us to call them?'

Margaret was about to say she could call herself. But she realised her handbag must be somewhere else. And her hand was hurting. Her legs were wrapped up in blanket. They were numb.

'Yes, please. Ask for Willie.'

'Yes, Madam.'

Within seconds, the connection had been made, and Willie came on. The paramedic held the mobile so Margaret could talk hands-free.

'Listen, Willie. There is nothing to worry about but I have had a bit of an accident. Paul has been taken to hospital with severe cuts. But I am alright. Tell everyone not to worry. Tell the hotel I will need special attention when I get there. I don't think I will be able to walk easily. I may need a wheelchair.'

Reggie the paramedic was impressed by this woman.

She was old, perhaps his granny's age. Well-dressed and posh. An American accent but so calm after such a serious accident.

'Oh, Mrs Drummond, I am sorry to hear about this. Let me come and collect you. Do you want me to tell the Boss. I can find him, wherever he is.' Willie was relieved that Margaret's bruises were small enough to only slow her down. He was now all eager to please, and wipe out any evidence of his role in this. He said a silent prayer that his chosen way—hiring a Chinese driver who was here illegally without a visa and driving a delivery van with no signs—had paid off.

'Well, he is in London, and I doubt he is thinking about me. But tell him just in case it gets into news before he hears about it.' Margaret had a hazy recollection of cameras flashing when she had been carried into her ambulance near the scene of the accident.

'Will do, Madam.'

Margaret shut her eyes with a sigh, as Reggie turned off the phone.

'Please, can you tell me if the other driver was hurt? Is he alright?' Margaret was solicitous as always.

'We think he ran away. Someone told the police that he seemed to be of Chinese origin.'

'Oh poor man. I do hope he is alright. Shall you let me go then?'

'One moment, Madam. Let me see about the traffic.' Reggie got out and walked over to the police car flashing its lights nearby.

8.55 p.m. London, the Archduke Restaurant, South Bank

The drunken party of fifteen women was found a table large enough for them. Lisa wanted a round table or at least an oblong one. With a rectangular table, you could not see everyone properly. But knowing their favourite client's preferences, the restaurant had found just what Lisa liked.

'Would you care for an aperitif, Madam, before you order?'

'I am not sure, Melvin. We have been at it solidly since the late afternoon. Oh, what the heck. I will have a *pernod*, as will my friend Miss Annie here. You can ask everyone what they would like.'

Lisa was determined to make this an occasion. Her mobile rang. She looked at it and found an unfamiliar number. Was this a newspaper hack?

'Hello, who is it?'

'Lisa, this is Margaret.'

'Darling, how are you? Have you reached Glasgow? Where are you calling from?'

'Listen, there is nothing to worry. I have just had a minor accident. It is nothing, just that my car was hit by a delivery van. I am bruised, but otherwise alright.'

'Oh Margaret. So where are you? In a hospital?'

'No, darling, just in an ambulance where a very nice young man has been taking care of me. I have told our office here to tell Matt, so he doesn't worry. If I have the energy for a long argument, I may call him myself. Don't you worry either. I am sure I will be alright. I will make the first night if I have to crawl.'

'Margaret, do take care. I will say a special prayer for you. Do you want me to ask Harry to come and see you wherever you are?'

'That's very sweet of you. I am sure Harry has bigger things on his mind. We have just been told that a riot has broken out at the game Harry is at and all over Glasgow there are clashes between the fans, especially near my hotel. They are trying to find me another hotel. But I am well looked after. Lots of love.'

9.00 p.m. Glasgow, Ibrox Stadium, the Directors' Dining Room

Harry wished he had bigger or just other things to do. He was being talked at by several people. The Rangers Chairman had quit haranguing his Celtic counterpart. He still thought the penalty was legitimate, as was the first red card and the next two, and while he did not say so, it just proved what animals Celtic fans were. Calum Kennedy was trying to fence Harry off from the others. He had planned to tell Harry a lot, mainly about himself, and his claim to proper honours. But his plan had gone awry.

'Prime Minister, let me sincerely assure you, that this is not typical nor normal. We are all shocked about the behaviour on the pitch, and in the stands. I am on the Scottish FA Executive, and, let me say, we shall take a most serious view of this. This sort of thing cannot be tolerated. I hope both teams are fined a large sum.' Calum could at least afford to show he was neutral between the two sides.

'How can you say that, Calum? It was not the fault of the home team,' the Chairman, who Harry thought was called Sir Archibald something, interjected.

'What you have to do is to suspend the other side for five games at least, or take away ten points next season.'

'I heard that. You can be sure we shall fight this to the highest courts if that happens. It was the fault of both sides. Don't you agree Prime Minister? You saw the game.' It was the turn of the Celtic Chairman.

'Gentlemen, I may be foolhardy in many things I do, but intervening between your two clubs on such a sensitive matter is not one of them. I say a word and my Party will be in wilderness for a generation. No, thanks.'

They politely laughed. Harry was still holding a pint of bitter someone had thrust in his hands when they arrived. It had been chaotic throughout. The Directors' Dining Room was heaving with people. Many were there without invitation. He had been taken into the inner room, and, before he could say anything, some one had said,

'This should calm your shattered nerves, Sir.'

Since then, Harry had taken one sip, and that was it. Foul stuff. He could see why he had to watch this rabble kick a ball about in a frenzied fashion, but not why he had to drink this muck. He was hoping Oliver would come and rescue him. Or Sarah.

'So when will the game resume? I am told football is a game of two halves.' Harry thought he had better keep the conversation on an even keel before the two Chairmen fall out again.

'Well said, Sir. We can find out for you. Normally, there is a twenty minute break, but given the circumstances, we cannot be sure. After all, we have not yet finished the first half. Let us hope we can resume quickly.' Sir Archibald got on his mobile.

Harry was relieved to see Oliver had made it to the inner sanctum. Oliver gave a thumbs up sign about the Statement having gone safely. Harry raised his pint glass and made a face. Oliver laughed and mouthed softly, 'See what I can do,' and went out again to where the bar was.

10.15 p.m. Vienna, the Gurtel

Terence had abandoned his taxi as it got near the Gurtel. Being a peripheral road circling inner Vienna, it was constantly carrying traffic along its four lanes. It was noisy but not dirty. Terence felt at home in this somewhat bleak and garish surroundings. The dinner with Sir Clive and his Lady was suffocating enough, so he did not stay a moment longer than polite. He wanted to walk a bit, and have another drink before he got to Rosa Giulia's, which was only fifteen minutes away. The bar he came to was called Casanova's. There were the usual strobe lights, and women were performing in a variety of outfits which were just lingerie while scouting around for punters to take them behind to the curtained rooms. Terence watched in an uninterested fashion. On the way over here, even in a short walk, he had been propositioned by women in feathers and fishnet stockings, but he had shrugged them off. His treat was special. He was prepared to wait. He liked Casanova's with its mixture of Italian and French arte-facts and women from every central European country you wished. Bertolt at the bar greeted him, but was too busy dishing out drinks and keeping an eye on the girls, to come and talk with him. Terence ordered a large brandy.

His mobile rang.

'Terence, can you talk?' It was Chris.

'Sure what's up? Did Harry fuck up then?'

'No. This is very important. It is too noisy your end. I can't hear you clearly. I need to talk to you in confi-dence. What I have to say is vital.'

'OK. Hang on while I find a quiet corner in this bar. Just wait. Tell you what—call me in five minutes, while I find some place...'

It was too far to go to Rosa Giulia's. The pavement outside had constant traffic passing on the Gurtel. Ter-ence looked at the performing women. The easiest way out was a room at the back. So he summoned the fresh-est looking woman. She was as near to a girl as he could see. She smiled and said,

'Would you like to take me to a *separee*? It will be three hundred euros.'

Terence was not bargaining. He said yes. Off they went with a wave to Bertolt. Terence was led to a narrow passage behind the door saying *Amore* with hearts and arrows. When they got in, it was a very narrow room with a bed, but also a tiny space with a *bidet* and a hose for washing yourself.

'I am Natalie. I speak English. You like fuck?' Saying this, she began to undress and fondle Terence.

Terence's mobile rang again.

'Sorry,' he said, as Natalie made a face. He then told her very slowly, 'This is important, but not long. I will be with you shortly. Why don't you do a show for me?'

That will keep her busy, he thought, and she will think she is earning her keep. Terence had no intention of staying beyond the phone call.

Natalie turned on the TV in the room but with the sound off. It was showing a porn film. She began gyrating and taking her scanty clothes off in some sort of a dance. Terence was busy trying to call Chris.

'OK. Tell me what is so important.'

'Terence, it is all over. They have got pictures this time. Very explicit. You with your C...' Chris spluttered over the words.

'What?' Terence's face went red. 'Who has?'

'*The Herald*. There is no doubt, and I tried to offer to buy them back but they won't play. They want your scalp.'

'I WILL SHOW THEM, THE BASTARDS. I WILL KILL MATT DRUMMOND.'

Terence was now shouting and flaying his arm about. Natalie was cowering in a corner, her skimpy dress crushed between her hands

'It is no good, Terence. I have seen the spread in to-morrow's *Herald*. You will be done for child molesting and worse. Do you even know what they get for incest with adults? Give up.'

'OH FUCKING HELL. OH NO, NO, NO.'

Terence went all red, and the next moment, he collapsed. Natalie let out a scream. Bertolt rushed in, fearing Natalie was being beaten. He saw Terence lying on the floor. A quick instinct told him what the problem was. He wrapped a big towel around Natalie and took her out first and found a *separee* which was not in use and told her to lie down. He came back to Terence and bent down to check his heartbeat. Nothing. Yet there was some sound, some shout. He picked up Terence's mobile.

'Hello, who is this? Listen, your friend has had a very serious accident.'

'What? Who is speaking?'

'The barman at Casanova Night Club. Your friend is dead. Heart attack, it looks like. He came here alone. I will have to call the police and...'

'Oh God, Oh God. Listen, do you know who he is?'

'No, but he comes once a year or so. Buys good drinks. Sometimes spends money with girls. But his favourite is another place near here. He is rich, yes? Does he have friends I can call here?'

'No, it is more than that. You understand Minister, yes? He is a Minister in Britain; very important. Can you get the British Embassy on the phone and tell them? His name is Terence Harcourt. Thank you. If he owes any money, the Embassy will pay. Thanks... Oh, and can you take my number, and call me later, and tell me what happened? Thanks again, I am sorry. I cannot help as I am in Scotland right now. Can you manage?'

'That is OK. We have all kinds of mensch here. We are used to this. The British often come to Vienna. Sometimes the excitement gets too much for them.'

9.20 p.m. Glasgow, Ibrox Stadium, the Directors' Dining Room

Oliver found Roger at the bar. Roger smiled and said,

'What can I get for you, Mr Knight?'

'How do you know my name?'

'Everybody knows your name. You are the Prime Minister's Press Officer. It says so in the Programme. Anyway, what would you like?'

'It is not for me, but can you make a Martini for the Prime Minister? An American style Martini, with gin?'

'Say no more, Mr Knight. I have read he likes a lot of gin and a touch of vermouth with an olive and some ice.'

'Well, I am impressed.'

Roger had to take a gamble on whether this was the only drink Harry would have. He reckoned even if the game was cancelled, his hosts would not let Harry get away without the dinner. It will have to be brought forward, but the Haggis was easy to do, even if for a posh dinner. So, at least two more drinks. Roger decided to wait and gave Oliver a clean Martini with an innocent olive.

9.25 p.m. Glasgow, outside the Ibrox Stadium

'Lex, stop the press.' Chris felt that, devastated as he was, he had to stop *The Herald* from coming out, even though Terence was beyond its mudslinging. He had to protect poor Catriona, her father's pet.

'What's happened? What did Terence say?'

'Terence is dead, Lex. He had a heart attack in Vienna.'

'When?'

'A few minutes ago. When I told him…'

'Where was he? What was he doing?'

'Enough, Lex. Let him be; he is dead. You and Matt Drummond have got what you wanted. Now leave him alone, and protect that girl's future. She is innocent.'

'How do I know you are not lying?' Lex could see his first edition going down the drain after half a mil and all the hard work.

'Because you know I would not lie about such things. I called to save your reputation, which would have been worse than mud if you had maligned a dead man. If you want, the British Embassy in Vienna can confirm. Do you want their number?'

'No. Leave it. Do us a favour. Give me a thousand words on Terence pronto. I will pay you five quid per word. I had better find out about the game and start a fresh front page.' Lex was never less than professional.

9.30 p.m. London, the House of Lords

Lettie Brighton was enjoying herself in the Peers'

Dining Room. She and her partner Matthew had invited some friends for dinner, and they were on the last course of pudding and brandy. The meal had been excellent, as she had expected. Her guests were American friends of her partner. They were special because Lettie had met Matthew at the house of Norman and Hattie at an post-theatre party while touring New York with the Royal Shakespeare Company. Matthew was then working on Wall Street and he had taken Norman and Hattie to see this stunning English actress playing Rosalind in *As You Like It*. Lettie had been impressed by Matthew and his cultured American friends. They came to London regularly to take in the theatre and who better but Lettie to direct them to the best plays in town. Along the way, Matthew and Lettie became fond of each other. Matthew relocated himself to London to be with Lettie. It had been nearly fifteen years now.

It was Hattie who was curious about Lettie's job.

'How did you get into this? Was it worth giving up your lovely career on the stage?'

Lettie was used to this question. She tried to vary the answer slightly each time she had to tell people her story.

'Oh, I did not plan to end up here. But, you know how it is. Political parties have to raise money. We did not do it in the old days but now we are all Americans. So the Party found me useful for fundraising and hosting dinners. That is how I met Elisabet. Do you know her? She is Harry White's wife and a brilliant theatre director. I am sure I can wangle a couple of tickets for you for her new play at the National.'

'Don't worry, we already got them. It is hot news in New York and tickets are selling fast. So did she get you the job?'

'Not quite. But through her I was put on the group which was writing the Arts and culture part of the manifesto. No one ever reads the manifesto except the nerds who only quote it to accuse the Party leaders of having betrayed it. But we have to do it at every election. After three defeats and three manifestoes, I was a veteran. So when we won, they needed bodies in the House of Lords. I said, what the hell? I can always get back to the stage when we are out.'

'You are not supposed to say that, Lettie. They will hear you,' Matthew interjected.

'I don't give a fig. I enjoy this job. They only come to gawp at me and when the charm wears off, I will be dumped like the rest of them.'

'Then you write your memoirs and make a killing.' Norman had his eye on the money.

'Who knows? Memoirs of political types only sell if you have been sacked or found in flagrante by some paparazzi. Now, who wants a liquer?'

Tonight the boys had enjoyed their Angus Beef Steak and the girls their Dover Sole. The girls had drunk Pinot Grigio and the boys some fine Australian Shiraz. But the last course had finally broken down all their resolutions of sensible eating. So the girls had gone whole hog for cheesecake and apple tart and the men were sticking to fresh fruit salad and strawberries and cream. After black coffee and liquers, brandy for the boys and chartreuse for the girls, Lettie was feeling quite pleased that she had given Norman and Hettie a good dinner.They should linger a bit longer and really savour the charms of the place, she had decided... They had plenty of time.

Lettie was waiting to see if the Opposition Front Bench wanted to hear the Statement on Libya. In such cases, the House of Lords had the choice whether it took the Statement being made in the Commons. The usual channels were sorting it out but not many Noble Lords lingered till late at night. Not after dinner, in any case. But all who were there would saunter into the chamber, if they took the Statement. As the Prime Minister's equivalent in the House of Lords, Lettie would have to read out the Statement. That would guarantee a near full house, even late at night. Few people knew about the Statement as yet. The Annunciator for the Commons was trailing the Statement as being read after the Division at 10.00 p.m. But nothing was said as to what the Statement was about and no indication of what the House of Lords would do. In any case, she could only read the Statement after Frank Thompson had got up in the Commons. So there was at least an hour and a bit before she would have to be at the Dispatch Box. No panic. She was going to enjoy her second helping of chatreuse... Her mobile rang.

Lettie was very embarrassed as other Noble Lords in the Dining Room looked mockingly aghast at this so-called bad behaviour by the Leader. She had to rush out, as mobiles were not allowed in the Peers' Dining Room. The call was from that sweet young Duty Officer at the FO.

'Baroness Brighton, I am sorry to call you at this hour.'

'Never mind, tell me, what is it Malcolm?'

'Bad news, I am afraid. The Vienna Embassy just called. The Secretary of State is dead.'

'Who Stein, the Austrian Secretary? Oh dear...'

'No, Madam. Our Secretary of State for Europe, Terence Harcourt.'

'What? OH MY GOD. How?'

'Heart attack it seems. In a bar. Rather suddenly. They are trying to contact his wife.'

'I had better go and tell them at the other end. Look, thanks Malcolm.'

Bloody hell. Terence Harcourt dead. How and why he was in a bar in Vienna, she would have to find out later. She went back in and called Matthew out, unaware of the tears running down her cheeks. Her American guests were disconcerted, while Noble Lords around looked at her curiously.

'What is it? Why are you crying?' Matthew put an arm around her.

'Terence Harcourt died of a heart attack in Vienna tonight. I had better go and tell Frank and Christine. Could you hold the fort for me, love? Take them in for extra coffee in the Guest Room, if you like. Give my apologies. I must run.'

9.35 p.m. London, 10 Downing Street

Christine was trying to get hold of Lettie as well. She wanted to know if she had got the Opposition to agree not to take the statement in the Lords. There were so many ex-Foreign Secretaries and ex-FO types there that there would be serious mauling of the Government policy. Lettie could handle it, of course, but even then Hansard would tell a sorry tale tomorrow. The policy community out there read the Lords Hansard before the Commons one.

9.37 p.m. London, the House of Lords

Lettie was running across the red carpets of the House of Lords, past the Pugin Room, and was soon on the green carpets of the House of Commons as she tried to reach Frank Thompson's office. Her mobile rang again. Another breach of protocol.

'Yes,' she said, somewhat peremptorily, her tone indicating that whoever it was should get off her mobile phone pronto.

'It is me, Christine. How did the negotiations go at your end? Are you taking the Statement?'

'Christine, it is Terence. He is dead. Of a heart attack. In Vienna.' Lettie was sobbing by now. 'He died in a bloody bar, for God's sake.'

'What? How did you find out? Let me look at the wires.'

'Our Embassy told the FO just minutes ago. I am off to tell Frank. I must rush. Bye.'

Christine could not believe what she had just heard. She loathed him of course, but never wished him dead. Poor Dorothy. Had anyone told her yet? Those three sweet pretty girls. Oh how sad. I must tell Harry, she thought.

9.40 p.m. Glasgow, Ibrox Stadium, the Directors' Dining Room

Harry had drained his glass. They had heard that the match was off. The SFA had decided that the referee could not carry on with a bandage half over his left eye. They were not going to provide a substitute referee. They would have to announce a fine for the clubs soon. In the meantime, there was still a battle raging on the ground between the two sets of fans and the police. Stabbings were already reported. Harry was relieved. This story would dominate tomorrow's papers in Scotland at least, and displace Libya to the back pages. That was one good thing. Now, how soon could he get away?

'No, Prime Minister. We would hate to see you go without our dinner. We have prepared sumptuous Scottish fare for you.' Calum was most insistent.

'Aye, it is Haggis, the best there can be with all the trimmings and lashings of whisky to wash it down with. We have to live up to our reputation for hospitality at Ibrox, Prime Minister.' Sir Archibald something wanted some credit for this event.

'What time will that be? We have to get to Belfast tonight.'

'I don't think that will be any problem. We can get you to the airport in no time at all.'

Oliver came in with a second glass of Harry's favourite.

'Thanks,' Harry said. 'What is the news?'

'I believe there are riots all over Glasgow. I was just

talking to the Commissioner and he reckons there must have been planeloads from Belfast, both Loyalists and Republicans, prepared for a punch up. They are looking at the flight records. It has never been this serious in the last thirty years. The match was being shown live and in every bar downtown and in every pub people watching it have gone out on a rampage. We will have to see how we can get out of here.'

9.45 p.m. London, the Ritz

They had just been served the desert. Matt Drummond was hoping to soften up the major shareholders before he told them of his expansion plans, for which he needed to raise more money. These were the hard-eyed mob, harder than himself or even Asha. The head waiter came and spoke to him discreetly. He was sorry, but he had another call from Glasgow. He had fielded the previous ones but this time it was his wife. Did he want to take it? Matt knew that Margaret would not call him for any trivial reason. Something must have happened. Had she got a new prognosis?

'Hello, Margaret,' he said.

'Sorry to get you like this, Matt. I just wanted to say, that if you hear about my car accident, it is nothing serious. I am bruised, and must use a wheelchair for a couple of days, that's all.'

'What on earth, Margaret? When did this happen and where are you?'

'Don't panic. I am in Glasgow for one night, and will return to London tomorrow for Lisa White's play at the

National. I just thought, you may worry if you heard it on the news or something.'

'Why should it be on the news?'

'Well, my chauffeur Paul died in hospital, and the van that hit us had the markings of *The Glasgow Times* which someone had attempted to paint over. So, the police are anxious to question Willie. I am sure there is nothing to it. Have a nice evening whatever you are doing.'

'I am having a working dinner, dear. As usual. Get well.'

He walked back to his dinner but his fertile brain was immediately working on the jigsaw puzzle of Willie, a delivery van belonging to his company and the accident. Who was behind this? he wondered.

As he joined the dinner again, he saw Asha trying to catch his eye as if to ask, what was all that about? He decided to ignore her. His shareholders were more important. He called a waiter and asked him to clear his plate away. He was no longer in the mood to eat. Once all plates had been cleared, they could start on the serious discussion.

The head waiter came back, and whispered that there was another call from Mr Pritchard, saying it was most urgent to speak to him. Matt was now angry. He was not used to his business dinners being interrupted like this.

'I am terribly sorry. I have to leave you again, but I shan't be long.' He bowed to the assembled company and left.

'What is it, Lex?'

'Sorry to get you like this from your dinner. But I just heard that Terence Harcourt died of a heart attack in Vienna, half an hour ago.'

'What? How? Did someone tip him off? Did you?'

'No, of course not. I just wanted to ask, if it is alright with you, to pull the planned edition with the pictures. We will throw together something else.'

'OK. Do as you like. But I want a full account of what happened.'

Matt went back into the dinner. Here were two events which were not according to what he had planned. Lex, he was sure, had warned Terence, and caused his death. His mobile record would have to be examined. But Margaret's accident was still puzzling him. Who would want to hurt her and from within his and even her own company. He stood at his seat and spoke sombrely.

'Gentlemen and Miss Chan, I have just heard that the Secretary of State for Europe, Terence Harcourt, died earlier this evening in Vienna.' He did not want to make eye contact with Asha.

The dinner broke up. All the institutional investors had to rush back and work out the impact of the news on the Bond markets. Tokyo would open soon.

They were left alone.

'What was the first call about, Matt?' Asha asked.

'Tell me frankly, now. Did you ask Willie to bump Margaret off?'

'What are you talking about, Matt? Why would I want to do that? How could I?'

'You are the only one I know, who has the sort of devious mind to do such a thing. Willie used a delivery van from the office but he had *The Glasgow Times* sign painted over. Unfortunately, not completely. The police will want to know who did this. I will be asked, and I am going to have to tell.'

'Is Margaret alright? Is she…?'

'She is bruised and concussed and in a wheelchair.'

'Thank God for that.'

'But her chauffeur, you know him. He works for our Glasgow office. Paul. He is dead.'

'But what has that to do with me?'

'My dear, Willie does not have the brains to stage an accident all by himself. Someone told him to have Margaret hit. Just hit; maybe not killed. Just to speed up her death, to debilitate her. It has to be you.'

'Nonsense. You have no reason to say that. You have no proof.'

'Ah, so you did it, but don't think I have the proof. You underestimate me. If you don't talk, Linda will.'

'Rubbish.'

'I pay her a second salary, twice what you pay her to keep an eye on all your movements. I am not such an old fool that I would be besotted by your lovely dark eyes, Miss Chan. We are through. Goodbye.'

'I'll sue you. I know all your tax fiddles. You will regret this.'

'You will be in jail, my dear. And, what is more, every one of my tax fiddles was arranged by you. Against your professional code of ethics. The Bar Council will not like what you do, Miss Chan. As I said, goodbye. I have work to do.'

Meghnad Desai

9.55 p.m. London, the House of Commons

Frank Thompson was aghast. Terence Harcourt, dead. He had better tell Austin, who could spread the news. This meant he had to draft a tribute to Terence, as well as make the Statement. Hell! Gideon was away, otherwise he could have helped. He had better ask the Library. He now wished he had not sent his PPS back to his constituency. But Rupert had a Scottish seat and was worried about his majority. So Frank had agreed to let him have Mondays off twice a month.

He dialled Austin's number. As expected, he wasn't there. So Frank left a message. Frank could not handle a pager, and would just have to wait till Austin got the message. In desperation, he did what he always did. He called Josephine, his wife.

'Josie, what's up?'

'Nothing much, darling. Had a hectic day as usual. I had to buy something for Elisabet's play tomorrow night. I hope you have not forgotten we are going. Then I had to make sure I had a slot with Jacques to come and do my hair. I have to look my best for you for the big night at the National tomorrow. I have had a nice bath and will wait for you to come home. What's up with you?' It was the simple pleasures of life that Josie liked, now that they had left the working class penury of the early years of their married life far behind.

'Oh, don't ask. I wish I could have a nice bath and curl up in bed.'

'What is it, darling? Why are you fretting?'

'You know I never like it when Harry is gone and I

270

have to stand in his place at the Despatch box.'

'But my sweet, you have done it before, and you know you are very good at it.'

Josie had met Frank when they were both children in Barnsley. She came from a miner's family as well, and had tried her best to keep up with Frank's rise to eminence. She had come a long way, but she remained a simple soul, though she took her privileges in her stride… But, above all, she stayed close to Frank and knew how stressed out he could get. She had to soothe him.

'Don't talk about it. Now Terence has just dropped dead, and in Vienna of all places.'

'Who? Terence Harcourt? Oh poor Dorothy. When did you find out?'

'Lettie Brighton just told me. Her Foreign Office got a message from our Embassy. Heart attack. I have to read out a tribute to him. Now, how am I going to do that?'

'Sweet man. You knew him, and you two have been in the same movement for some twenty five years together. You quarrelled a lot, but you were fighting for the same things. He started a poor man like you. Only he married a rich woman, and you got stuck with me, penniless as I was, all your life. Just speak from your heart. Don't be pompous or sarky like Harry. Just say what a great guy he was. Leave the long obituary to someone else.'

9.58 p.m. London, across Hampstead Hill

Ian was happy. He was walking up from Pond Street

to his home at Frognal. He varied his path depending on his mood. He had had a long day with a lot of
drinks, so a longer route was to be preferred. It was a
lovely evening, warm and pleasant. The twilight had
gone, but from the heights of Hampstead you could
see some glow in the far distance. He had crossed Hav-
erstock Hill and walked along Lyndhurst Road. That
way took him on to Fitzjohn's Avenue. Then, to make
it interesting, he had strolled downhill along Arkwright
Road. He was just turning into his front garden when
the door opened and Hilda came out.

'There was a call from Marcus, love. They want you
as soon as possible. I am sorry. Would you like a quick
cup of tea?'

It was not usual for Hilda to be concerned about calls
from Marcus. Normally she regarded all Ian's friends
and employers as bad news. They always led him into
unhealthy habits. She did not see why he had to work
this late in his seventies. Her own practice gave them
enough to live on and more.

'Why does Marcus want me? I have just been there
all day,' Ian fibbed a bit.

'Terence Harcourt dropped dead of heart attack
in Vienna. No doubt boozing, overeating on Wiener
Schnitzel and gobbling sachertorte. When will they
ever learn?'

Hilda's mind did not reach the more devious reasons
behind Terence's heart attack.

'What on earth is happening? Terence at such a young
age? I saw him last month, and he was fine. Anyway, let
me have a cup of tea and call them. I want a taxi. I am

not going back to the bus stop.'

'I am sorry darling. They offered to send a taxi. Knowing you, I agreed that while you would not be best pleased, you will go if they send a taxi. There should be one in five minutes, so you had better have your cuppa.'

Ian crossed to his favourite chair in the living room while Hilda went in to the kitchen and Ian could hear the hiss of the kettle being put on. The phone rang.

'Hello, who is it?' Ian asked.

'Ian, I am glad I found you. This is Frank Thompson.'

'Well, this is a surprise, the Deputy Prime Minister himself! What's up?' Ian used Frank's gambit.

'I guess you have already heard about Terence. Have you?'

'I just heard as I came home. Hilda told me.'

'Well, I need you to help me with my tribute to Terence. I have a Statement to make on Libya as we were talking about. But I should start by saying something about Terence. I wish Harry was here.'

'Listen Frank. Young Marcus is sending me a taxi to go to *The News* office. I will ask them to take me via the House and en route I will scribble something and I will bring it to you. Hope I get there on time. After that I will need to rush to Marcus. You may need to provide me with police outriders so I can get there quick, OK?'

'You are a pal. Anything you ask for is yours. Another day like this and you can have my job, I am telling you.'

9.59 p.m. Glasgow, Ibrox Stadium, Directors' Dining Room

Oliver's mobile rang. It was Christine.

'Have you heard? Terence died of a heart attack in Vienna. The news came just a while ago via our Embassy. He was in a shady bar with some woman. Our Embassy is trying its best to keep the reptiles off. Tell Harry. He will have to make a statement. He'd better sound sorry.'

Bloody Matt Drummond, Oliver thought. He was sure he knew what had caused Terence's death. He sidled up to Harry, and whispered in his ear. Harry was genuinely shocked. He immediately clapped his hands demanding silence.

'Listen, please. I have a very sad announcement to make. It is sad for Scotland and it is sad for the whole country. We have just heard from our Embassy in Austria that the Secretary of State for Europe, Terence Harcourt, who was in Vienna in connection with an EU ministerial meeting, has died of a heart attack.'

A sense of shock swept over the gathering. One of the fur clad women began sobbing into her drink.

'Terence was a brilliant Cabinet minister, a consummate politician at British and European levels, a doughty fighter for justice and the rights of ordinary people. I have lost a good friend, Scotland has lost a great son and our country has lost an outstanding political leader. Our sympathies go to Dorothy and their three lovely daughters. I request you to observe a minute's silence in his memory.'

In that one minute's silence, Oliver savoured what a fantastic politician and impromptu speaker Harry was. Sarah was also crying, but she did not know why. She hardly knew Terence, but Alan had told her a lot about him, not all flattering either. But she felt as if she had lost a close friend. Perhaps it was just the tension of it all. She wished the day would end. She wanted to get out of the place.

As did Harry, of course. He needed space to think clearly about the political implications of Terence's death on his position, for Scotland and for the Party's fortunes. Who would he pick to replace Terence? He needed to talk to Oliver and Christine. He had to get out of here.

The silence continued beyond the minute. There was a palpable sense of incredulity mingled with grief. Among the more senior people one could see that they knew Terence and were thinking, there but for Grace of God go I. Then suddenly Jamie, who was in tears, began to sing '*Flowers of Scotland*'. Soon the entire crowded room was joining in. Harry had to keep still, and appear to be mouthing the words of this song he did not know. Nor did Sarah, but Oliver did of course. Sarah looked admiringly at the distraught Jamie and held his hand. She was deeply moved by his gesture.

The song ended. There were murmurs of appreciation for Jamie. Then Harry spoke again.

'There is no question of us sitting down to a dinner now. Let us go all of us to our tasks. Terence would want us to. He had a sense of duty to the last day of his life. When something like this happens you realise how lucky one is to be alive. We all need to meditate on this sad event each of us by ourselves. I hope you don't mind if we now go. Let me thank you for your hospitality for me and my staff, Oliver Knight and Miss Disney.'

'Thank you for coming to Ibrox, Prime Minister.' Calum had decided to take over. 'We are very sorry that the game was interrupted, and then came this sad news of our comrade's death. But, I am sure, I speak on behalf of all of us here that we hope you will come back on another occasion, and grace us with your company.'

'Well said,' Sir Archibald wanted to have the last word.

'OK, let us go. Where's Barney?' Harry asked.

'I am here, Prime Minister.'

'So can we go?'

'Let me contact our police escort. They are somewhat overwhelmed now as fights have broken out all over the city.' He took out his mobile.

Harry gestured to Sarah to join him. She came, followed by Jamie. She tried to be casual and professional.

'Prime Minister, this is Dr Jamie Hencke. He is a proper medical doctor and has been kindly looking after me all evening.'

'Thank you for that, Jamie. What do you do?'

'Sir, I work for Mr Crawford in his Glasgow office. I was hoping to come to London to work for Mr Harcourt. But, sadly, that will not happen now.'

'Why not? Come. What were you going to do for Terence?'

'Sir, he had asked me to come and look at the European experience on health insurance to help ease the financing problems of the NHS. I am just finishing a Master's degree in Health Economics for that reason.'

'Listen. Do come. Just give my office a call. You know Sarah now, so you are on the inside track. If she asks me, I have no choice but to say yes. You can work on the same problem in my office. OK?'

If nothing else, he could take Sarah off my hands when I am fed up with her, Harry thought. Barney was off his phone.

'Sir, can we talk by ourselves?'

'Come into this ante room, Prime Minister.' Calum had taken over the place.

Oliver followed. Harry asked Sarah to join them. She came quickly. Harry ever so lightly brushed himself against her. Sarah was thrilled. Harry whispered in her ears.

'Stay close. I have dropped my contacts. Can't see a thing.' Sarah laughed.

Harry called Oliver over. Drawing him close he said, 'That and this riot will at least take the heat off Libya. Tell Christine, whoever is on *Newsnight* must put Terence before Libya. Poor Terence. Mind you, that is the best way to go if you have to. Quickly.'

'And just in time for *Newsnight*, as well.' Oliver thought of his angle.

They all gathered into the inner office where Oliver had been before.

Calum asked Barney whether he should stay or go.

'I don't mind you staying, sir. I just did not want everyone to be listening to what I have to say.'

'What's the problem, Barney?' Harry knew there must be something serious.

'Sir, the Chief Constable sends his apologies. He was going to be here for the dinner but he has been called away. He says the situation is much more serious than I thought. They have now come across evidence that the riot was predictable, if not pre-planned. They had seen two plane loads come from Belfast: one, a loyalist group and the other, a republican group. These were chartered flights. Also, buses came over on the ferry from Ulster. Strathclyde Police have intercepted some mobile phone traffic. There is a possibility, no more, but still it is there, that some people have a plot to attack your car, even perhaps to kill you. I am sorry to be so blunt, sir. But the Chief Constable says he cannot provide you with full security transfer to the airport. There is a lot of trouble at the airport as some of these gangs have headed there. He is sorry, but these are the worst riots he has known.'

'So what does he advise?'

Harry was cool and factual. Sarah was numb with fear. Oliver was incandescent about the bloody Northern Irish.

'Sir, he hopes that a Police helicopter will be available within an hour when he expects the trouble to have calmed down. Then they can take you to your flight.'

'Well, it is ten right now. We won't get to Belfast at this rate till midnight. I wish things were faster. Where is the nearest RAF base?'

'Prime Minister, can I suggest a quicker way? My

helicopter can be summoned immediately, and take you to wherever you wish to go. It is a six-seater Eurocopter twin squirrel aircraft. Fast and comfortable. Why not go to Belfast directly and avoid the airport?' Calum Kennedy saw his chance of doing a favour to the PM, and reclaim some goodwill despite a completely disastrous evening.

Harry turned to Oliver and Barney.

'What do you reckon?'

'Sounds fine to me. It will get us out of here and we can avoid the ride from the airport in Belfast as well. Barney?' Oliver was impatient.

'If it is fine with you, sir, I am happy to come along. Or, if you like, I can see about the RAF facilities.'

'OK, let us take Calum's offer. Thanks a lot. That will sort out our problem.'

'I am delighted, Prime Minister. I can get the 'copter here in ten minutes.'

'Fine. While we are waiting, we'd better get back in there and join our shattered colleagues.' Harry was now feeling generous about his Scottish hosts. He also wanted to see how they were taking Terence's death. Would it help in the elections to the Scottish Parliament?

So they moved out, leaving Calum to bark his orders to his personal assistant. Harry decided now was the time to be effusive to Sir Archibald something who had lost his game, his reception and even the dinner.

'Now, Sir Archibald, we are all set. Hopefully, Calum Kennedy will get his helicopter to come here. But I am afraid that means you have to suffer our presence for another ten minutes. I hope you don't mind.'

'Prime Minister, how can you say that? We are sorry to send you off without a taste of Scottish hospitality. It has been a difficult and now a sad day. But may I ask you and your party to join me in a farewell drink. How about a large malt whisky, the nectar of Scotland?'

'Can I be very rude and say no to the whisky? I will, however, have another of the excellent Martinis that I had earlier. It was just perfect for my taste buds.'

At the bar, Roger felt it had been a fitful night. Much less drinking than he had expected. They had hired waiters to help him who were carrying the usual beers and whiskies, leaving Roger to do the fancy stuff. Now the dinner was cancelled and here was the end of the evening coming. Would Harry have another drink? Suddenly, he saw Sir Archibald approach.

'My dear fellow, can you make one last one of your Martinis for the Prime Minister. He loved your last effort. Tell you what, if it is so good, make me one as well. I will wait here so you don't need to carry them.'

Roger saw the complication at once. He would now have to hand the specially made Martini to Harry himself. He could not possibly rely on this old fool to hand the drink to Harry.

'No need, Sir. I will bring them to you in a trice. The Prime Minister needs your company.'

Sir Archibald was thankful as he realised that Calum had stolen a march on him. So he had better get his share of PM's time. He hurried back. Roger was quick. He had to manipulate his two bottles of olives and re-member which was which. His private special olive was a shade darker than the clean one. His deft hands moved fast and within minutes he had the two Martinis ready. Calum walked up to him.

'Jesus, Roger, I had forgotten you were here to-night. Let us have a large malt, will you? My favourite, please.'

'Te Bheag, isn't it? Sure.' Roger pulled out a bottle of Te Bheag which only the afficianados drank. 'Calum, there you are. Can I ask you to do me favour? This Martini is for Sir Archibald and this one for the Prime Minister. Can you take them in please. But keep them separate. They are different recipes. The Prime Minister is very particular.'

'OK, you old rascal. Just for old times' sake. Now, tell me again, which is which.'

Roger realised that Calum was beyond the driving limit, and would fail a breath test by a mile. The risk was too great. He would rather be recognised by Harry than kill Sir Archibald. Anyway, Calum could not carry three drinks.

'Don't worry, you old Stalinist. I will do it.'

Roger went into the large group surrounding Harry. A path was cleared for him. He gave the clean drink to Sir Archibald, and almost simultaneously the special one to Harry. Sir Archibald was feeling expansive.

'Prime Minister, this is the man who made you your perfect Martini. Indeed, he has converted me to it now. It is Roger, isn't it?'

'Yes Sir.' Roger wanted to be away as soon as he could. But he did not reckon with Harry. For a politician, every new person is a hand to be shaken, a potential vote to be bid for. He took Roger's hand and with his blue eyes that Roger recalled to this day, looked into Roger's eyes. Shit, this is it. He knows who I am.

'Nice to meet you Roger. Thanks for a finely made Martini. Let me say, if I come here again, I want you to be here to make me another one.'

Harry kept on staring at Roger. Roger was not to know that Harry could not see him well. His myopia was such that Roger was just a blur.

'Thank you, Prime Minister.' Roger withdrew with alacrity.

Calum gulped his drink down. His mobile was ringing. He answered it and said,

'OK. We are ready. If we get down to the ground, the 'copter will land there in just a minute. It is all clear but watch your steps as there are broken bottles about.'

Harry looked at his drink. Should he abandon it? He hesitated. Then, he drank it down in a single gulp and, as a result, swallowed the olive whole. He hated that, but then he had to move fast. Oliver, Sarah and Barney were already going down. Calum stayed with Harry and kept on plugging his case.

'It is a state of the art machine, Prime Minister, and Angus Stewart is an experienced pilot who has done fifty thousand miles. You are in good hands. You should be in Belfast in no time whatsoever.'

'This way, if you want to avoid the Press, Prime Minister.' Oliver was anxious to get away. They went down a long dark tunnel, and emerged on the pitch, where just an hour ago, fights had raged. It looked like a battlefield. The Rangers cleaning staff were picking up the broken glass the best they could with the floodlights as their only help. With the helicopter landing, a lot of things, including paper, were flying about. Angus Stewart was standing at the foot of the helicopter. He was holding one door open. He shook hands with Harry.

'Welcome to the Queen of the Clyde, Prime Minister. I am Angus Stewart, your pilot.'

'Thank you Angus. This is Sarah and this here is Oliver Knight. Barney Jones will also be travelling with us for security.' As he said that Harry put his arm around Sarah and helped her up, making sure that they would be together at the back. Oliver and Barney knew their place and got in the front leaving a row of two seats between the boss and themselves. Harry waved to Calum and mouthed Thanks, but the noise was too great for anyone to hear much. Even before they were off, Harry's hand had slid under Sarah's dress. Sarah sidled closer to him and whispered, 'Don't be shocked but no panties, clean forgot.' Harry laughed.

10.00 p.m. London, House of Commons

Bong—This is the ten o'clock news from the BBC.

Bong—First the headlines.

Bong—Terence Harcourt, the Secretary of State for Europe, has died of a heart attack. We look at the implications for the Government.

Bong—Riots in Glasgow at the match between Rangers and Celtic. Two dead and dozens injured.

Bong—Is America about to bomb Libya? Is Britain's RAF going along?

First, Terence Harcourt. Our correspondent, Nyta Roberts, reports.

Frank was relieved. Watching the BBC in his room just before he voted in the Division lobbies, he wanted to see if the Libyan news had leaked out. This meant that the news would be known only when the Americans made their announcement at five o'clock their Eastern time. So far, the BBC had not picked anything up. So even if CNN picked it up and reported it as breaking news, and then the BBC's Washington Correspondent called London, the BBC would not report it till after, say, ten past. So, by the time Mary got to *Newsnight*, they would have only the tiniest amount of information. Even better, if *Newsnight* started with Terence or the punch-up at Ibrox. And Libya got squeezed out. If Frank had been a praying type, he would have done so now.

Eric came to him in the Division lobby.

'Frank, Can I have a word with you?'

'Eric, nice to see you in our lobby. What's up, tell me?'

'Are you announcing a US attack on Libya? Is HMG going along? If so, I am bound to ask you some searching questions following your statement. I thought it best to warn you.'

'Fair enough. Eric, you are a gentleman. As you know, it would be a breach of privilege if I were to tell you what was in my Statement before I told the House. But ask me what you wish. It is a free country.'

10.05 p.m. Glasgow, Glencoe Hotel

Margaret was watching BBC news. She had arrived at the hotel where the ambulance had brought her. This was in the university area across the river from where she had the accident. It was up on the hill. The hotel was very comfortable and her suite was the best they had. Margaret had been taken up in her wheelchair. They had given her a maid, who was exclusively to help her. She had some soup and bread, and now was ready for bed. But she could not sleep yet. Much had happened to her, and tomorrow was going to be crowded. She had to sort it all out in her mind. Watching the news was the best way to settle her mind. She did not want to watch Rainbow, the channel that LDNC owned, since she hated commercials during news. So BBC it was.

They were still on Terence Harcourt's sudden death. Margaret had never met him, but knew vaguely that Matt hated his guts, though not why. Matt had his own collection of loves and hates. That boyish-looking BBC Political Editor was saying that this might increase Harry's control over the Party, and drive the rebels further into isolation. Then, they moved on to the Glasgow scene with the riots. Margaret started browsing through the recent issue of *The New Yorker* she had carried with her. She hated to see the ugliness of all that violence.

10.02 p.m. Glasgow, Ibrox Stadium, Directors' Dining Room

Roger started clearing up and packing up. He had

breathed a sigh of relief that Harry did not recognise him. But if Harry had eaten the olive as he liked to do in his last drink, Roger had no more than an hour to get out of town. Harry seemed to have left early. Roger did not know where or how. The noise he had heard of the helicopter could have been the police or it could have been Harry. Roger did not care anymore. He had to go.

'That was a very fine drink, young man, and the Prime Minister appreciated it as well. Can you make me one more for the road?' It was Sir Archibald.

Roger had no choice. He nearly chose the poisonous olive jar but refrained. He was in enough trouble as it was. He had to avoid doing anything which might raise suspicion. The place was crawling with police.

'Would that be just for yourself or for the PM as well?' Roger thought it best to feign ignorance of what had happened to Harry.

'No. The Prime Minister has rushed off. Mr Kennedy kindly made his private helicopter available. He hopes to be in Belfast in an hour or so. I do hope he repays us a visit. We need to show him some real hospitality. I hope you will be available then to mix our drinks. Pity about the haggis though.' Sir Archibald was still sore about the wasted food.

Roger gave him the drink. At least for an hour or so, the news about Harry would not be known, and if he died on the way to Belfast or in Belfast, that would make for an even longer delay before the Law came chasing Roger. He had to get out. Roger called over Billy who was one of the waiters at the Bar and told him to hold the fort while he went to the toilet. Billy agreed but was puzzled that Roger went off clutching a jar of olives. He just shrugged his shoulders. It was a rum world. How was he to know that Roger was just destroying evidence?

10.15 p.m. London, the House of Commons

Frank was relieved. Ian had given him a beautiful short text to read out. It mentioned Terence's Northern Irish background and his progress through Glasgow University, his battle to wrest power from the Old Guard, his early promotion during the Wilson Callaghan years, his role as Deputy Leader under Stan and finally his marriage with Dorothy. Frank knew all this but he could not have written it as well as Ian. He must tell Josie to invite Ian and Hilda for dinner at Chevening. Frank and Josie had Chevening as their weekend residence. The lovely old house belonged to the Foreign Office. But Nick Davies wanted to be in Wales as much as he could, so he gave it up to Frank.

'Tell you what, Ian. You must never retire. The world and I need you to be around,' Frank said. The clock was at quarter past ten and the Division would end soon. Frank had come out quickly to meet up with Ian. Now he debated if he could risk a drink before his Statement. Habit proved superior to reason.

'Let me buy you a pint for that. I owe you a big dinner, but that will have to be arranged between Josie and Hilda. Come, lad.'

It was pleasant on the Terrace but the gloom at Terence's news was palpable. Austin joined them with a scotch in his hand.

'In the memory of a great Scotsman. What a tragedy. How will the Party cope?'

'The Party will have to learn how to cope. Harry has the more immediate problem of finding a successor.'

'Have you spoken to Dorothy?' Austin asked.

'Oh, yes. She was very badly cut up. All she kept on saying was "my poor lambkins". He was such a lovely father. After a few minutes of her crying, I had to politely say I will get in touch with her about the funeral. She said to get in touch with Terence's secretary, that Adrian Andrew. I can't get hold of him on his mobile. So I have asked the switch board to track him down.'

'Just how did he die? What was he doing in Vienna?' Ian asked.

'He was attending a European Ministerial meeting on costs of enlargement. Boring hard work if you ask me, but someone has to do it. He had dinner with our Ambassador and then suddenly phut. Off he goes.'

'I hear he was in some bar or other.'

'You don't want to listen to the reptiles. They are sniffing around for a scandal.' Frank wanted to put a lid on this line of inquiry.

'Frank, I almost forgot.' Austin was on Frank's wavelength and changed the subject. 'The Tories say that they would like to do the tribute to Terence first as a separate item so their tributes don't get mixed up with some argy-bargy over Libya. The Lib Dems are happy to go along with that, given they think they are going to win big in Scotland. Is that alright with you?'

'To tell you frankly, I prefer it all in one go. If they

like, they can pause for breath between their tribute to Terence and their comment on Libya. I don't want the media accusing us of bringing Libya so late in the night, it doesn't make the papers tomorrow. What with the punch-up in Glasgow and Terence, if we get Libya also in, it would get less space on the front pages. Anyway, that is how Harry would play it, I am sure. So, can you unwind it?'

'Oh, how did Harry cope with the punch-up in Glasgow?'

10.20 p.m. Aboard the Queen of the Clyde

Harry was all over Sarah. It was all he could do to stop himself from nuzzling her bare back and lovely white shoulders when they were in the big room with everyone looking. But as soon as they were in the helicopter, he could not wait even for the take off. Nor, for that matter, could Sarah. So she helped him by easing the straps off. She took his mouth to herself and then to her nipples. His hands had worked their way deep into where she wanted him. They had slid further down so they could not be seen by the front rows. The noise was so loud that Sarah's moaning was inaudible to anyone else. Sarah had her hands busy with removing Harry's belt and then his zip and she was just about to get where he wished. Harry was nuzzling Sarah's neck and kissing her full on the mouth, and stroking her breasts. Suddenly, he slumped and slid along the seat, and onto her lap, his hands limp and hanging loosely.

'Harry, Harry, are you alright?' Sarah was shouting,

but still no one at the front looked back. She tried to stand up, adjusting her dress, to attract the pilot's attention, but she was thrown back as the helicopter lurched. Sarah screamed. She hadn't looked where they were going ever since they got in. Now, suddenly, she saw a big white surface in front of the helicopter. The pilot was shouting and swearing. The helicopter lurched up quickly, but came down again with a swift jolt. Oliver and Barney were thrown off their seats.

Angus Stewart was trying to get his vehicle to rise higher. It was dark and he could not see clearly. Earlier in the evening, he had been watching the Old Firm game on TV with his mates. He knew Calum Kennedy was staying in town, and assumed there was no chance of his being called for duty tonight. So, a few beers had been had between friends. When the call came from Calum's assistant that he had to go quickly, he could not possibly plead any excuse. He was supposed to be on duty 24/7, and drinking was not allowed on the job. But still, there was the game, and he so loathed Celtic that he wished to see them thrashed. So, he got together with the lads and had a lovely time, then quickly washed his mouth with Listerine and came to Ibrox. The air was foul as it always was in Ibrox so Calum did not notice his breath, not that Calum's was any sweeter. The woman at the back was screaming but, oh shit. Oh shit, he had hit something.

10.25 p.m. London, Heathrow Hilton

Adrian was enjoying his room service at the Heathrow

Hilton. He had come away as soon as he got his cash. He needed time to think how to convert his money in ways he could use it. He reckoned airport hotels would be least surprised to be paid cash for hotel rooms, especially if he took a big suite. He also had to figure out if he had to leave the country and go after that. He had to see what Lex did with his photographs, and how Terence reacted. He had to hide somewhere safe, and what better place than the Heathrow Hilton. So, he had spent the day lazing around. He lingered in his jacuzzi for a long time sipping champagne, and then snoozed for a while. It was time to throw caution to the winds. It was years since he had not worried about money. He had given up such luxuries as a five star hotel. Now, at least for a bit, he could indulge. For a short time, he would allow himself to drink some decent stuff.

He had woken up hungry. It was nearly ten in the evening. So he had been asleep for six or seven hours. He ordered room service to bring him their best grilled salmon with salad and another bottle of Bollinger. He then settled down to watch the news.

As soon as he heard the news on BBC, his first instinct was to call Dorothy. He was one of the few who had her mobile number. Adrian reactivated his own mobile which he had switched off once he left LDNC.

'Dorothy, I am so sorry to hear…'

There were sobs on the other end. Adrian waited patiently. Then Dorothy spoke,

'Where are you, Adrian? I need you to be here. We all need you. Terence is gone, and I have no friend but you. Can you get here soon?'

Adrian was taken aback. Of course, Dorothy had no idea what part he had played in Terence's death. How would she know, and now of course, unless Roddy was to talk, no one would ever know. So, he was clean and kosher. Here was Dorothy, desperate for his company. He had thought she would be with her relations or friends. But, in many subtle ways, he had made Dorothy dependent on himself. Adrian would have to go. He could break it gently to her that he was not gay. What was more, he could be there and destroy the evidence by removing the cameras.

'Dorothy, I am in London. I will get to Heathrow first thing and find a flight to Edinburgh. I will call you as soon as I get a flight reservation. Don't worry. I will be there.'

'Oh thank you, thank you, Adrian. I always said to Terence I could rely on you. You come from such a solid good family. These things matter when the time comes. Thank you, thank you, Adrian. Come as soon as you can.'

Adrian called the reception.

'Hello, Mr Andrew. What can we do for you?'

'Can you tell me if you know any airline taxis who can fly me to Edinburgh now?'

'Sure, Sir. Just give me a couple of minutes.'

Adrian was pleased that he had done nothing precipitately.

10.25 p.m. London, the Archduke

Kath slid down her chair, and onto the marble floor

with a clatter. As a fashion model, she was used to a strict regime in eating and drinking. This long bout of drinking and eating and talking and singing had finally gone to her head. Everyone broke out in hysterical laughter.

'I guess that's curtains for us, sisters. We'd better get on our broom sticks and fly back home.' Lisa was pissed, but perfectly in control of the situation It was just half past ten, but the Archduke was quite empty as Monday was always a slow day. So the staff were waiting patiently for this drunken rabble to wrap up their dinner. Lisa stood up and raised her glass.

'To Ubu and stupid men and husbands everywhere. Till tomorrow.'

'Down with kings and Presidents and leaders everywhere. Up with Lisa,' Annie responded.

Lisa summoned the waiter and asked for the bill.

10.25 p.m. London, the House of Commons

Frank Thompson stood up at the Dispatch box and began.

'With permission, Mr Deputy Speaker, I wish to make a Statement on behalf of My Right Honourable Friend, the Prime Minister, on Her Majesty's Government's policy on North Africa. But before I do that, I hope you will allow me to say that it is my sad duty to inform the House of the sudden death of the Right Honourable Member for Renfrew, the Secretary of State for Europe, Terence Harcourt.'

Ian was shaping his obituary in the news office, but,

just in case, he had the Parliamentary Channel on. He wanted to see how Frank fared, and also how the Libya Statement went down with the Commons, especially on Government backbenches. He was also looking up the cuttings file on Terence that they had helpfully provided. He had his previous draft in front of him, but that had been done before Terence became Secretary of State for Europe. He had a lot to do and not much time to do it in.

10.25 p.m. Glasgow, Ibrox Stadium, Directors' Dining Room

Roger had flushed the olives down the toilet. It had been a busy evening, and there was no danger any one would notice what he had put down. As the remaining people went home, they would be stopping by and using the facilities, so his olives would be accorded a fast forward passage into the local drains. He then went back and made sure Billy saw him. He said good night to him and asked him to clear up. He had just one more thing to do, and that was to collect his money from Alex, who made all these informal transactions for the club.

'What a pity, Roger. We could have won that fair and square. Who knows, the League may yet award it to us. That will make it one more nail in the coffin for those bastards.' Alex's tolerance earlier in the afternoon was gone. Roger cared more about the discretion with which he handed over the money.

'Well, that is life, Alex. Thanks. Take care how you go.'

'There are a lot of mad buggers out there. Mind how you go too, Roger.'

There was indeed one man who was very mad but in the American not in the British sense. Red was furious that Harry White had escaped his clutches. He had his device in place and it would have been triggered off by the car's motion itself. Within minutes of the car starting, Harry and all who travelled with him would have been blown up. Then this had to happen. Now, the police were swarming all over and people were pouring out of the posh parts of Ibrox. In the general melee, he had no time to deatch the device. But Red could not see any point in killing an innocent Government chauffeur if he was travelling without Harry White. He took out a beer bottle from the rucksack and hurled it at the windscreen and then ran for his life.

Roger was out of the building, and now he was walking rapidly, as running would only attract attention. He did not see Red nor anyone else very clearly. His eyes were befuddled with fear and he was in a desperate hurry. There were people and police in a chaotic melee. The police were trying to disperse fans as quickly as they could, but there were shouts and sounds of fighting all around…he had to be careful. He had to get a taxi to take him to the airport, and then off to Dublin, if a flight was still available. There were no taxis, however. There was not even a bus. He kept on walking. Police had cordoned off large areas around Ibrox…he was beginning to worry how he would get away. Suddenly, he heard a horn behind him. It was Calum in his Rover.

'Where are you going? It is murder out there. Can I take you somewhere?'

Oh shit, Roger thought. What is to be done now? So he took the line of least resistance.

'Drop me off where I can get a bus or taxi to get to the airport. I have a late flight to catch. Thanks, Calum.'

'You won't get out anywhere tonight. The airport is flooded with police. They are expecting trouble since a lot of the gangs have come over from Belfast. I doubt if any flights will leave tonight. Wait till tomorrow. Let me drive you all the way home. It is a rough night to be travelling by public transport in Glasgow. Tell my driver where you live.'

10.25 p.m. Glasgow to Ayr on the A77

'OK, kids, we will stop at the next junction, and take you to the Little Chef. You have been very good so far,' David Byrne said.

He was now driving back from the aborted game to their home in Ayr. The nightmare of the match was over. The kids had been frightened, but they had not said a word. He was so proud of them. He got into the car park ahead of many others, who were also running. He drove off as soon as he could, and headed south out of Glasgow. But the traffic was bad, and at many places, there were police roadblocks to thwart the rioters. It was not until after nine thirty that they were on the stretch of A77 which was congestion free. Now, after having driven for an hour, he felt relaxed.

Robbie and Alastair had been exemplary. They had sensed that their dad was worried about them. They had remained silent through the ordeal, and clutched their dad's hands tightly through the twenty minutes it took them to get out of Ibrox. Now he was feeling a bit relaxed and thought he had better tell Sophie they were alright. Sophie would have seen the news on TV, and would be worried. So David parked his car in a layby and called her and told her how good and helpful the twins had been and so brave. Not once had either of them cried or complained. David let the twins talk to their mum, and proudly told her that not once had they asked their Dad, Are we there yet? So, Sophie agreed they should be rewarded, and told David to take it easy, drive carefully and give the kids another treat. The next rest stop was not far away, and there would be a Little Chef there.

'Look, Robbie, a helicopter,' Alastair said.

Robbie was back to reading his comic. He did not immediately look up.

'Robbie, look it is going to hit the hills.'

Robbie looked up from his book. David Byrne looked up. He was just about to start the car again. He had been aware of a distant noise of the helicopter in the last ten minutes, but had taken no note. Now suddenly the air seemed to be ripped apart by the sound of metal smashing into the rocky face of the hill. There was a blaze of fire and then an eerie silence. The noise stopped, and it looked like the helicopter had crashed. He told the kids to stay there, and dialled 999.

10.30 p.m. London, the House of Commons

'Mr Deputy Speaker, I turn now to the question of Her Majesty's Government's policy on Libya. As Right Honourable and Honourable Members know, Libya has been the subject of UN Resolutions which have asked the country's leadership to stop aiding and abetting terrorism in the region. We have given Libya ample chances to comply with the UN Resolutions, but the response so far has been poor.' Frank had done his tribute to Terence Harcourt and was now on to the dreaded subject of Libya.

Eric stood up.

'On a point of order, Mr Deputy Speaker.'

'The Right Honourable Member for Nonesuch North knows that no point of order can be allowed during a Statement.' Sir Reginald Bassett,the Deputy Speaker, was firm.

'Is it in order that the Right Honourable Gentleman tells the House a blatant lie?'

'I warn the Right Honourable Gentleman that he is out of order. I shall overlook his breach of parliamentary behaviour this once. I warn him, if he persists, I will have no option but to name him.' Sir Reginald was losing his cool.

Frank was glad of that interruption. Every minute wasted kept the news from off the air. He wished he had more interruptions from all sides.

'Mr Deputy Speaker, tonight at twenty two hundred hours, American F-16 aircraft were launched from their base to attack Libyan airport facilities and Libyan planes in retaliation for the terrorist attack by Libyan aircraft on US aircraft carrier USS Ronald Reagan. RAF aircraft were engaged in support of the US F-16 as refuelling reserves.'

10.30 p.m. Glasgow, Glencoe Hotel

And now on BBC2, Newsnight with Jeremy Paxman.

Margaret saw the futuristic platform move around, and, on the screen, there was Jeremy Paxman. It was obvious from the sardonic twist of his mouth that he was going to enjoy savaging whichever Minister he had in his sight tonight. Margaret had already seen the Libyan bombing announcement trailed on BBC 1 news.

The headlines played out on *Newsnight*.

America bombs Libya as RAF planes assist with refuelling.

Terence Harcourt, Secretary of State for Europe, has died in Vienna.

Riot and mayhem at the Old Firm game in Glasgow. Was there a plot to attack the Prime Minister?

Good Evening. The American Government announced at ten o'clock British time that American planes have taken off from their base in Fakenham in Norfolk. RAF planes are engaged as refuelling reserves. As I speak, the Deputy Prime Minister, Frank Thompson, is making a statement to the House of Commons from where our correspondent, Nyta Roberts, reports.

There was a cut to Nyta standing in the Central Lobby.

Yes, Jeremy. Frank Thompson is still making his state-

ment. The unrest on his back benches was already evident when he was twice interrupted by Eric Thor, whom the Deputy Speaker, Sir Reginald Bassett, had to warn that he could be expelled from the Chamber. The mood here is a mixture of sadness about the death of Terence Harcourt and anger that, once again, Britain has been found playing second fiddle to American policy in the Middle East. Over to you, Jeremy.

Thank you, Nyta, for that. The American attack on Libya will cause major ructions in the country, and even perhaps in the Government. With me to discuss that question is Mary Duggan, the Defence Minister.

'Mary Duggan, what possible ground in international law can you claim for this blatant and unprovoked attack on Libya? Is Harry White again playing America's lapdog?' Jeremy was not one to start softly.

'This is total nonsense, if I may say so, Jeremy. But, before I answer your question, let me say how sorry I am about Terence Har...'

'Hang on. We shall come to that later. First, about Libya, if you don't mind.'

'Of course, I mind. I have lost a valuable comrade.'

'With the greatest respect, Secretary of State, can we deal with Libya first, and then talk about Terence Harcourt.'

'I am not going to be bullied like this. Good manners require that we mourn the loss of a high-ranking British politician, an outstanding Scotsman.' Mary was determined to have her way.

'Don't you think we should mourn the collapse of British sovereignty in matters of foreign policy, before we do that, Secretary of State?'

'There is no collapse of any kind. If you recall, Jeremy, we were joint movers of the UN Security Council Resolution which denounced Libya.'

'Which was only passed because Russia and China abstained, and even then it was eight for and five against.'

'What matters is that we have UN backing for our actions.'

'Tell me, how does the Government, or should I say, how does Harry White get away with such illegal actions?' Jeremy was enjoying himself.

Mary Duggan was just getting into her element. But before she could answer, Jeremy put up his hand to silence her.

'Just a minute', he said. 'We have some breaking news.' His face indicated that something serious had happened. He pressed his ear phones closer. It looked like minutes passed in silence but it was just thirty seconds. Jeremy was solemn when he resumed.

'We have just heard from our Glasgow studios that the helicopter carrying the Prime Minister and Oliver Knight, his Press Officer, has crashed near Kilmarnock. As of now, we don't know whether the Prime Minister is injured or safe, nor do we know who was travelling with him. We go immediately to our Glasgow newsroom, and talk to George Trump. George, what is the latest?'

George was in the BBC Glasgow newsroom.

'Jeremy, all we know as of now is that a driver on the road to his home in Ayr from Glasgow, saw the helicopter crash in the south uplands. This is just along the A77. He called 999 and a rescue team is on its way and should be there any minute now. I have spoken to our sports correspondent Ivan Lawrence, who was at Ibrox. He told me the Prime Minister managed to avoid the Press and took off in a private helicopter. He could not confirm this, but the helicopter may have belonged to the Scottish media magnate Calum Kennedy. It is not clear as of now why the Prime Minister was taking a private helicopter, and where he was going. He had been in Glasgow addressing a party rally and then watching the game at Ibrox, which, as you know, had to be cancelled even before half time due to crowd violence. Police have made several arrests and there is a rumour that many of the rioters have come across from Northen Ireland for the occasion. It has been a bad day all around for Glasgow and for Scotland and indeed for the United Kingdom, what with the riots and the death of Terence Harcourt and now this.'

'Thank you George. It has been a terrible day for Scotland and now it seems for the nation. Mary Duggan. This is indeed a shock, won't you agree?'

Mary Duggan had gone completely white. She tried to speak twice, but no word came out. Jeremy saved the day for her and said,

'Let us go again to Westminster and Nyta Roberts. Nyta?'

'Jeremy, the House is in some state of shock. The Deputy Speaker was given the information by the Clerks on the table, who were told by the Serjeant at Arms. He was himself distraught as he read out the message. John Altrincham, the Conservative Deputy Leader and Foreign Affairs Spokesman was just about to reply to Frank Thompson's Statement when the Deputy Speaker interrupted him and read out the news. He then suspended the proceedings for fifteen minutes while they try to ascertain what has happened precisely in that crash. I saw Frank Thompson sitting on the Front Bench and he was in tears. Austin Mills was also hiding his face in his hands. It is a shocked House of Commons tonight, Jeremy.'

'Thank you, Nyta.'

10.50 p.m. Glasgow Road to Kilmarnock

It was a very noisy scene. Five ambulances had converged on the site where the helicopter had crashed. The local police from Kilmarnock and Ayr and Prestwick had rushed to the scene. The Glasgow situation meant that all across the region, police and ambulance staff were stretched. This was the last thing they expected or needed. The fire which had ignited had been hosed down but the difficult task of rescuing the bodies remained.

David Byrne had got out as soon as he had called 999. He told the children to sit in the car and locked it from outside. He told them not to speak to anyone nor open the door. He had some experience of emergencies. He had tried to get close to the main body of the helicopter. There were bits scattered everywhere. He felt the heat as he reached near. But he could also see someone scrambling to get out. He had shouted, 'It is alright. I am here. Grab my hand.' A tall man covered with blood dragged himself on his knees and grabbed David's proffered hand. It was Barney.

'Thanks, mate. Can I use your mobile? It is the Prime Minister in there.' David gave him the mobile. Barney called an emergency number while David tried to shift the broken shafts of metal to create a passage through the debris. He could hear someone moaning inside.

'Hi, this is Barney Jones. We are on the...'

David said A77 near Kilmarnock.

'On the A77 near Kilmarnock. This is red alert. It is the Prime Minister's team. We had a crash. Send all help. Immediately.'

Barney handed the phone back to David and said, 'Let us see what we can do.'

They heard an ambulance arriving and the siren of a police car.

10.50 p.m. London, along the Strand

Lisa was in the mini bus taking the women home. She had taken the locals to Waterloo or to Victoria from where they could get home. Kath lived in trendy Hoxton. At the moment, she was just getting home having dropped off Annie last at the Savoy. She looked at her mobile and saw six missed calls and five text messages. She had forgotten that she had switched her phone to 'silent' mode when they left the Archduke. As she put the ringtone on again, her mobile phone rang immediately. Lisa saw it was Margaret calling from her own phone this time.

'Margaret, how are you darling? Are you alright? I

won't forget to pray for you tonight. Margaret, why are you crying?'

'Lisa, darling Lisa. How can you not know—such a terrible thing has happened. It is Harry. His helicopter has crashed. I am afraid I will be praying for both of you.'

'Is he, is he…? Oh God. I had my phone switched to silent and they must have been trying to call me. What is the news?'

'We don't know yet. The BBC has just heard about the crash, but no one knows anything more. He was in some private helicopter. He was probably trying to get to Belfast, away from the mess that Glasgow is in.'

'Why? What has happened?' Lisa just wanted to keep talking.

'Haven't you heard anything? It has been a terrible evening. You have been in your post-rehearsal dinner, of course. Well, the match here broke up because of some violence on the pitch, and then the fans fought each other. Four people have died, and many injured. Fighting is still going on all over Glasgow between rival fans. And we heard earlier that Terence Harcourt died of a heart attack in Vienna, where he had gone for a Euro meeting. Poor Dorothy. Anyway, I hope it all turns out alright for you. I will pray for you.'

'I must call Dorothy and give her my condolences. Those girls as well. Oh, what a tragedy. You are a friend, Margaret. We will all have to pray tonight. I had better call up Christine and find out about Harry.'

10.50 p.m. London, *The News* **office, Long Acre**

Ian called Hilda.

'Have you heard, Hilda?'

'Yes, my dear. I reckon you will be very late back tonight.'

'I think you are right. Sleep well.'

11.00 p.m. Glasgow, the Robertson Estate

The car stopped by the estate. Roger got out and thanked Calum.

'Don't mention it, Roger. Stay put, now. Don't go out anywhere tonight. That's a good man.' Calum was most solicitous of his old mate. He was feeling generous. Despite the abrupt end to the football, he'd had a good evening and had made an impression on the PM. His mobile phone rang.

'Hello. Oh God. What? When? We will get there.' Roger thought it best to slink away and not ask what it was. Calum rushed off without waving.

Roger was quite confused. Having got this far, he had no choice but to go up to the flat and face Dierdre. Hopefully she would be asleep, and ask no questions. Roger had to think about his escape strategy carefully. He did not know how soon he could get out of town.

He rang the bell. Samantha opened the door. She was small for her age but had lively brown eyes and a sallow complexion.

'Hi, Roger. How's things?'

Before he could answer, Dierdre appeared in her nightie.

'Have you heard, Roger? It is your friend, Harry White. He is probably dead.'

'What? How did that happen? Who says?'

'He was in some helicopter, and it crashed. Just outside Kilmarnock. It is on the news. Come and see.'

Harry possibly dead in a helicopter crash? How amazing. Did that mean they would never find out? Would the body be recovered and examined by doctors? Would they discover the poison he had administered? Roger's head was now swimming. He slumped on a chair. Harry was dead. He tried to recall Melissa's face. He wanted to tell her, I did it for you, but everything seemed distant and hazy.

'Are you alright, Roger? You look worn out. You shouldn't work so hard. I wish you could take it easy. Go off on a holiday somewhere.' Dierdre was really concerned.

'God, I could do with a holiday. Let's try and get out of here, and go off somewhere. Shall we? Where do you think?'

'You choose. It is your holiday and I am afraid you will have to pay for it.'

'Don't worry about that. I made good money tonight. Why don't we go somewhere near? Like Dublin. We can set off tomorrow. Will you come Sam?'

'No. Sorry, I've got too much on. But you and Mum go. You both could use a holiday. When did you last have a holiday, Mum?'

11.10 p.m. London, Drew House, 38th Floor

Lex was in despair. He had never seen a night like this. He had scrapped the Terence Harcourt edition. A lot of money down the drain. Those pictures would now remain in the strong box forever. He had prepared a new front page with pictures of the referee Peter Houston with a bandage across his brow just above his eyes. Across his face was a big bold headline in red letters: SAVAGES. Inside, there were full-page pictures of the riot in Glasgow, but he had restored the nude on Page Three... Gisella, as she was called, was holding a football in her hands. A balloon from her lips said Gisella thought it was wrong for fans to attack referees, and that Paul Houston (whom she had never laid eyes on) was her hero.

He had put the news of Terence Harcourt's death in a small entry on the top right hand corner beside the masthead and continued the story on page 9 with the article Chris had sent in. The first print run had gone for outstation delivery by ten thirty. Now he had to rethink the front page. Should he take Paul Houston off the front page? Would Harry White be found alive and unhurt? The first pictures of the helicopter were beginning to be shown on Rainbow, which was there before anyone else. Good for our side, Lex thought. He knew that the Rainbow pictures would be fed through to him. The question was: could this be the night two big political figures bite the dust? How soon could he wrap up the next print run?

11.25 p.m. London, 10 Downing Street

The phone rang and Christine answered immediately. She had been holding Lisa in her arms. Lisa had come back to Downing Street and found Christine waiting. Christine normally went home by nine but today she had been staying back to deal with the aftermath of Terence's death. She had all the three TV sets on with BBC, CNN and Rainbow watching the news as it broke. She was preparing a note for Harry about what the choices were for replacing Terence, and the impact of his death on Scottish elections. She also had to monitor the media about Libya, but that story had begun to fade because of Terence's death. Then, she heard about the crash. She tried to contact Lisa, but her phone just kept ringing... So she stayed behind.

Lisa was pale, but still bearing up stoically. Christine hugged her as soon as she came in, and Lisa broke out into sobs. Christine had to say soothing words, though she had little hope herself about Harry's fate. Nothing was spoken. Lisa knew Christine was fiercely loyal to Harry. She also knew that, for all practical purposes, Christine was Harry's one constant mistress. Lisa had never minded. She and Christine were similar people. They had come from humble backgrounds, were able and good looking. They had faced a lot of criticisms for being stroppy as well. Christine was like a sister, a big sister for Lisa. Now, more than ever, they clung to each other, waiting for the news they hoped would never come.

'Yes, this is 10 Downing Street. Christine Brown here.'

Meghnad Desai

It was Police Superintendent Richard Erskine.

'I need to speak to Mrs White, please.'

'She is here but you can tell me. I am the Prime Minister's Special Adviser.'

'No, madam. I must speak directly to Mrs White.'

Christine knew what was coming, as did Lisa. Lisa took the phone.

'Yes, this is Elisabet White.'

'Madam, I am sorry to say this on the phone. Someone should come personally and say this. But I want to tell you before it is announced on the TV news channels. I am Richard Erskine of the Strathclyde Police. As you know, we have just had news of a crash of the helicopter in which your husband was travelling. We have recovered his body. I am afraid the news is very bad.'

'Tell me, please. I do want to hear.' Lisa was calm.

'We found the body with some difficulty, as we also recovered other bodies. The doctor on hand has tested his pulse and heartbeat. I am sorry to say there is no hope. Your husband, the Prime Minster, is beyond recovery. He died in the crash. I am sorry to have to say this.'

'Thank you, inspector. I know it cannot be easy for you to say this. Can you speak to my friend Christine Brown as well.'

Lisa passed the phone to Christine.

'Tell me about the other passengers on the helicopter—Mr Knight and Miss Disney. Also Barney Jones, the PM's Security Officer,' Christine said.

'Madam. Barney Jones has escaped unscathed. We have taken Mr Knight and Miss Disney in an ambulance

310

to the nearest hospital in Kilmarnock. Barney Jones was able to identify them, and confirm their names for us. The pilot, Mr Angus Stewart, has sadly died as well.' Richard Erskine had to be careful in what he could assert.

'Tell me, are the two survivors very badly injured?' Christine was now feeling responsible for Sarah being caught in the crash.

'I could not honestly tell you Madam. They were unable to move on their own but quite aware of what had happened. Mr Knight was most anxious to speak to the assembled newsmen, but we had to forbid that. It would have been too risky to delay their removal to a hospital. Would you like the number of the hospital?'

Five months later

October, 10.30 a.m. London, 10 Downing Street

Frank Thompson could never get used to working in 10 Downing Street. He had tried his best not to move Lisa White from her home. But Lisa was insistent. Rules, she said, were rules. She had taken just twenty-four hours more before she moved out. She went through the first night of her play stoically and received a standing ovation. And, it was not just out of sympathy for a newly widowed woman. The play itself was a success. The reviews all made clear that they were praising *Ubu Roi* on its merits, and not on Lisa's bereavement woes. But, after that first night, she moved out, and took a flat in Kensington. Fiona Hartley, Roscoe Hartley's wife, had come to her rescue, and rented her one of the three flats that her family owned in London, besides unlimited access to their country mansion.

There was a double funeral for the Party to deal with. But it decided to have Terence Harcourt's funeral first. Jamie Hencke went to Vienna to bring the body back. Dorothy, accompanied by Adrian Andrew and her three children, had stayed behind, and was on hand to receive the body, when it arrived at Edinburgh. A huge crowd gathered at the airport and all along the route to the Edinburgh Castle, where permission had been given to put his coffin on display for people to pay their respects. It was as if all Scotland had decided to turn up for the event. The funeral took place on the Friday following, and Dorothy could not complain that her Terence had not been given the most splendid send-off.

It took longer to arrange Harry White's funeral. The crash had to be investigated, even if only for insurance purposes. But the posthumous examinations had been quick and Christine orchestrated the detailed arrangements to bring the body back to London. Lisa wanted a private funeral away from the political and media crowds. Her will prevailed, and Harry White was cremated very quietly at Mortlake, and according to his wishes, his ashes were scattered at the Fenners cricket ground in Cambridge. He always said that, but for his myopia, he could have been a Cambridge blue and played there. Now he could be there forever.

The Party had asked unanimously for Frank Thompson to take over as Prime Minister. The Conference at Brighton later in September was more like a wake than the usual ideological gang warfare it used to be. Comrades were still in a catatonically depressed state about the double death of Harry White and Terence Harcourt.

Even his worst detractors were glad to see Oliver Knight when he attended the Conference. He was in a wheelchair still, after four months. Oliver had received a two million pound contract to write his memoirs, but he had been too fragile to put pen to paper or finger to laptop. Frank had gone back to an old-style Cabinet with the Treasury back in a powerful position and European affairs in the Foreign Office. He decided he could not hold two portfolios as Harry did. So he said to Nick Davies that he had to sober up and take over as Chancellor, and Nick had quietly gone off to the Priory to seek a cure for his depression and alcoholism. Now, as Deputy Prime Minister, he was getting ready to walk along with John Altrincham at the State Opening of Parliament tomorrow.

Christine came in to Frank's office. She had agreed to smooth his transition as Prime Minister. They had agreed that she would go after the Queen's Speech. She had been put on the list for Peerages for her services to politics. Lisa had refused a title, as she was not at all interested in being cast as the Party Widow. She was going to tour Europe with her production of *Ubu*, and then settle in Glasgow where her friend Margaret had decided to live.

'Are you happy with your diary then today, Prime Minister?' Words such as Prime Minister were still difficult for Christine to say and for Frank to hear.

'Aye, Christine. I have the egregious Calum Kennedy to see in the afternoon. I don't know what I can say to him, except that we don't blame him for what happened. He persists.'

'You know why. He was hoping Harry would give him a Peerage. All his plans came unravelled that fateful night at the Ibrox.'

'Well, until Gideon tells me that he recommends Calum, I am not going to proceed. He is now First Minister, and so I intend to leave all Scottish matters to him. Less to worry for me. Anyway thinking of that, how is Sarah doing? Is she better?'

'Yes, she should be out of the hospital next week, we hope. But, she is alright and in good spirits. She did not enjoy attending the inquest but she bore up. She still feels guilty that she survived and Harry did not. But I tried to tell her that so did Oliver and Barney. Only the pilot died besides Harry.'

'So will she be back at her job? She has the right to resume, and I could do with someone who knows this place.' As a former trade unionist, Frank had not forgotten Sarah's rights to resume her job.

'I will ask her. She has a new boyfriend now. The doctor James Hencke, who accompanied Terence's body back from Vienna. I believe he was Terence's protégé.'

'Aye, I met the lad. Terence was going to bring him to London to work with him. Oliver told me that when Jamie met Harry after they heard about Terence's death, Harry said he could come anyway and work here at No 10 for him. I came across him at the Party Conference. So I renewed the promise. Don't know if he is coming though.'

'Well, it will all depend on her. If she comes back, so will he.'

'That is a piece of good news. What else?'

'Oh yes. You have the Chief Police Constable of Strathclyde to see you in five minutes.'

'What does he want? Do I tell him we don't blame

him either?'

'Something like that I guess. Maybe a gong was to come to him and has got delayed due to that fracas that evening.'

'Aye, everyone wants gongs and honours. All except poor old me. I wish I was back at number two.'

'Now Frank—I hope you don't mind me calling you that—this is no time for self pity. You are where you are because of all your work and your ability. Remember, Harry too got where he was, not because Stan died but because his time had come. Now, it is your time. *Courage, mon ami.*'

'Thanks for that, Christine.'

Christine kissed Frank on his cheeks and went out. She was soon back.

'Prime Minister, the Chief Police Constable of Strathclyde, Douglas Mackie.'

'Hello, Commissioner, come in. Have a seat. Thanks, Christine. So, Chief Constable, what's up?' Frank's conversational gambits had survived his promotion.

Douglas Mackie waited for Christine to leave. He then shut the door behind him and sat down.

'Prime Minister, I do hope our communications are secure, and that we cannot be overheard because I have some very sensitive information to give to you. It is only for your ears. It is about the Prime Minister's death.'

'You mean Harry White, since I am still here.' Frank thought he had to put the pompous ass in his place.

'Oh, yes, of course, Prime Minister. It is about the verdict at the inquest. Although it concluded that the ex-Prime Minister died as a result of injury in the helicopter crash, we have further evidence that he was poisoned. We believe he was given a poisoned substance, an olive, as part of a drink. We believe we know who gave him the drink, though we don't have a motive yet. We would like your permission to pursue the line of inquiry.'

Frank thought for a minute. Christine was right. Harry White was dead and should be allowed to rest in peace. Now his time, Frank Thompson's time, had come.

'Forget it, Chief Constable. The man is dead. He only needs to die once. Leave him be.'

The Chief Constable was surprised, but he hid it well.

'Is that your final decision, Prime Minister?'

'Yes, it is final.'

Douglas Mackie thought for a while he should stick to his guns. As a policeman, he hated to see a case remain unsolved, and this one was especially important. But then he asked himself whether some advantage would not come to him if he listened to the new Prime Minister.

'Yes, Prime Minster. Thank you.' Saying that, he saluted and made a smart exit.

THE END

Walter Raleigh's statue has subsequently been moved from its original place.

Beautiful
Books